SACRIFICE

KARIN ALVTEGEN is one of Scandinavia's most acclaimed and bestselling crime writers. She was born in Jönköping, Sweden, in 1965 and had a varied career, including work in set design for film and stage, before she started to write. She won Sweden's most prestigious crime novel award, the Glass Key, for *Missing*. Her novel *Shadow* was shortlisted for the CWA International Dagger 2009. She is the great-niece of Astrid Lindgren (author of the Pippi Longstocking series), and lives in Stockholm. Her books have been translated into 27 languages.

STEVEN T. MURRAY has been translating from Nordic languages for over thirty years. He is the prize-winning translator of Henning Mankell's Kurt Wallander books.

Also by Karin Alvtegen

Missing
Betrayal
Shadow

KARIN ALVTEGEN

SACRIFICE

First published as *Shame* in Great Britain in 2006 by
Canongate Books Ltd, 14 High Street,
Edinburgh EH1 1TE
Originally published in Sweden as *Skam* in 2005 by
Natur och Kultur, Stockholm
Published by arrangement with the Salomonssen agency

This paperback edition published in 2012 by Canongate Books

1

British Library Cataloguing-in-Publication Data
A catalogue record for this book is available on
request from the British Library

ISBN 978 0 85786 196 2

Typeset by Palimpsest Book Production Ltd,
Falkirk, Stirlingshire
Printed and bound in Great Britain by
Clays Ltd, St Ives plc

www.canongate.tv

To my brave giants
August and Albin

Dear God,
take away all the war and all the violence and
everything that is unjust
and make it so that all the poor people have money
so they can buy a little food. Then make it so that
all evil people turn nice and nobody I know gets
really sick or dies.
Help me to be smart and nice so that
Mamma and Pappa
can always be proud of me.
So that they will love me.

AMEN

1

I swear upon my honour that in my work as a physician I shall strive to serve my fellow man with humanity and respect for life as a guiding principle. My goal shall be to preserve and promote health, to prevent illness, and to cure the sick and alleviate their suffering.

She had failed. The man who would soon die sat in the chair facing her, completely calm and still, with his aged hands resting in his lap. She sat with her eyes lowered to his voluminous file. Almost two years had passed since his first visit. Her assiduous attempts to cure him had amounted to nothing, and today she was forced to admit her defeat. To give him the news. It always felt like this. It was never a question of age or the fact that the disease was incurable, or that the lack of medical advances in research was not her personal failure. It was a question of life. Life, which she had not been skilful enough to save.

He gave her a friendly smile.

'You mustn't take it so personally. We all have to die one day, and this time it's my turn.'

She felt ashamed. It wasn't his job to console her, really it wasn't, but in some way he had clearly managed to see straight into her thoughts.

'I'm old and you're young, think of that. I've lived a long life and lately I've actually started feeling quite satisfied. At my age, you know, there are so many people who have already passed on that it starts to get quite lonely down here.'

He fidgeted with a well-worn wedding ring on his left hand. It was easy to move it around; his sinewy fingers had grown gaunt over the years since the day it was slipped on.

It was always the hands that attracted her gaze in these situations. How strange it was that all the experience and knowledge that had been infused into them through all the stages of life would soon be lost.

Forever.

'But sometimes I wonder what He was actually thinking, I mean everything else is so ingeniously worked out, but this dismantling you're forced to go through, He should have done it a little differently. First you have to be born and grow up and learn, and then when you start to get into the swing of things it's all taken away from you again, one thing after another. It starts with your eyesight and it just goes downhill after that. Finally you're back just about where you started.'

He fell silent, as though pondering what he had just said.

'But that's what's so clever about it all, when you think about it. Because when nothing works the way it should anymore, then it doesn't seem so important in the big picture. You start to feel that maybe it's not such a stupid idea to die after all, and finally have a chance to rest a little.'

He smiled again.

'It's just a shame that it goes on for so long, all that dismantling.'

She had no reply, no suitable words to offer to his musings. The only thing she knew was that the dismantling didn't apply to everyone. Some were snatched away in mid-stride, even before the assembling was finished. And there was no rhyme nor reason to who was selected.

Whom the gods love die young.

There was no consolation in those words.

In that case, God must hate the ones who were left behind. Why else would God think that His own well-being justified the devastation that death left in its wake?

She didn't want to be hated by God. Even though she didn't believe in Him.

'But you know what's the best of all? Now I'm going to go home and pour myself a glass of really good wine, since I haven't been able to drink anything for such a long time. I have a bottle I've been saving for a special occasion, and I suppose today could be considered one.'

He winked at her.

'So, every cloud has a silver lining.'

She tried to return his smile but wasn't sure she really succeeded. When he made a move to stand up she sprang out of her chair to give him a helping hand.

'Thank you for everything you've done. I know that you put up a good fight.'

She closed the door behind him and tried to take a deep breath. The air in the room felt stale. She saw by the clock that there was a little time left before she had to leave. Some papers on her desk were out of order, and she went over to tidy things up. Her hands flew across the desk, and when everything was in neat piles she hung up her white coat and put on her overcoat. She was annoyed to see that there was still plenty of time, but she'd rather be on her way than spend any more time here.

Because it was impossible to run fast enough when what you were running from came from inside.

'Hi, it's Mamma. Just wondering what time you're going to pick me up. Call me as soon as you get this.'

The message was on her voicemail when she turned on her mobile phone on the way to the parking lot. It was ten past five, and she had agreed to pick her up twenty minutes from now. Why she had to call and agree on the time again was a mystery to her, but not doing so would be a bad choice in this situation.

'Yes, hi, it's me.'

'When are you coming?'

'I'm on my way, I'll be there in fifteen minutes.'

'I have to stop by Konsum and buy some new candles.'

'I can do it on the way if you want.'

'All right, but buy the 110-hour ones this time. The last ones you bought burned down too quickly.'

If her mother had even the tiniest clue about how these constant visits to the cemetery tortured her, she wouldn't pretend that it was because of some kind of stinginess that the candles she bought didn't last as long as promised. She would gladly buy candles that burnt for a whole lifetime if anyone made them. But they didn't. The 110-hour candles were the most you could get. And since her mother had sold her car because she didn't dare drive anymore, it was Monika's eternal assignment to ferry her to the cemetery and light new candles as soon as the old ones had burnt out.

Twenty-three years ago. He had already been dead longer than he had been alive. And yet he was the one who took up the most room.

Who took up all the room.

There were a couple of cars in the lot but the cemetery seemed to be deserted.

My beloved son
Lars
1965–1982

She never got used to it. His name on a tombstone. His name belonged at the top of the list of results from some sports competition. In some newspaper article about the most promising young hockey players. When she couldn't impress someone any other way, she could always mention that she was Lasse Lundvall's little sister. He would have been forty this year, but to her he was still her big brother, two years older, the one his pals looked up to, the one the girls all chased, who was always successful in everything he tried.

His mother's pride and joy.

She wondered how things would have turned out if their father had stayed and lived with them all those years. If he hadn't already left the family while Monika was in her mother's belly, and her mother had been spared all those years of loneliness. Monika had never met him. Sometime during her teenage years she had written him a letter and received a brief, impersonal reply, but their plans to meet had fizzled out. She had wanted him to be more eager, wanted him to be the one to urge them to meet. But he hadn't done it, and then his pride took over. She certainly didn't want to make a fuss. And then the years passed and he slipped back out to the periphery.

The candle, as expected, had burnt out, and she saw her mother's displeasure at the thought that it had stood there extinguished on the grave. She quickly took the matches from her pocket, cupped her hand to protect the flame, and lit another candle. So many times Monika had stood here and seen her mother's hands lighting the match, watched the flame growing stronger in the plastic holder until finally it found its way to the wick. Hadn't her mother ever been struck by this thought? That it had all started with just such a little flame? That it had been the cause of all the destruction? And yet she had to keep coming here and re-light the flame as soon as it went out. It would burn here on the grave in triumph over its victim.

They headed back to the car. With one last sigh her mother had turned her back to the grave and started walking. Monika had stood there a moment, read his name for the millionth time and felt the familiar helplessness. What does a sibling do who gets the chance to live her life, when the one who seemed to have the best prospects has lost his? What did she have to accomplish to deserve this chance? To justify the fact that she was still alive?

'You'll come over and have a bite to eat, won't you?'

'I can't today.'

'What else do you have to do?'

'I'm just going to meet a friend for dinner.'

'Again? I get the feeling you're always out these days. It can't be possible to do your job properly if you're out running around like that in the middle of the week.'

She dreamed about it sometimes. Sometimes she was awake when she imagined it. A high fence, completely white with a black, wrought-iron gate. A locked gate that would only open when she gave permission.

'Who are you going to meet?'

'Nobody you know.'

'I see.'

She closed her eyes for a second when she climbed into the driver's seat. She hadn't yet said anything about the course she had to go to next week, and now it was too late, now that her mother was already in a bad mood. No candles would be lit on the grave unless her mother took the bus out there, and this was no sort of news to give her when she was already in a bad mood.

Monika put on the indicator and drove off. Her mother sat with her face turned away, looking out the side window.

Monika gave her a quick glance.

'I'm giving a lecture at the library on the twenty-third, about the welfare fund we have at the clinic. You're welcome to come if you like, I can give you a ride.'

A brief silence, as she possibly considered . . .

Imagine if she, just once . . .

Just one time.

'Oh, I don't know.'

Just once.

They sat in silence for the rest of the ride. Monika slowed down and stopped with the engine running in front of the driveway. Her mother opened the door and got out.

'And I bought chicken for dinner.'

Monika watched her back disappear through the front door. She leaned her head back against the neck rest and tried to see Thomas's face before her. Thank God he existed, that he was the one she had found. His sincere eyes, that looked at her with an expression that she had never seen before. His hands, which were the only things that ever made her come close to anything that might resemble calm. He had no idea how important he was to her, and why would he? She had never really used the right words.

The truth was that he had become essential.

But the mere thought of how important she had allowed him to become filled her with utter terror.

2

It was pure coincidence that she noticed it, and that was actually thanks to Saba. The post basket on the door underneath the letter-box had been screwed on by one of those people from home care; why they had bothered to take the time and effort was completely beyond her. She realised of course that it was so that she would be able to reach her mail, but since she never got any it was a sheer waste of taxpayers' money. Especially the way they were scrimping on everything these days. Occasionally a notice would arrive from the bank or somewhere, but since it wasn't so urgent for her to read that type of correspondence, it didn't justify the expense. Nor was she interested in any daily newspaper; there was enough misery on the TV news in the evenings. She would rather save her disability pension for something else. For something she could eat.

But now there was a letter lying there.

A letter in a white envelope with handwriting on the front.

Saba had sat down by the door with her tongue hanging out and looked at the white intruder; maybe it had an odour that was only apparent to her superior senses.

Her glasses were on the table in the living room, and she wondered whether it was worth sitting down in the easy chair. With all the weight she had put on in recent years it had become so hard to get out of it that she avoided sitting down unnecessarily, especially if she knew that time was limited.

'Do you want to go out for a bit before I sit down?'

Saba turned her head to look at her but showed no great desire. Maj-Britt moved the easy chair closer to the balcony door and made sure the picker-upper was within reach. That way she would be able to open the door without getting up. They had fixed things so that Saba could go out by herself for a while on the lawn. The home help had helped her unscrew one of the bars in the balcony railing, and she lived on the ground floor. But soon they would have to unscrew another one to make the opening bigger.

With a grimace she sank into the easy chair. Whenever her knees had to bear her entire weight for a few seconds they always gave in. Soon she would have to get herself a new easy chair, a higher model. The sofa was already impossible to use. The last time she sat on it they had to send for reinforcements from Security to get her up. Two hefty young men.

They had taken hold of her, and she was forced to submit.

She didn't intend to allow that kind of humiliation again. It was disgusting when anyone touched her body. The loathing she felt at the mere thought made it easy to stay away from the sofa. It was bad enough that she had to let all those little people into her flat at all, but since the alternative was to go out herself, she had no choice. To tell the truth, she was dependent on them, no matter how repugnant it was to admit it.

They would come storming into her flat, one after the other. Always new faces that she never bothered to put names to, but they all had their own key. A quick ring of the doorbell which she never managed to answer and then the door would pop open. They had probably never heard of personal privacy. Then they would invade the flat with their vacuum cleaners and buckets and fill up the refrigerator with their reproachful looks.

Have you already gobbled up everything we bought for you yesterday?

It was remarkable how obvious it was, the way people's attitude changed with each added pound. As if her intelligence decreased at the same rate as her physical bulk increased. Overweight people had slightly less intellectual prowess than thin ones, that seemed to be the prevalent belief. She never refuted them but instead ruthlessly exploited their stupidity to gain advantage, knowing precisely how to act to make them do what she wanted. She was fat, after all! Handicapped by obesity. She couldn't help acting the way she did, she didn't know any better. That was the message they projected every second they spent in her vicinity.

Fifteen years ago they had tried to talk her into moving to sheltered housing. So it would be easier for her to get out. Who said she wanted to go out? Not her, at any rate. She had refused and demanded that instead they adapt her flat to her size. Take out the bathtub and put in a roomy shower, since they were always nagging her about how important hygiene was. As if she were a little girl.

The letter had no return address. She turned it over and read the front. 'Please forward.' Who in the world would address a letter to her childhood home? She felt a pang of conscience when she saw the address. The house up there that was falling apart. The garden that would probably be impenetrable by now. The pride and joy of her parents. That was where they had spent any spare time they had after their devoted commitments to the Congregation.

How she missed them. To think it was possible to leave behind such a void.

'I tell you, Saba. You would have liked my parents, you would. It's a shame you never got a chance to meet them.'

She hadn't been able to go back there. Couldn't face the shame of showing herself up there, not the way she looked, so the house would have to stay the way it was. There was probably no hope of getting much for it, way out there in the sticks. It must have been the Hedmans who forwarded the letter. They had stopped writing to ask whether she intended to sell the house or at least do something about the furniture, but she assumed that they still looked in at regular intervals. Maybe mostly for their own sake. It might not be very pleasant living next door to a dilapidated and deserted house. Or else they had cleared it out on their own initiative and had stopped communicating because they had a guilty conscience. You couldn't trust anybody nowadays.

She looked around for something to cut open the envelope with. She couldn't possibly wedge her finger into that tiny gap. But the claw on her picker-upper worked just fine, as usual.

The letter was hand-written on lined paper with

holes down one side and looked like it came from a college notebook.

Hi Majsan!

Majsan? That was a bit familiar.

She swallowed hard. Deep in the convolutions of her brain a tiny scrap of memory detached itself.

She instantly felt a desire to stuff something in her mouth, the need to swallow something. She looked around but there was nothing within reach.

She resisted the temptation to turn over the sheet of paper to see who had written it; or maybe it was just the opposite, maybe she really preferred not to know.

So many years since she had last heard that nickname.

Who had travelled down through the years, uninvited, and forced themselves in through her letterbox?

I know you must be wondering why I'm writing to you after all these years. To be honest, I have to admit I was a little hesitant to sit down and write this letter, but now at least I've decided to do it. The explanation will probably sound even more peculiar to you, but I might as well tell you the truth. I had such a strange dream a few nights ago. It made a big impression, and it was about you, and when I woke up there was something inside me that told me to write this letter. I have learned (at long last and after hard lessons) to listen to strong impulses. Well, so much for that . . .

I don't know how much you know about me and how my life has turned out. But I can imagine that people talked about it a good deal back home, and I understand perfectly if you don't want to have any contact with me. I'm not in touch with anyone in my family or anyone else from back home. As you can tell, I have plenty of time to think about things here, and I think a lot about when we were growing up and everything we took with us from those years, and how much it affected us later in life. That's why I'm so curious to hear how you're doing these days! I sincerely hope that everything worked out and you're doing well. Since I don't know where you are now or what your married name is (for the life of me I can't remember Göran's last name!) I'm going to send this letter to your childhood home. If it's meant to reach you I'm sure it will. Otherwise it will just circulate around for a while and keep the post office busy which I'm sure would be a good thing since I hear they're having hard times.

In any case . . .

I hope with all my heart that in spite of your difficult years growing up your life has turned out well. I never fully understood until I was grown up what an awful time you must have had. I wish you all the best!

Drop me a line if you feel like it.

Your old best friend,
Vanja Tyrén

She heaved herself up out of the chair. The sudden burst of anger gave her an extra push. What sort of nonsense was this?

In spite of your difficult years growing up?

She'd rarely seen the like of such impudence. Who did she think she was, really, assuming she had the right to send her such condescending statements? She picked up the letter and read the address written at the bottom of the page, and her gaze fixed on the words: Vireberg Institution.

She could hardly remember this person, who clearly was locked up in Vireberg, but who still thought she had the right to sit in judgement over her childhood and thus by extension her parents.

She went to the kitchen and yanked open the refrigerator door. The cocoa package was already on the kitchen worktop, and she quickly cut off a chunk of butter and dipped it in the brown powder.

She closed her eyes as the butter melted in her mouth, soothing her.

Her parents had done everything for her. Loved her! Who knew that better than she did?

She crumpled up the paper. It ought to be against the law to send letters to people who don't want to get any mail. It was impossible to tell what that person was after, but to let her insult stand unchallenged was more than she could bear. She was going to have to reply in her parents' defence. The mere thought of having to communicate with someone outside the walls of the flat without choosing to do so herself made her cut off another chunk of butter. The letter was an attack. A blatant assault. After all these years in voluntary isolation someone had suddenly clawed their way through her arduously erected barriers.

Vanja.

She could remember so little.

If she made a real effort she could call up some scattered images. She recalled that they had hung out together a bit, but no real details surfaced. She could vaguely remember a messy house and the fact that sometimes the yard outside looked like a junkyard. Nowhere near as neat as her own home had been. She also thought she could recall that her parents hadn't approved of their friendship; and there, you see, for once it turned out that they were right! How they had struggled. She got a huge lump in her throat when she thought about them. She hadn't been an easy child but they refused to give up on her; they did their best to help her get on in life even though she was so difficult and caused them so much worry. And then this person comes along more than thirty years later, wondering how *they* had been affected by their upbringing, as if she were looking for an accomplice in her own failure, someone to blame for it. But who was the one sitting in prison? What nerve to come here with her veiled insinuations and accusations when she was the one who was locked up. She could only imagine the reason why.

She braced herself against the worktop when the pain in her lower back started up again. A sudden stab that almost made her black out.

Yet she really didn't want to know anything. She wanted to let Vanja remain buried in the past and let the dust she was stirring up settle again.

She glanced at the kitchen clock. Not because they ever bothered to be punctual, but they should be coming in an hour or two. She opened the refrigerator again. It was always stronger when something she didn't want to acknowledge was attempting to intrude on her consciousness.

The compulsion to stuff herself in order to shut up what was screaming inside.

3

He claimed that he loved her. In fact, everything he said and did indicated as much. And yet it was so hard to accept the words. That she was the one he loved.

What he tried to get her to believe was that he found her unique, that she of all the people in the world was the one he valued most, the one who was most important to him. The one he would under no circumstances ever betray and would always protect.

It was so hard to accept the words.

Because why should she be the one that a man like Thomas would love? Eligible bachelors were scarce when you started pushing forty, and you only had to take one look at him to figure out that he must be a desirable catch. Yet it was probably his mind that had captivated her first. His self-deprecating sense of humour that made her laugh in the strangest situations. Only a man who was so completely sure of his masculinity could laugh so heartily at himself. And only a man who had dared acquire some knowledge of himself would realise what was worth laughing at. She had never met anyone like him before. He possessed a curiosity and a voracious appetite for learning something new, understanding more. Always ready to abandon his entrenched views; if someone else suddenly seemed more reasonable, he would always try to look at things from new angles. Maybe this was one of the reasons for his success as an industrial designer, or maybe it was a consequence. His unusual talents and liberal way of thinking took their conversations to unexplored heights, and sometimes she even had to make an effort to keep up with him. She found it incredibly stimulating.

Intellectually he was fully her equal. Men like that were scarce.

So why was she the one he happened to fall in love with?

There had to be a catch somewhere. But no matter where she searched she couldn't find it.

Of course there had been other men. There were plenty of brief relationships in her past; other ambitions had guided her choices, and she hadn't put energy into trying to extend them. The long years in medical school had demanded her full attention. Getting a B on an exam was a failure, getting an A was a must to feel satisfied, and sometimes even that didn't help. She would prefer her professors to throw themselves across their desks out of sheer rapture over her marks and her brilliance, but she had been forced to realise that this was not at all easy to achieve. There were many talented students. That's why she had always been filled with a sense of inadequacy, that she wasn't good enough. And this made her work even harder.

One by one all of her contemporaries had vanished into marriage and family life, while she, to her mother's dismay, had maintained her single status. It didn't happen so often anymore, now that it was almost too late, but for years her mother had assiduously informed her of her great disappointment that she would never have any grandchildren. And deep inside, in that place where neither her mother nor anyone else was ever allowed, Monika had shared that disappointment.

It wasn't always easy to live alone. Whether it was a cultural thing or not was impossible to say, but somewhere in the human mystery there still seemed to be a basic striving for connection. Her body spoke its unequivocal language. After months in solitude it begged to be touched. And she had no obligations to anyone. So she could initiate a little love affair just to brighten up her life for a while, but she never let her emotions take over. She permitted herself only restrained pleasure, and the relationship was never given the opportunity to become very important. Not on her part at least. A heart here or there had probably been hurt by her actions, but she had never allowed anyone to come anywhere near the core where little Monika lived, where she scrupulously concealed all her fears.

And her secret.

Sex was easy. It was genuine intimacy that was hard.

Sooner or later the balance would always be upset. They would start ringing too often, wanting too much, revealing their expectations and long-term plans. And the greater the interest they showed, the cooler she became. She would observe suspiciously their growing enthusiasm and then cut off the relationship completely. Better to be alone than to be abandoned.

Some of them had called her the Ice Queen, and she took it as a compliment.

But then she met Thomas.

It happened on a train, in the dining car. She had been to visit some friends at their familial idyll in the countryside one weekend, and took the train so she could use the extra time to read up on the new findings about fibromyalgia. On the trip home a gloom settled over her after having observed for forty-eight hours what was missing in her own life. How petty everything had become. She was the type of person who lived her life but who still hadn't managed to make anything out of it. But on the other hand, how happy did someone like her have the right to be?

She had gone to the dining car to have a glass of wine, and had ended up staying at one of the tables, on the seat nearest the window. He had sat down across from her. They didn't say a word, scarcely exchanged a glance. They had both gazed out at the landscape rushing by. And yet her entire being had been aware of his presence. A peculiar sensation of not being alone, the feeling that in the silence they shared they were still keeping each other company. She couldn't remember ever experiencing anything like this before.

She stood up when she saw they were approaching the station where she had to get off, and gave him just a quick glance before she went back to her seat to get her bag. On the platform he suddenly came running to catch up with her.

'Wait! You really have to excuse me, but . . .'

She stopped in astonishment.

'You probably think I'm crazy, but I just felt that I had to do this.'

He looked embarrassed but then he gathered up his courage and continued.

'I just wanted to thank you for keeping me company.'

She didn't say a word, and he looked even more self-conscious.

'I mean, we sat across from each other in the dining car.'

'I know. Thank you too.'

His face broke into a big smile when he realised that she recognised him. He sounded almost excited when he went on.

'Excuse me again, but I just had to find out whether you felt it too?'

'What?'

'Well, sort of . . . I don't really know how to say it.'

He looked embarrassed again and she hesitated a bit, but then she nodded slightly and the smile he gave her should have made her run a thousand miles away out of sheer self-preservation. But she just stood there, unable to do anything else.

'Wow!' he said.

He looked at her as if she had suddenly popped right up out of the platform, and then he started digging around in his pockets. He pulled out a wrinkled receipt and looked around, grabbing the first person who came by.

'Excuse me, do you have a pen?'

The woman stopped, set down her briefcase, opened her handbag, and took out a ballpoint pen which looked quite expensive. He quickly scrawled something on the receipt and held it out to Monika.

'Here's my name and number. I really ought to ask for yours but I don't dare.'

The woman with the briefcase had a smile on her lips when she got her pen back and walked away.

Monika read the note.

Thomas. And a mobile number.

'And if you don't call I'll never go to another Hugh Grant movie for the rest of my life.'

She couldn't help but smile.

'So don't forget, you're carrying his entire acting career on your shoulders.'

She had hesitated for a few days. Followed her usual pattern, not wanting to look too eager, but to tell the truth he had been in her thoughts the whole time. Finally she managed to convince herself that it really couldn't hurt to contact him. They only had to see each other once. The fact that her body was hungering to be touched also made it easier to press those ten numbers on the phone.

On the third day she sent him a text message.

'Guilt feelings about Hugh becoming intolerable. Can't stand the responsibility.'

Her phone rang a minute after she sent the message.

That same evening they had their first dinner together.

'*Columba livia*. Do you know what that is?'

He smiled and filled her glass.

'No.'

'That's what carrier pigeons are called in Latin.'

'Animals aren't my strong point, but if you have some body part you're not sure about, I'm sure I can help you.'

She could hear how it sounded the instant the words came out.

'I mean, tell you what it's called in Latin.'

She could feel herself blushing, and that was certainly something out of the ordinary for her. She could see that he noticed it too and that it put him at ease.

'My grandfather had a pigeon roost when I was little; he kept carrier pigeons. I used to stay with him and Grandma in the summertime, and I was always allowed to help out in the pigeon roost. Feed them, let them out when they had flight training, band them, everything really. It was a whole little science in itself.'

He seemed to sink into pleasant memories, and she took a moment to study him. He really was a beautiful person.

'When I say that Grandpa had a pigeon roost, I mean that he really lived for those birds. Grandma may not always have thought it was so great, but she let him keep them. You know how a carrier pigeon finds its way home?'

She shook her head.

'They follow the magnetic fields.'

'Oh really? I thought they navigated by the stars, I read that somewhere.'

'Then how do they find their way in the daytime?'

'Well . . . I haven't stayed up nights thinking about it.'

The waiter cleared the table, and they assured him that the food had been delicious and that they didn't want dessert but would like a cup of coffee. Monika had almost forgotten the pigeon lesson when he suddenly brought it up again.

'Do you know why they always fly home and don't fly off somewhere else?'

She shook her head.

'Homesickness.'

He leaned forward.

'They stay together for life, a pair of pigeons. They're faithful to each other the whole time, so no matter where you let one of them loose, it will always fly back home. One of Grandpa's pigeons had apparently flown into a high-tension wire, because its legs were gone when it returned, but it still came home, by God, home to its life partner.'

She pondered his story. 'I almost wish I were a pigeon instead, at least if you ignore the part about the legs.'

He smiled.

'I know. When I was little I used to think that when I grew up one day in some terribly distant future and met my wife, it would feel just like that, like a sort of magnetic field. That was how I would know I had chosen the right one.'

She brushed away some invisible crumbs from the tablecloth, because she felt like she wanted to ask but at the same time she didn't for the life of her want to seem too pushy.

'So was that how it was?'

'What?'

She hesitated a bit, because she realised that she didn't really want an answer. Then she fidgeted with her napkin a bit.

'When you met your wife.'

He took a gulp of wine.

'I don't know.'

She could feel the disappointment in her stomach. The way it contracted when she realised that he was married. One of those cowards without a wedding ring. She never got involved with married men.

'I felt the magnetic field, I really did. But the part about the wife is too soon to say.'

Another waiter interrupted the moment and asked if everything was all right. They both nodded without taking their eyes off each other, and he quickly withdrew.

'So now you probably have a better understanding of my behaviour there on the platform. Since it was the first time I ever felt that magnetic field, I just had to do something about it.'

What a strange man she had met. On the way here she had been open to the possibility that they might spend the night together. As the evening went on she grew more and more doubtful. Not because she didn't want to anymore, but because she felt that she wanted it too much. But when the matter was finally mentioned, it was his decision.

'I don't think I'll ask you to come home with me tonight.'

She stood quite silent. They had stopped under the awning outside the restaurant to keep out of the rain.

'This isn't something I want to fritter away. It feels much too good for that.'

She had never met anyone like Thomas. They said good night and he promised to call her the next day, but his first message appeared on her phone after only eight minutes. That night the keypads on their mobiles grew hot with use, the art of communication reached unimaginable heights, and she found herself lying there smiling to herself in the dark when she read his ingenious messages. Inspired by the challenge, she did her best to come up with equally witty replies. By five a.m. she was forced to concede defeat.

'Life and the night are approaching each other with haste. Never are dreams so close as now.'

She was finally speechless.

And he had gone up a notch or two.

And wait they did. In the time that followed they explored each other. Slowly but surely, inside and out. Two lonely people who were cautiously approaching their innermost hopes about everything they had always lacked, what they had always dreamed they would find someday in their lives. Each conversation was an adventure, each discovery a new opportunity to plumb the depths. She knew that she had never before entered that place where her feelings had now led her. Everything was enveloped in benevolence. Bit by bit she got to know him, and none of what he told her or confessed dampened her interest. On the contrary.

Step by step they came closer to the moment, and both of them were brave enough to admit that they were as nervous as teenagers, middle-aged though they were.

But, as usual with Thomas, everything fell into place quite naturally. One Sunday afternoon they just couldn't hold out any longer.

And she realised that she was actually a virgin.

She had had sex many times. But she had never made love before.

The experience was revolutionary, overpowering, so far from her normal intellectual domain. To be completely and utterly dissolved and merge, not only with another body but in an absolute presence. For a brief time to be blessed with clear vision, to discern the simplicity in the immense mystery of the meaning of life. Overwhelmed by the desire to let down all defences, reveal her vulnerability, and in complete confidence put herself at his disposal, let happen whatever was going to happen. She had never been so close to her innermost core. Where there was no turmoil and no loneliness.

But when Monday came, fear had taken her over once more.

She didn't communicate the whole day. When she listened to her voicemail after the last patient had gone, he had left three messages and sent four text messages. She should have been annoyed. If everything had been as usual, his interest would have been the death knell for their relationship. Instead she only grew more afraid. 'You're just being a coward' didn't help. Not even 'Look at it as a challenge'. Her normal ways of tricking herself weren't working, not this time; the challenge involved risks that were much too great. She was still scared out of her mind. If he dumped her she'd never survive, to have let him in so close and then end up abandoned. It was dangerous to make herself dependent on something that couldn't be controlled. To reveal herself as profoundly as his intimacy demanded made her more vulnerable than she could bear.

At twelve thirty that night, when she had still not replied, he was standing outside her door.

'If you don't want to see me anymore you can tell me to my face, you know, rather than hide behind a mobile that you've switched off.'

For the first time she saw him angry. And she could

see how worried he was, how he fought against his own fear.

She didn't say a word, just moved into his embrace and began to cry.

She was lying on his arm. Outside the bedroom window it was starting to become light. She lay as close as she could but it still didn't seem close enough.

'Do you know what Monika means?'

She nodded.

'The one who warns.'

'Yes, in Latin. But in Greek it means the lonely one.'

He turned his head and stroked her forehead with his index finger.

'I don't think I've ever met anyone who tries at all costs to live up to her name.'

She closed her eyes. The lonely one. That's how it had always been. Until now. And now she wasn't brave enough to let herself be rescued.

He sat up and turned his back.

'I'm scared too, don't you realise that?'

He had read her thoughts. He had the ability to see straight through her. It was one of his many qualities that she appreciated, but also feared in equal measure. He got up and went over to her bedroom window. Her eyes wandered over his naked skin. How beautiful he was.

'I've always been able to weigh the pros and cons, go back and forth about how I should behave, and get dragged into all those stupid games people play so they don't seem too eager. But that won't work with you. I've longed so much to be hit by something like this, to feel so much that it seems I just don't have any choice.'

She wanted to say something but she couldn't think of a single word. All the words that would have been suitable were inaccessible, deep inside some cranny, because she had never before needed them.

'I only know that I've never felt anything like this before.'

He stood there just as naked as his confession. She got up and went over to him, stood behind him and slid her arms through his.

'So don't ever leave me alone with a silent phone again. I don't know if I could stand it.'

He was the most courageous man she had ever met.

'I'm sorry.'

For one dizzying instant she dared to feel total trust, and take comfort from the feeling of being loved through and through. She felt the tears rising again, felt something black and hard inside her begin to dissolve.

He turned round and took her face in his hands.

'I ask only one thing, and that's for you to be honest, that you tell me the truth so I'll understand what's happening. As long as we're honest then neither of us has to be afraid. Don't you think?'

She didn't answer.

'Don't you think?'

Only then did she nod.

'I promise.'

And at that moment she meant it.

They were supposed to have dinner that evening. The following morning she had to leave town to attend the course, and she was already missing him. Four days. Four days and four nights without his presence.

Her mother had been upset. Not about the course itself, but about the fact that the grave would be dark for several days. Monika had promised to hurry home. She would pick her up at three on Sunday when she returned.

She spent a long time going through the clothes in her wardrobe. Actually she had already decided what she was going to wear, knew so well what he liked best, but she wanted to check one last time that she wasn't mistaken. On the way past the window she stopped by one of the orchid plants and pinched off a withered flower. The others still stood in their full splendour, and she regarded their perfect creation. So insanely beautiful, in such absolute symmetry, so utterly without shortcomings or flaws. And yet he had compared her to them when he noticed them in the bedroom window, so he wasn't that smart after all. An orchid was perfect. She wasn't. He had the ability to make her feel unique, both inside and out, but only when he was there and she could dwell in his compelling gaze. When he wasn't there, the other took over, what she knew was inside and wasn't worth loving. Swiftly and ruthlessly it would take back the ground it had lost.

She hesitated in the doorway as she was leaving. If she left this minute she would get there right on time. What would happen if she arrived late? Quite a bit late. How annoyed would he be? Maybe it would make him realise that she wasn't as wonderful as he imagined. Then maybe he would finally reveal his hidden side, expose that flaw that she was convinced he must have somewhere. Show that he only loved her as long as he thought she was perfect. She turned off her mobile and sat down on the hall bench.

She made him wait forty-five minutes. Soaked to the skin he stood in the middle of the square when she finally came running up. He had refused to leave their meeting place.

'Finally . . . God, how worried I was, I thought something had happened.'

Not one mean word. Not the slightest hint of irritation. He pulled her to him and she hid her face against his wet jacket and felt ashamed.

But she wasn't completely convinced. Not deep inside.

They slept together at her place that night. When morning came and she had to leave soon, he lingered and held her in his arms for a long time.

'I've worked out that you're going to be gone for a hundred and eight hours, but I'm not sure I can hold out for more than eighty-five.'

She crept closer to him and rested in another dizzying moment. She wanted to stay this time, and for once allow life itself the opportunity to make the decision.

'You know I'm coming home soon, pulled by magnetic homesickness.'

He smiled and kissed her on the forehead.

'But whatever you do, watch out for those high-tension wires.'

She smiled and saw by the clock that it was high

time she left. She had so wanted to say those three words that were so difficult to utter. Instead she put her lips lightly to his ear and whispered.

'I'm so glad I was the one who became your girl pigeon.'

And at that moment neither of them in their wildest dreams could imagine that the Monika who was just about to leave would never ever come back.

4

It took four days before she managed to gather her thoughts enough to begin to formulate an answer. The nights were filled with restless dreams, all taking place near large bodies of water. Enormous shapes hovered beneath the water's surface like black clouds, and although she stood on land she perceived them as threatening, as if they could still get at her. She was thin again and could move unhindered, but something else had prevented her from moving. It had something to do with her legs. Several times she awoke just as a giant wave came rolling in towards her and she realised that she wouldn't be able to escape it.

The big pillow behind her back was wet with sweat. She wished she could lie down properly. For just one night, to be able to lie down and sleep like a normal person. That possibility no longer existed. If she lay down she would be suffocated by her own weight.

It had been so many years since she had written a letter. She got one of the little people to buy her some stationery on the first day, but then she hid it in the top drawer of the desk. The letter she had to answer was in there too, smoothed out after having been crumpled up, and every time she passed the desk her eyes were drawn to the elegant brass fittings.

*   *   *

In the past few days some more fragments of memories had surfaced from the depths. Brief images in which Vanja was present. Vanja laughing on a blue bicycle. Vanja deeply engrossed in a book. She had distinctly seen her dark-brown ponytail, always tied back with a red elastic band. And then a vague image of the woodshed back home, whatever that had to do with the whole thing. Small shards that refused to fall into place. Small objective fragments utterly devoid of emotional content.

She had emptied the refrigerator. She had eaten everything. On three occasions the urge had been so strong that she had to call the pizza delivery. The menu said half an hour, but just like all the other idiots they were never on time.

To think that something that was empty could hurt so much.

The letter was still occupying her thoughts. Most of all she would have liked to tear it up and throw it away, but it was too late. She had read the words and they had become etched inside her and were now impossible to ignore. And, worst of all, her anger was starting to subside and suddenly leave room for something else. An obscure feeling of dread.

Alone.

That feeling hadn't bothered her in a very, very long time.

The nights were the worst.

She tried to convince herself that she didn't have anything to be afraid of. Vanja was locked up and couldn't reach her; if another letter showed up she could toss it away unread. She mustn't let herself be lured into the trap again.

But no amount of clever words helped. And she realised that it really wasn't Vanja who scared her. It was something else.

On this morning she had got up early, before it was even light. She never dared get into the shower when there was a risk that the little people might catch her unawares. It was so hard to dry off properly between all the rolls of fat, and she knew how the eczema on her back must look. The itching told the tale. If they saw it they would sound the alarm, and never in her life would she permit anyone to rub lotion on her. She owned two dresses that she always wore. Ankle-length tents with holes at the top. She had had them made fifteen years ago, and she didn't want to think about the fact that one of them would soon be too small.

After Saba had had her morning walk on the lawn and the balcony door was locked, Maj-Britt went to the kitchen and sat down at the table. She looked at the clock. It should be three or four hours before anyone showed up, but what did she know? They came and went pretty much as they liked. But, to be honest, she was eagerly awaiting them today. Her empty stomach was screaming to be filled. And despite the reproachful glances she had ordered extra provisions.

Hi, Vanja.

She really had no desire at all to say hi to her, but how else did you start off a letter? And how did you refute implied insults without revealing how upsetting they were? She wanted to sound cool and unperturbed, show that she was above all the embarrassing things that a confused inmate thought she was entitled to write.

As you guessed, I was surprised by your letter, to say the least. It took a while before I remembered who you were. As you said, some years have passed since we last saw each other. Both my family and I are doing fine. Göran is working as a department head in a big company that makes appliances and I work in the banking industry. We have two children who are both studying abroad now. I am quite content with my life and have only happy memories of my childhood. Mother and Father passed away many years ago, and I miss them terribly. That's why we no longer drive up there very often, but prefer to take our holidays abroad. So I haven't talked to anyone and know nothing about you or your fate. But I understand from your address that you wound up in trouble.

Tonight Göran and I are going to the theatre, so I will have to close now.

Best wishes,
Maj-Britt Pettersson

She read over what she had written. Exhausted from the effort, she decided that it would have to do. Now she just wanted to get it out of the flat and mailed so that she could put the whole thing behind her.

It had irked her to write his name.

The home help arrived at one o'clock today; a new one, someone she had never seen before. Another one of those young girls, but at least she was Swedish. The kind who went about dressed in suggestive sweaters with the bra straps showing. And then they were surprised that rape was on the increase. When young girls dressed like whores, what were the boys supposed to think?

'Hi, my name is Ellinor.'

Maj-Britt looked with distaste at her outstretched hand. Never in her life would she dream of shaking it.

'I don't suppose you've been informed of the routine in this household?'

'What do you mean?'

'I hope at least you took along the correct shopping list when you went to the store.'

'Yes, I think so.'

The intruder kept smiling, and this irritated Maj-Britt even more. She took off a worn denim jacket decorated with small colourful plastic buttons with slogans printed on them; they gave the garment an even more slovenly appearance, if that were possible.

'Shall I put the stuff in the fridge or do you want to do it yourself?'

Maj-Britt scrutinised her from head to toe.

'Just put the bags on the kitchen table.'

She always put away the food herself, but she could no longer lift the heavy bags. She liked to know where all the food was stored. In case she was in a hurry.

When she was left alone in the hall she took a look at the small plastic buttons. With her thumb and forefinger she gingerly pulled out the jacket and snorted as she examined them. DON'T KEEP SILENT! STOP THE TORTURE. FEMINIST – DAMN RIGHT! IF I AM ONLY FOR MYSELF – WHAT AM I? A candle wrapped in barbed wire with the legend RIGHTS FOR ALL. A multitude of small self-righteous messages about this and that, as if she had taken on the responsibility of changing the world all by herself. Oh well, it would pass when she got a little older and understood the way things worked.

She heard the little person go into the bathroom and fill a bucket with water.

It took about half an hour for her to finish. Maj-Britt stood by the balcony door and waited for Saba to come in. Outside in the playground stood a father pushing his child on a swing. The child, who couldn't be much more than a year old, whooped with laughter each time the swing changed direction and fell back towards the father's outstretched arms. She had often seen them there. Sometimes the mother came along too, but she seemed to suffer from some kind of pain, because sometimes the man had to help her up after she had been sitting on the park bench. Saba stayed near the balcony and never paid any attention to the people she met outside. And Maj-Britt would send the home helps out to pick up the dog shit; she didn't want any complaints from the neighbours about letting Saba out alone.

She opened the balcony door to let Saba in. At the same moment a window opened on the second floor across from her, and the mother of the kid in the swing stuck her head out.

'Mattias, there's someone on the phone asking if you want a ride to the course you're taking. Something about car-pooling.'

That was all Maj-Britt heard, because now Saba

was back inside and there was no reason to keep the door open. She pulled it shut. When she turned round, Ellinor was standing in the room.

'I can take her out for a while if you like. I did the cleaning so fast that I have time for a short walk.'

'Why should you do that? She's just been outside.'

'But I thought she might want to go for a longer walk. It might be good for her to get some exercise.'

Maj-Britt smiled to herself. This was a bolder move than most of them made, but there would still be some way to get rid of her.

'Why do you think she needs that?'

'A little exercise is always a good thing.'

'For what?'

Maj-Britt could see her gaze waver. She was suddenly searching for a better choice of words, and that was certainly needed. The objective was to make her opt for no words at all.

Maj-Britt didn't take her eyes off her.

'What do you think would happen if someone didn't get any exercise?'

Now she was finally speechless.

'Maybe you think someone might get fat, if they didn't exercise?'

'It was just a suggestion. I'm really sorry.'

'So what you're saying is that it would be dangerous to get fat. Am I right?'

So. This one shouldn't be any problem in future.

Ellinor had already opened the front door when Maj-Britt handed her the letter.

'Could you post this for me?'

'Of course.'

Her eyes scanned the address with curiosity just as Maj-Britt had foreseen.

'I didn't ask you to deliver it in person. Just stick it in a post-box.'

Ellinor put the letter in her handbag.

'It was nice meeting you. I'm the one coming next time too, so we'll be seeing each other again.'

When she received no reply, she closed the door behind her. Maj-Britt looked at Saba and sighed.

'We can hardly wait, can we?'

It turned out as she had anticipated, only easier. As soon as the letter was out of the flat, the walls managed to regain something of their old ability: to provide a boundary between herself and everything out there she didn't want to deal with. She felt safe again.

She had two days to be happy. Then Ellinor was back again, and Maj-Britt understood right away that she hadn't managed to shut her up as properly as she had intended. The girl wasn't in the flat more than a few minutes before her torrent of words caused another deep rift.

'Say, is it okay if I ask you a question? I know you don't like to talk to any of us who come here, but . . .'

She had both asked the question and answered it herself. Why should Maj-Britt have to join in her conversations? She caught Saba's eye, and they were in agreement. They had to see about getting this person replaced.

'That letter that I posted . . .'

She didn't even have to finish her sentence before Maj-Britt wanted with all her heart to get her out of the flat so that she could open the refrigerator undisturbed and select what she was going to stuff in her mouth.

'Was it *the* Vanja Tyrén?'

Maj-Britt was trapped again. Once more her long since forgotten 'best friend' was trying to force her into something against her will. She didn't intend to permit it. She didn't intend to reply. But it was no use. When Ellinor didn't get an answer she just kept going on her own, and the words she said made the cracks grow to huge holes exposing her to the hostile outside world.

'The Vanja Tyrén who killed her entire family?'

5

Leadership – tools and methods that produce results.

She had agreed several months earlier to take the course, a long time before Thomas had come into her life. At a time when any of the infrequent breaks in her monotonous daily life had been more than welcome. Back then she had looked forward to the trip.

Now everything was different. Now she didn't know how she was going to make it through the four days.

A pharmaceutical company had offered to pay her course fee. Not for a moment had they managed to convince her that they were worried about her leadership skills or ability as a boss to motivate her staff. Perhaps they were worried about her ability to motivate her staff to select their company's brand of medicine when they were writing prescriptions, but both sides participated in the game. It wasn't the first time that a pharmaceutical company had shown some of the clinic's doctors a little extra appreciation. Nor would it be the last.

She didn't consider herself a particularly good boss, but as far as she knew the staff in her department were satisfied. Her poor leadership qualities seldom had any effect on them; on the contrary, she was the one who usually took on the most extra work. Delegating tedious tasks had always gone against the grain; it was easier to do them herself and avoid resentment. She always felt a need to compensate in some way if she asked them to do something, keep them in a good mood. But actually it was more about ensuring continued goodwill towards herself. So that nobody would think badly of her.

In her role as a physician she had more self-confidence. If she hadn't been regarded as highly skilled and goal-oriented, she never would have been offered the job four years ago. The clinic was under private management with a foundation as the primary shareholder, and to be offered a position as head surgeon was a clear endorsement. There were nine departments in the building, and she was the head of General Surgery. Even so, her leadership skills could definitely use some work, and in her former life, the one before she met Thomas, she would have thrown herself into the assignment wholeheartedly. Now it no longer felt so important. Thomas thought she was fine the way she was, despite all her shortcomings. Right now she just wanted to enjoy that feeling.

Except that there was one shortcoming she hadn't revealed yet.

The nastiest, lowest of them all.

She stood at the bus station and waited. Thomas had given her a lift there, and despite the fact that they had been urged to keep their phones turned off during the four-day workshop, she had promised to call him every night. Now she was sorry she hadn't taken her own car. A woman she didn't know had called and offered her a ride, saying she had got Monika's name and number from course management. And why not? At least that's what she thought when the matter first came up. Now she wished she could have the time to herself, that she could sit all by herself and enjoy the giddy feeling she was experiencing. Everything was suddenly transformed into a sense of warm, exhilarating anticipation. Things were perfect, she didn't need anything else. If this was what they called happiness, then she suddenly understood all human striving for it.

She looked at the clock. It was already eight-thirty and the woman had promised to pick her up at twenty past eight. It was almost 200 kilometres to the course venue, and if they didn't get going soon they would arrive too late for the first session. She always prided herself on being punctual, and she felt a slight pang of annoyance.

She turned round and glanced over at the newspaper kiosk. Involuntarily she scanned the placards with the headlines from the evening papers.

'13-YEAR-OLD girl held as SEX SLAVE for three months.'

And then its competitor alongside:

'8 out of 10 diagnosed incorrectly. A COUGH can be a DEADLY DISEASE. Test whether you are affected.'

She shook her head. One might almost imagine that the newspaper publishers were trained in neurophysiology. Appealing directly to their buyers' primitive alarm systems was a foolproof method of catching their attention. It lay embedded deep inside the ur-brain, and as in all other mammals its purpose was to search its surroundings constantly for possible danger. The placards acted as one big warning signal.

A potential threat that had arisen. But someone who was afraid needed to be informed *why*, not merely *how*, and especially not in disgusting detail. It wouldn't put a stop to any fears; on the contrary, and consequently she suspected that the evening papers' placards had a greater effect on the tenor of society than people realised. No one could avoid them, and what else could the readers do with all the fear that was constantly being forced upon them but hide it away in some nook and let it lie there, to be mixed with a suspicion of foreigners and a general feeling of hopelessness?

The fact that people bought newspapers that used placards like this was the triumph of the primitive ur-brain over the intelligence of the cerebral cortex.

A red van came driving at high speed from the direction of Storgatan, but she didn't pay it much attention. Painted on the side was BÖRJE'S CONSTRUCTION in big letters. If she remembered correctly, the woman had introduced herself as Åse. The van slowed to a stop with the engine running. The woman behind the wheel was in her fifties and leaned across the passenger seat to roll down the side window.

'Monika?'

She grabbed the handle of her suitcase on wheels and walked towards the van.

'I thought it might be you. Hi, I'm Monika.'

The woman shifted back over to the driver's seat and hopped out. She held out her hand to Monika and introduced herself.

'I'm sorry you had to wait, but believe it or not my car wouldn't start. Jesus, what a hassle. I had to take my husband's van instead, and I hope it's okay. I've tried to shove the worst of the junk off the seats.'

Monika smiled. It would take a lot more than a van to dampen her spirits.

'No problem at all.'

Åse took her bag and tossed it in the side door of the van. Monika glimpsed a metal rack with carpenters' tools on it and a firmly secured table saw with a round blade before Åse slid the side doors shut.

'It's a good thing there are only two of us. I tried to get hold of some others from around here, but luckily they'd already organised lifts, otherwise they'd have to lie in the back of the van.'

'So, there are others going from here?'

'Five of them. All I know is that some are from the Council and some from KappAhl, I think, or one of the big department stores, anyway I can't remember.'

Monika opened the door and climbed into the passenger seat. A green pine air-freshener dangled from the rear-view mirror. Åse followed her gaze and sighed.

'I dearly love my husband, but he has never had particularly good taste.'

She opened the glove box and tossed the pine tree inside. The aroma still lingered, and she rolled down the window before she put the car in gear and drove off.

'Okay.'

The word was accompanied by a relieved sigh.

'Finally, we're on our way. A couple of mornings like this a year are liable to shorten your life expectancy.'

Monika looked out the side window and smiled. She already felt like calling Thomas.

* * *

The course venue looked like it had once been a boarding-house. Yellow with white corners and a newly built annexe next door with all the hotel rooms. The journey here had been full of laughter and wise insights. Åse had proven to be both witty and funny, and perhaps humour was a necessary trait, considering she was head of a treatment centre for drug-addicted girls in their early teens.

'I don't really know how I stand it, hearing all the things some of those girls have been through. But every time I realise that I've had a hand in helping some of them move on and break their addiction, it's all worth it.'

The world was full of heroic people.

And those who wished they were heroic.

On the schedule they had received in the mail, it said the course would begin with a reception and the introduction of the leaders and participants. The rest of the afternoon they would learn how to motivate their co-workers by 'understanding people's basic needs'. Monika could feel her interest flagging. She wanted to go home, and as soon as she got her key and checked into her room she rang Thomas. He answered right away, even though he was in a meeting and really couldn't talk. And afterwards her motivation to 'understand people's basic needs' was even less.

She already knew all about it.

'Well, now you know who I am, so it's time for all of us to find out who you are. Your names are on your name tags, so you can skip that part. But the rest of us have no idea what you do.'

Twenty-three newly arrived participants sat in a circle and listened intently to the woman standing in the centre. She was the only one who seemed comfortable in this situation; those seated looked around the circle rather self-consciously. Monika was struck by how obvious it was. Twenty-three grown people, all in leadership positions, several wearing suits, had suddenly been hauled out of their comfort zones and were bereft of any kind of control. As if by magic, twenty-three scared kids now sat there instead. She felt it herself; the discomfort crept through her body, and not even the thought of Thomas made her plight feel more bearable.

'With regard to the course content for this afternoon, I have a proposal and a request about what I'd like you to tell us about yourselves, so I thought I'd start with a little exercise.'

Monika met Åse's glance and they exchanged a brief smile. Åse had told her in the car that she had never been to a 'personal development' course before and that she was a bit sceptical. It was the session about how to handle stress that had appealed to her.

The woman in the centre continued: 'To start with, I'd like you all to close your eyes.'

The participants glanced uncertainly at each other, mutely wondering what this was about before they retreated one by one into darkness. Monika felt even more vulnerable now, as if she were sitting naked on her chair and no longer knew whose eyes to hide from. The leg of a chair scraped on the floor. She was sorry that she had let herself be talked into coming.

'I'm going to say six words. I want you to pay attention to your thoughts and above all notice the first specific memory that comes to mind when you hear them.'

Someone coughed to Monika's left. Only a faint whirring from the air conditioning broke the silence.

'Are you ready? Then we'll begin.'

Monika shifted position on her chair.

The woman paused at length between the words to give them time to sink in.

'Fear . . . Sorrow . . . Anger . . . Jealousy . . . Love . . . Shame . . .'

A long silence followed, and Monika was all too conscious of both her thoughts and the specific memory they had evoked. Six thoughts, straight as an arrow, which mercilessly forced her towards the precise memory she wanted to forget most of all. She opened her eyes to break the spell.

The urge to get up and leave was overwhelming.

Most of the people around her remained sitting with their eyes closed; only a few had fled from the experience behind their eyelids. Now their shameful gazes met, only to rush on in a desperate search for a way out.

'Are you ready? Then open your eyes.'

Their eyes opened and bodies shifted. Some were smiling and others looked as though they were reflecting on their thoughts.

'Did it go well?'

Many nodded while others looked more doubtful. Monika sat quite still. She did not reveal with any expression what she was feeling. The woman in the centre smiled.

'It's been said that these six feelings are universal and that they're found in every culture on earth.

Since we're going to talk about people's basic needs in the next exercise, it would be rather stupid not to make use of our expertise. I think that what you were thinking of just now when we did this was the event, or at least one of the few events, that has been most crucial in your lives and that has influenced you most.'

Monika clenched her fists and felt her nails pressing into her palms.

'When you introduce yourselves, if there's anyone who wants to tell the rest of us what they were thinking about, you're more than welcome to do so. But I can't force you, of course, and above all I can't check that you're telling the truth.'

Scattered smiles, even laughter from some of them.

'Who wants to start?'

No one volunteered. Monika tried to make herself invisible by sitting utterly still and looking at her lap. She had come here voluntarily. At this moment that was impossible to comprehend. Then she sensed a movement to her right and saw to her horror that the man next to her was raising his hand.

'I'll start.'

'Fine.'

The smiling woman moved closer to read his name tag.

'Mattias, go ahead.'

Monika was having heart palpitations. By raising his hand he had instigated a natural starting sequence and suddenly it would be her turn next. She had to think up something to say.

Something different.

'Okay, well, I'll do as I've been told, like the

obedient student I am, and skip all the formalities and such and get straight to the important stuff.'

Monika turned her head and stole a glance at him. Just over thirty. Jeans and a polo shirt. He looked around the circle as a means of greeting everyone, and for a second their eyes met. His whole being radiated self-confidence without being full of arrogance. Merely a healthy sense of self that made the others relax. But it didn't help her.

He scratched the back of his neck for a moment.

'For me it wasn't a specific event I thought of, but a process that continued for several years. But I didn't need to do this exercise to know that the most important moment in my life was when my wife took her first hesitant steps again.'

He paused, picked at something on the arm of his chair and cleared his throat.

'It was a little more than five years ago now. We were quite advanced scuba divers in those days. Pernilla, that's my wife, and I, were out with four friends diving in a shipwreck when the accident happened.'

It was evident that he had told this story many times. The words came loosely and easily and nothing was hard to admit.

'There was nothing particularly special about that day, we had made dives like this hundreds of times before. I don't know how many of you know anything about scuba diving, but for those who don't know you always dive in pairs. Even if you're in a group, you always have a buddy to watch out for during the dive.'

A man in a suit on the other side of the circle

nodded, as if to show that he also knew about diving rules.

Mattias smiled and nodded back before he went on.

'This time Pernilla was diving with another friend. My buddy and I had probably been down for three-quarters of an hour, and we were the first ones up. I remember that I took off my gear and that we talked a little about what we had seen down there, but by then too much time had passed and the only ones who hadn't come up were Pernilla and Anna.'

Now something changed in his tone. Maybe a person could talk about a really difficult experience as many times as he liked without it getting any easier. Monika didn't know. How would she know?

'I hadn't been at the surface long enough to go back down, and the others tried to stop me, you know how it is with nitrogen uptake and all that, but the hell with it, I decided to go down again. It was as if I sensed that something was wrong.'

He paused, took a deep breath, and smiled apologetically.

'Please excuse me, I've told this many times but . . .'

Monika couldn't see who was sitting to the right of him, but she could see a woman's hand. The hand was placed over his in a gesture of sympathy and then vanished from view. Mattias showed with a nod that he appreciated the support and then continued.

'Anyway, I met Anna halfway down and she was completely hysterical. Well, we couldn't talk but we signed to each other and I understood that Pernilla was stuck somewhere in the wreck and her air had almost run out.'

Now the self-confidence came back into his voice. As if he really wanted to make everyone understand. And share his experience. He sounded almost eager when he continued.

'I don't think I've ever been that scared in my life, but what happened was so strange. Everything suddenly became crystal clear. I just had to go down and get her, that was it, there was no other thought.'

Monika swallowed.

'I don't know if it's true that there is some kind of sixth sense that gets switched on in situations like this, but it was as if I could sense where she was. I found her straightaway inside the wreck.'

Now the words were flowing again. He waved his hands in the air to emphasise what he was saying.

'She was unconscious, lying half-buried under a pile of debris that had fallen on top of her; I remember every detail as if I'd seen it in a movie.'

He shook his head as if he too found the whole thing inconceivable.

'Anyway, I got her up to the surface, but after that all my memories are gone. I remember almost nothing; the others had to tell me what happened.'

He fell silent again. Monika pressed her nails harder into her palms.

Everything he had done that she hadn't.

'Her spine was injured when that wall collapsed on her. I was in the decompression chamber, so the first 24 hours I couldn't be with her, and that was really unbearable.'

He picked at the arm of his chair again and this time the pause was longer. Nobody said a word. Everyone sat quietly, waiting for the rest of the story; letting him have all the time he needed. Then he raised his eyes from the arm-rest and his expression was sombre. Everyone understood how serious the accident had been, and what marks it had left on his life. When he went on, his tone was objective and matter-of-fact.

'Well, I don't want to talk all afternoon, but to cut a long story short, she fought for almost three years to learn to walk again. And if that wasn't enough, it turned out that our insurance premium had arrived two days late, so the company refused to pay anything during her entire rehabilitation. But Pernilla was fantastic; I don't understand how she had the guts. She worked like a dog during those years, and it was just so tough not to be able to do anything but stand by her side and give her encouragement.'

Then he looked around the circle and smiled again.

'So, the day she took her first steps I can honestly say were the best in my whole life. Along with the day our daughter Daniella was born.'

It was utterly still. Mattias looked around and finally he was the one to break the respectful silence.

'Well, that little episode was what I thought of.'

Spontaneous applause broke out, increased, and would not stop. The sound rose like a wall around Monika. The woman who led the course had sat down on an empty chair while he talked, but when the applause began to die down she stood up and turned to Mattias.

'Thank you for an incredibly gripping and interesting story. I would just like to ask one question if that's all right?'

Mattias shrugged amiably and said, 'Yeah, of course.'

'Now, afterwards, can you sum up what you feel about the whole thing in a few words?'

He only had to think for a couple of seconds.

'Gratitude.'

The woman nodded and was about to say something else, but Mattias spoke first.

'Actually, not just because Pernilla recovered, even though that may sound strange.'

He paused, formulating the right words to use to make it all comprehensible.

'It's a little hard to explain, but the other reason is actually quite selfish. I realised afterwards how grateful I am that I reacted the way I did and didn't hesitate to go back down.'

The woman nodded.

'You saved her life.'

He almost interrupted her.

'Yes, I know, but it's not just that. It's being aware of how you would react in a crisis situation, because you have no idea before you're in it – that's something I really understood after the accident. What I mean is that I'm incredibly thankful that I reacted the way I did.'

He smiled a little, almost embarrassed, and looked down at his lap.

'No doubt all of us dream about being that hero when it really counts.'

Monika felt the room closing in on her.

And any second now it would be her turn to speak.

6

She couldn't move. She was sitting on a chair and she was thin, but for some reason she couldn't move. A nauseating taste in her mouth. Something reminded her of the kitchen at home but she was surrounded by water with no horizon. There was the sound of footsteps coming closer, but she couldn't tell from where. A single urge, to run, to escape the shame; but there was something wrong with her legs so she couldn't move.

She opened her eyes. The dream was gone but not the feeling it left behind. Thin, sticky threads of her consciousness held on to it and tried in vain to put it into context.

The pillow behind her back had slipped to one side. With great effort she managed to heave herself out of bed and onto her feet. Saba raised her head to look at her but lay down again and went back to sleep.

Why had she suddenly been dreaming so much? The nights were filled with dangers, and it was hard enough to sleep sitting up without having to worry about what her mind was going to do when she relaxed her grip.

It must be the fault of that little person. The one who had been coming over lately and had such a hard time keeping her mouth shut. Maj-Britt hadn't asked to know, but Ellinor had told her anyway. Without being asked she had let the words flow out of her mouth, and every one of them had penetrated into Maj-Britt's reluctant ears. Vanja was one of the few women in Sweden who had been sentenced to life in prison. Fifteen or sixteen years ago she had suffocated her children in their sleep, slit her husband's throat, and then set fire to the house where they lived in the hope of killing herself in the blaze. At least that was what she claimed afterwards, having survived with serious burns. Ellinor didn't know much more than that; the little she knew she had read in a Sunday supplement. A report on the most closely guarded women in Sweden.

But what she remembered and recounted was more than Maj-Britt ever wanted to know. And as if that weren't enough, the little person refused to stop plaguing her, trying to weasel out of her how she knew Vanja and whether she knew any more details. Naturally she hadn't replied, but it was distressing that the girl couldn't keep her mouth shut and just clean, which was the only reason she was in the flat in the first place. But she just wouldn't shut up. Such a constant stream that you might almost think her speech organs had to be kept busy for the rest of her body to function. One day she had even brought along a potted plant, a dreadful little purple thing that didn't flourish – maybe it didn't like the smell of bleach. Or else it was the sub-zero temperature on the balcony at night that it didn't appreciate. Ellinor insisted that she was going to complain at the shop and ask for a new one, but thankfully it didn't appear in Maj-Britt's flat.

'Is there anything you'd like me to buy for next time, or should I just follow the usual list?'

Maj-Britt was sitting in the easy chair watching TV. One of those reality shows that were on all the time these days; this one was about a group of scantily clad young people who had to win the right to keep their room at a hotel by procuring as quickly as possible a roommate of the opposite sex.

'Earplugs would be nice. Preferably the yellow ones made of foam rubber you can get at the chemist's, the kind that workers use in noisy jobs. They swell up and block the entire ear canal.'

Ellinor jotted it down on the list. Maj-Britt glanced at her and thought she saw a little smile under her fringe, just above her plunging neckline where her breasts were about to pop out of her jumper.

This person was going to drive Maj-Britt crazy. She couldn't figure out what exactly was wrong with her, since she didn't let herself be provoked. Never before had she felt such a wholehearted desire to get rid of someone, but all of a sudden none of her usual old tricks was working.

'Whatever happened to that nice Shajiba? Why doesn't she come by anymore?'

'She doesn't want to. She and I traded work schedules because she didn't dare come here anymore.'

Oh, really. Shajiba might not have been so bad after all. Right now she looked like an absolute dream.

'You'll have to tell her that I really appreciated her work.'

Ellinor stuffed the shopping list in her pocket.

'Then it was a shame that you called her "nigger whore" the last time she was here. I don't think she took it as a sign of your appreciation.'

Maj-Britt went back to the TV.

'It's not until you have something to compare things to that you can see clearly.'

She glanced in Ellinor's direction, and now she was smiling again; Maj-Britt could have sworn that it was a little smile she saw. There was quite clearly something wrong with this person. Maybe she was even mentally handicapped.

She could imagine what the gossip was down there at the home care office. How hated she must be as a User. That's what they were called: not patients or clients, but Users. Users of home care. Users who required the help of little, repulsive people because they couldn't manage without it.

Let them say what they liked. She enjoyed playing the role of The Big Fat Ogre that nobody wanted on their work schedule. She didn't care. It wasn't her fault that things had turned out like this.

It was Göran's.

On the TV, one of the female participants had just lied to a gullible girlfriend and started to take off her shirt in order to tempt a potential roommate. The lowest types of human behaviour had been suddenly elevated to desirable entertainment by people who degraded themselves in full view of the public. They filled the TV schedule, they were on every channel, all you had to do was click through with the remote. And they all tried to outdo each other with their shocking behaviour in order to keep their viewers. It was disgusting to see.

She seldom missed a single episode.

Out of the corner of her eye she noticed that Ellinor was standing watching the TV. A little exasperated snort was heard in the room.

'Jesus. Dumbing-down has really taken over.'

Maj-Britt pretended not to hear. As if that would help.

'Do you know that people in all seriousness sit and discuss those programmes, as if they were something important? The world is going under out there, but people say the hell with it and get involved in stuff like this instead. I'm sure there's a conspiracy behind all this shit; we're supposed to become as stupid as possible so that the powers that be can do as they like without having us complain about it.'

Maj-Britt sighed. Just think if she could have a little peace and quiet. But Ellinor wouldn't stop.

'It makes you sick to watch it.'

'So don't watch.'

Admitting that she partially agreed with her was out of the question. She would rather justify a cholera epidemic than admit that she shared an opinion with this person. And now Ellinor was really wound up.

'I wonder what would happen if they shut down all the TV stations for a couple of weeks, and at the same time saw to it that people couldn't drink any alcohol. Then at least the ones who didn't go right out and hang themselves would be forced to react to what the hell is going on.'

No matter how much Maj-Britt disliked using the telephone, soon there would be no other alternative; she had to ring the office and get this girl replaced. She had never had to do that before. They had always seen fit to leave on their own.

The thought of a mandatory telephone conversation made her even angrier.

'Maybe you should apply to join them. With those clothes you wouldn't even have to change.'

It was quiet for a moment, and Maj-Britt kept watching the TV.

'Why would you say something like that?'

It was hard to tell whether she sounded angry or sad, and Maj-Britt went on.

'If you ever passed by a mirror and glanced at yourself then you wouldn't have to ask such a dumb question.'

'So what's wrong with my clothes, in your opinion?'

'What clothes? I haven't worn my glasses in so long that unfortunately I haven't been able to see any.'

It was quiet again. Maj-Britt would have liked to see if her words had hit home, but refrained. On the TV the credits had begun to roll. The programme was sponsored by NorLevo, a morning-after pill supplier.

'Can I ask you one thing?'

Ellinor's voice sounded different now.

Maj-Britt sighed.

'I have a hard time believing that I could actually stop you.'

'Do you enjoy being so mean, or is it only because you feel you're such a failure?'

Maj-Britt felt to her dismay that she was blushing. This was outrageous. No one had ever talked back to her before. Nobody had dared. And to presume that she regarded herself as a failure was an insult that could get this loathsome little person sacked.

Maj-Britt turned up the volume with the remote. She had absolutely no reason to reply to an insult.

'I'm proud of my body and I don't think there's any reason to try and hide it. I think I look great in this shirt, if that's what's making you so upset.'

Maj-Britt still didn't shift her gaze from the TV.

'Well, it's up to you whether you want to walk around looking like a whore.'

'Right. Just like it's up to each of us to decide whether to lock ourselves in a flat and try to eat ourselves to death. But that doesn't mean that a person has no brain. Or what do you think?'

That was the last thing either of them said that day. And it annoyed Maj-Britt to bursting point that Ellinor had had the last word.

As soon as she was alone she called the pizza delivery.

Six days had passed since she sent her reply. Six days to let her feeling of repugnance slowly but surely fade away; or at least it no longer bothered her more than she could stand. She had enough to think about with being annoyed at Ellinor. But then one morning she again heard a noise in her useless letter basket, and before the flap on the letter-box snapped shut she knew that it was another letter from Vanja. She could feel it through the whole flat; she didn't even have to go to the door to have it confirmed.

She let the letter lie there, and avoided looking towards the door when she passed by in the hall. But then Ellinor arrived, of course, and beaming with happiness she stuck it right under Maj-Britt's nose.

'Look! You've got a letter!'

She didn't want to touch it. Ellinor put it on the table in the living room, and there it lay while Ellinor cleaned and Maj-Britt sat silently in the easy chair, pretending it wasn't there.

'Aren't you going to read it?'

'Why's that? Do you want to know what's in it?'

Ellinor kept cleaning and exchanged a few words

with Saba instead. The poor beast couldn't escape, and Maj-Britt saw her quietly lying there, suffering.

Maj-Britt got up and headed towards the bathroom.

'Does your back hurt?'

Would this person never learn to shut up?

'Why?'

'I just noticed you grimacing and putting your hand there. Maybe it's something a doctor should have a look at.'

Never in her life!

'Why don't you just see about finishing the cleaning here and then pack up and leave. Then you'll see how much better my back will feel.'

She locked the bathroom door behind her and stayed in there until she was sure that the unpleasant little person had gone.

But her back did hurt, she couldn't deny it. The pain was always there, and it had been more pronounced lately. But never in her life would she consider undressing and letting herself be examined by someone who would touch her body.

The letter lay there. For days and nights, consuming every molecule of oxygen in the flat and making Maj-Britt long to get out of there for the first time in ages. She was incapable of throwing it away. She could see that it was a thick letter this time, considerably thicker than the first one. And it lay there like a reproach and shrieked at her day and night.

'You have no backbone, you fatty! You can't resist reading me!'

And she couldn't either. When the refrigerator was empty and the pizza delivery had closed for the night, she had no more defences. Even though she didn't want to read a single one of the words that Vanja had written.

Hi, Maj-Britt!

Thanks for your letter! If you only knew how happy it made me! Especially hearing that you and your family are doing well. Yet another sign that it's the voice of the heart we should listen to! The last time I saw you, you were pregnant and I remember how you suffered at having to go against your parents' will when you married Göran. It makes me so glad that everything worked out and that your parents finally saw reason. No one should die without resolving matters, it's so hard for those who are left behind. If you only knew how I admired your decisiveness and your courage and I still do!

I often think about our days growing up. Just think how different our situations were. At my house it was always a mess as you recall and we never knew what sort of state my father would be in when (and if) he came home. I never said it straight out, but I was so ashamed in front of the rest of you and especially you. But I also remember that you always wanted to come to my house to play, and you said you had a good time there, and that made me so happy. I have to admit I was a little scared of your parents. They talked a lot about the congregation that you all belonged to and how strict the rules were. At my house there really wasn't anyone who talked about God. Something in between your house and mine would probably have been best, at least as far as spiritual nourishment was concerned!?

Remember the time we played 'doctor' in your woodshed and that Bosse Öman was there? We must have been ten or eleven, I think, weren't we? I remember how scared you were when your father discovered us and Bosse said that the game was your idea. I still feel ashamed that I didn't take the blame myself that time, but we both knew that you weren't allowed to play games like that so it probably wouldn't have done any good. It was such an innocent game, the kind all children play. You weren't at school for several weeks after that, and when you came back you wouldn't talk about why you'd been gone. There was so much I didn't understand because our families were so different. Like that time several years later, it must have been when we were teenagers, when you told me how you used to pray to God to help you take away all the thoughts you didn't want to have. We all thought about boys at that age so I probably didn't understand how you suffered, I must have thought it was just a little odd. And you were so beautiful, you were always the one the boys were interested in and I was probably jealous of you because of that. But you prayed to God that He would crush you and teach you to obey and . . .

Maj-Britt dropped the letter to the floor. From the depths of everything she had forgotten, the nausea came rushing in like a berserker. She wrenched herself up out of the easy chair but made it no further than the hall before she threw up.

7

You're a doctor. You can handle this. Tell them anything!

Twenty-three expectant faces were turned to her. Monika's mind was a blank. Only one memory erupted like a boil from the nothingness and made all invented fantasies impossible. The seconds passed. Someone smiled encouragingly and someone else sensed her torment and chose to look away.

'If you like we can skip to the next person now and you can speak later. If you would rather think about it for a while, that is . . .'

The woman gave her a friendly smile, but being pitied was more than Monika could stand. Twenty-three people were thinking at that moment that she was weak. If there was anything she had devoted her life to, it was to being regarded as the exact opposite of that. And she had succeeded. She heard it often. How colleagues on the job said that she was so capable. Now she was sitting with twenty-three unknown people and had just been granted special treatment because of her weakness. Everyone in the room viewed her as an ordinary, second-rate person, incapable of carrying out the task that Mattias had executed in such a brilliant manner. The need to reclaim her position was so strong that it succeeded in conquering her indecision.

'I only hesitated because the memory I thought of also dealt with an accident.'

Her voice was steady and deliberately a bit indulgent. Everyone's gaze turned back to her. Even those who had turned away in discreet sympathy.

The woman who was subjecting her to this had the bad taste to smile.

'It doesn't matter. The point was for all of you to free-associate, and often it's the strongest experiences that come up first. Please, tell us whatever you like.'

Monika swallowed. Now there was no turning back. All that remained were tiny corrections to the truth if she couldn't bear it.

'I was fifteen years old and my big brother Lasse was two years older. He was invited to a party at his girlfriend Liselott's house while her parents were away, and since I had a small crush on one of his friends who was going too, I managed to convince him to let me come along.'

She was aware of her own heartbeat and wondered if anyone else could hear it.

'Liselott lived some distance away, so we decided to sleep over. Our mother probably wasn't entirely aware of what went on at parties like this, that we drank a lot, I mean. And even if she suspected it, she wouldn't have thought that my brother and I would be involved. She had quite a high opinion of us.'

There was no danger yet. So far it was possible to meander cautiously alongside the truth.

Because so far, it was possible to live with it.

'Some of the kids took a sauna that night. Quite a lot of drinking was going on, and afterwards no one shut off the sauna heater.'

She paused. She remembered it so well. She even

remembered Liselott's voice although it was so long ago now and she never heard it after that night. *Monika, could you go down and turn off the sauna?* And she had said yes, but all that beer was whirling round in her head and the boy she had had a secret crush on for so long was finally showing some interest and she'd promised to wait there on the stairs while he was in the bathroom.

'Then all of us who were staying over decided to go to sleep. There were three others besides Lasse and me. We slept wherever there was room to lie down, on sofas and beds and everywhere. Lasse slept upstairs in Liselott's room and I was downstairs.'

Her newly won boyfriend had gone home. Lasse had already fallen asleep in Liselott's room. Monika, dizzy with infatuation and beer, went to lie down on the sofa right outside their closed door.

On the second floor.

On the hallway at the top of the stairs.

She had never admitted to anyone where she had slept that night.

'I woke up around four, I think, because I couldn't breathe, and when I opened my eyes the house was already in flames.'

The terror. The panic. The terrific heat. Only one thought. To get out of there. Two steps over to the closed door but she hadn't hesitated. She simply rushed down the stairs and left them to their fate.

'There was smoke everywhere and even though you think you can find your way around a house, it's a whole different matter when you can't see a thing.'

The words gushed forth in a desperate attempt to finish this task as quickly as possible and escape.

'I crept over to the stairs and tried to go up but it

was already burning too fiercely. I tried to scream to wake them but the noise of the fire was deafening. I don't know how long I stood there by the stairs trying to climb them. Time after time I was forced to retreat a couple of steps and then try again. The last thing I remember is a fireman carrying me out of there.'

She couldn't go on. To her dismay she could feel herself blushing, felt the colour of shame spreading across her cheeks.

She had stood there in safety outside on the lawn and watched how the heat made the glass in Liselott's window explode. As if turned to stone, she had slowly but surely realised that he would never get out. That he would remain inside in the trap she had set. She had stood there, alive, and watched the malicious flames destroy the house and those who were left inside. Her handsome, happy big brother who was supposed to be so much braver than she was. Who never would have hesitated to take those two steps to save her life.

Who should have lived instead of her.

And then all the questions. All the answers that even then were distorted by her despair over the truth. She had been sleeping in the living room on the ground floor! Liselott had promised to turn off the sauna heater! Weeks of terror that one of the kids who had gone home might have heard her promise to turn off the sauna or seen her upstairs on the sofa. But her statement was allowed to stand unchallenged, and with time it had become the official story about what happened.

'What happened to your brother?'

Monika couldn't get the words out. She hadn't been able to then either, when her mother came rushing across the lawn with only a robe over her night-gown.

The top floor had collapsed and the firemen did their best to extinguish the flames that refused to be brought under control. Someone had called her and she had rushed out and jumped into her car.

The clearest image that remained in Monika's mind was her mother's face when she spat out her question, her eyes wide with terror because of what she already knew but refused to comprehend.

'Where's Lasse?'

It was impossible to answer. Impossible to utter the necessary words. It couldn't be true, and as long as nobody said it, it was still not reality.

She felt her mother's hands on her shoulders, the fingers making her sick to her stomach as her mother tried to shake an answer out of her.

'Answer me, Monika! Where is Lars?'

A fireman came to her rescue and it only took him a couple of seconds to say the words that made everything irretrievable, that meant nothing would ever be the same again.

'He didn't make it.'

Each syllable slashed down between then and now, irrevocably. The past, so unsuspecting and naïve, was forever sliced away from the future.

And that was when she saw it. She could sense it in her mother's eyes as she stood there in her night-gown, desperately trying to protect herself from the merciless words. She saw what would become the greatest sorrow in her life, and what she would spend her whole life trying to change.

But never could.

Her mother's grief over Lasse's death was deeper than the joy she was able to feel that Monika was still alive.

8

'And if your right hand causes you to sin, cut it off and cast it from you; for it is more profitable for you that one of your members perish, than for your whole body to be cast into hell.'

She opened her eyes. It had been her mother's voice. She pulled her hand close and was disgusted by what she smelled. As soon as she could, she got up and went to the sink in the bathroom, washed herself with soap and let the hot water rinse away the sickening vomit.

It was all Vanja's fault. Her letter had opened up small channels that Maj-Britt could not control, small trickles of thoughts that she didn't want to deal with sneaked in, and she wasn't able to keep them out. As long as the threat had come from the outside she could master it with her old tricks, but now it was coming from inside, and years of defence were levelled, leaving the battlefield wide open.

Impure thoughts.

At an early age they had come to her, she never understood from where, suddenly they were just there inside of her. Crawling like black worms out of her brain and making her want things that were unthinkable. Sinful. Maybe it was Satan tempting her after all, the way they said. She could remember it now, what they had said.

She didn't want to remember!

Suddenly she was being forced closer and closer to the screen that protected her, and when she got close enough it was possible to make out details on the other side, details that shouldn't be allowed to exist. Trickle after trickle came seeping through the tiny channels, piecing fragments of memory together into a whole. Fragments that rooted out everything she thought she had managed, once and for all, to forget and leave behind her. Next to the words that Vanja had written they had wound their way into her consciousness. No one would fight by her side this time. Her parents were dead, and their Jesus had abandoned her long ago.

She had prayed and prayed but never managed to share their faith; God had not wanted her prayers. She gave up everything to show her obedience and to be embraced by His love, but He never answered. Never showed her a single word or sign that He was listening, that He saw her struggle and her sacrifice. He silenced her because she was not worthy. He rejected her and left her alone with her filthy thoughts.

She went into the kitchen. There was a little left of the meat she had seared, and she cut off a piece and placed it on her tongue. The meat was seared just on the surface. When she leaned back in bed again she let her saliva soften and warm the morsel of meat before she closed her eyes and swallowed.

A brief moment of pleasure.

Several times she had woken with her hands over her crotch, and the shame she felt was blood-red. Why had she been born in a body with such sick desires?

Why had their God not been able to love her? Why had He punished her parents when she had been willing to sacrifice everything?

One night she hadn't awakened until it was too late. She had woken up in the midst of her shame.

And her mother had spoken to her in her sleep.

They saw what she had done.

A large hall. She sat on a chair and the water all around her was back. She couldn't move. There was something wrong with her right leg, something about the leg made it impossible for her to escape. A noise frightened her and she looked up. He was standing right in front of her in a black suit, he was so enormous that she couldn't even see his face. She wanted to flee, but there was something about her right leg that prevented her. Behind him lay a severely wounded man on the floor, and his white clothes were cut to ribbons. Blood gushed from spike holes in his hands, colouring the water red, and he looked at her and appealed for help.

The voice of the huge man boomed like thunder.

'Jesus died on the cross for your sins, because your hands seduced you and because of your unclean desire.'

She heard sounds behind her. People had gathered, they were there because of her, because of what she had done. Their eyes burned into the back of her neck.

'There are three forms of love – our love for God, God's love for us, and erotic love, which turns us away from God.'

The water was seeping in from all sides. Her parents sat some distance away with their hands folded. They looked up adoringly at the man who was speaking, beseeching him for help.

'The shame of desire is that it is independent of will. Virtue demands complete control over the body. Do you understand, Maj-Britt?'

Her name echoed between the walls but she could not reply. Something was suffocating her. People behind her whom she could not see were placing their hands on her head.

'Before the Fall, Adam and Eve could propagate without desire, without the lust that has now been forced upon us; their whole bodies were under the control of the will.'

The water was continuing to rise. The wounded man on the ground vanished beneath the surface and she wanted to rush over and help him, but she couldn't. Her leg and all those hands held her back. Soon her parents would vanish too; they would drown because of her, because she had forced them in their despair to come here for help.

'You must learn to cultivate and nurture your relationship with God, to cleanse your filthy soul. A true Christian refrains from the damnation of sexuality. What you have done is a sin; you have strayed from the true path.'

With a mighty noise the walls came crashing down and the room was completely filled with water. Her parents sat quite still in their grief and let the water wash over them. She could no longer breathe, couldn't breathe, couldn't breathe.

When she woke up she was lying on her back. She tried to roll over on her side but her body prevented her. The big pillow had slipped onto the floor and she was abandoned, trapped by her own weight. Like a beetle on its back she tried in vain to regain control, but the strain used up the last oxygen in her lungs. She was going to suffocate. She would die here, outwitted by her own body, the body that all her life had been her prison, both thin and fat. Now it had won. At last it had won what it wanted and conquered her, forced her to yield and give up.

They would find her here. That Ellinor would discover her tomorrow and tell the others that she had died lying in her own bed, suffocated by her own fat.

Shamed forever.

With one last effort she managed to roll over on her side and then fall to the floor with a hard thud. Her left arm was trapped under her but she didn't feel the pain, only the relief when air found a narrow passage down to her lungs.

Saba barked uneasily and wandered back and forth. Saba. Dear Saba. Her faithful friend who was always there when she needed her. But now Saba could do nothing. Maj-Britt would remain lying here until Ellinor came, but at least she wouldn't be dead.

The hours passed slowly. Her left arm went to sleep after a while, but she didn't dare move, didn't dare risk landing on her back again. Finally she was forced to move. With a minimum of effort she managed to free the blood flow down into her arm. Worse was the pain in the small of her back. The pain that had been throbbing lately; often it hurt so much that she had a hard time moving at all.

She was lucky. Ellinor came early. The clock by the bed showed only a little past ten when she finally heard the key in the door.

'It's only me!'

She didn't reply; Ellinor would find her soon enough. She heard the food bags being laid on the kitchen table and Ellinor saying hello to Saba, who had left her side when the front door opened.

'Maj-Britt?'

The next moment she was standing in the bedroom doorway. Maj-Britt could see that she was alarmed.

'Shit, what happened?'

She squatted down by her side but still hadn't touched her.

'Jesus, how long have you been lying here like this?'

Maj-Britt couldn't speak. The humiliation she felt was so deep that her jaws refused to move. Then she felt Ellinor's hands on her body and it was so ghastly that she wanted to scream.

'I don't know if I can manage to get you up. I'll probably have to call security.'

'No!'

The threat caused a spurt of adrenaline and Maj-Britt reached her arm up towards the bedstead to try and get a grip.

'We'll manage by ourselves. Try to shove the pillow in behind my back.'

Ellinor worked as quickly as she could, and in a moment Maj-Britt was in a half-sitting position. The pain in her lower back made her want to scream, but she gritted her teeth and refused to give up. They kept on going. One pillow after another was forced in and it took them almost half an hour, but they did it. Without the security men and their awful touching. When Maj-Britt sank down in her easy chair, panting, and it was all over, she felt a strange emotion.

She was grateful.

To Ellinor.

She wasn't required to do that; according to the rules she should have called in security. But Ellinor hadn't, for her sake and together they had done it.

The words came from deep inside.

'Thank you.'

Maj-Britt didn't look at her when she said it, or the words would have stuck in her throat.

Not much was said during the next hour. The feeling that they had suddenly become a team, that their common experience had forced Maj-Britt to lower her guard, felt threatening. She was indebted now, and that could easily be exploited if she didn't stay on alert. This did not mean that they were friends, far from it. She had Saba, after all, and needed no one else.

She couldn't face dealing with the bags of food, and she heard Ellinor start to unpack them and open the refrigerator door.

'Wow, what a lot of food is left.'

'I can finish eating it all if that would make you feel better.'

She bit her tongue, that wasn't what she meant to say, but the words had come out by themselves. She regretted saying them, but the mere thought that she wanted to take them back disturbed her. She was indebted. In future that would be intolerable.

Ellinor appeared in the doorway.

'I was just surprised, that's all. I mean about the food. You aren't sick or anything, are you?'

Maj-Britt looked at the letter. That was where it

came from. All she had left unread, and the things she *had* read but had never wanted to see. Not even food soothed her anymore.

'Is there something you want me to buy for next time?'

'Meat.'

'Meat?'

'Just meat. Forget about the rest of it.'

She was back in her easy chair while Ellinor cleaned around her; Maj-Britt was doing her best to pretend she didn't exist. She was aware of Ellinor's worried glances but didn't care. She knew that she wouldn't get her wish fulfilled; buying nothing but meat was something that Social Services would never agree to. She had waged a long battle to get any extra rations of food at all, but this would definitely cross the line.

But meat was the only thing that could deaden the thoughts that had now invaded her again.

Ellinor was at the front door when she suddenly turned round and came back.

'You know, I think I'll leave you my mobile number on the nightstand by your phone. If it should happen again, I mean.'

She disappeared into the bedroom but came right back.

'I'll see you the day after tomorrow then.'

She vanished into the hall and when she opened the front door she called back towards the flat, 'By the way, I put the earplugs you ordered on the kitchen table. See you!'

Maj-Britt didn't answer, but to her dismay she felt like crying. A thick lump in her throat made her frown and she hid her face behind her hand until Ellinor had gone.

Ellinor was puzzling. Maj-Britt could not for the life of her understand the friendliness that never diminished no matter how she behaved. There was every reason to be suspicious, because there must be something that Ellinor was expecting in return. She was like one of those advertising flyers that came through the letter-box, some even printed in type that looked like handwriting, as if it were sent solely to her. *Dear Inga Maj-Britt Pettersson. We are pleased to make you this fantastic offer.* The better the deal seemed, the more reason to be suspicious. There was always a catch, carefully concealed in the gush of kindly language; the harder it was to discover, the greater reason for caution. Nothing was ever done out of sheer kindness. There was always a profit motive. That's how the world worked, and everyone did their best to get a piece of it.

Ellinor was like an advertising flyer.

There was every reason to mistrust her.

She took the picker-upper and reached out for the letter. It had been lying like a magnet there on the desk, waiting for her to capitulate. Now she could no longer resist it. Her hands trembled as she unfolded the rest of the letter.

I'll never forget the time I questioned your father's faith. Now I don't understand how I dared. We had just read in school that Christianity wasn't the biggest religion in the world, and I remember how surprised I was by that. If there were more people who believed in a different God then maybe they were the ones who were right! Jesus, how angry he was. He explained that those sorts of thoughts would land me in hell, and even though I didn't believe him, it took a long time to get over his words. It was the first time I experienced God as a threat. He said that everyone who didn't acknowledge Jesus Christ as the Son of God was not welcome in the Kingdom of Heaven, and I wanted so much to ask about all those people who lived before Jesus was born. Whether it wasn't a little unfair to them, since they hadn't even had a chance, but I never dared ask. It was enough to have been damned once that day.

I always thought it was so strange that we human beings were 'sinful' and that in church we were supposed to pray to God to forgive us our sins whether we thought we had committed any or not. I remember you tried to make me understand that it wasn't only sins we committed consciously that counted, but also the original sin we were born with. 'Through the carnal conception because of our sinful seed.' I will never forget those words. They were so upsetting that I didn't reject them until many years later when I realised that 'the carnal conception' was the only way for us to propagate. I decided that God probably wanted us to do it, since He had taken so much trouble creating us.

When we were growing up, sex was something that boys were 'unfortunately' interested in and that we girls understood that sooner or later we would 'have to learn to tolerate', but that we absolutely mustn't 'give in'. We weren't supposed to wonder why it got so confusing when we reached our teens and boys were the only thing we thought about and we actually wanted to 'give in' a little, of our own free will. I wish that amongst all the warnings and all the scare propaganda they had added a little footnote and explained that it's quite natural for all people to feel desire and want to reproduce.

Another strong memory from my childhood was the time we found those magazines in your father's desk drawer. For the life of me I can't remember what we were doing in there, but I assume it was my big idea. I was always the one who decided we should do things we weren't supposed to do. Those magazines were quite tame by today's standards, but finding them at your house was like discovering the sign of Satan in the church, and you were utterly terrified. You were convinced that someone had broken into your house and put them there, but nothing on earth was going to make you say anything to your parents. Do you remember how we put the magazines on the floor and then hid under the bed? I can still picture your mother's legs when she came into the room, and her hand when she picked them up. And I especially remember how upset we were afterwards when she just put the magazines back where we found them.

Now that I'm an adult I think it says a great deal about how strong our desires actually are, when not even your father with his strong faith had the power to resist them.

Today the times seem to be quite different, at any rate that's the impression I've got from TV and magazines. Now sexuality has to be so awfully 'accepted' that it seems to have been transformed into a commercial leisure activity which requires both a manual and assorted equipment. But from this distance it seems mostly to be a matter of realising yourself and developing your ability to have stronger orgasms, and the fact that there should be a little love thrown in doesn't seem to be that important. It all seems a bit sad. But what do I know, here in my prison celibacy?

My, how long this letter has gone on, but I'm so glad that we have made contact again. I knew that it was fate that my letter would reach you!

Now it's time for lights out, and tomorrow I have an exam. I've been given the perk of 'studying long distance' (a strange expression, but in my case you couldn't think up a more fitting description). I've finished 15 modules in theoretical philosophy and have just begun my second year in the history of religion. If only I pass the test tomorrow!

Give my warmest greetings to the rest of the family!

All best wishes,
Your friend Vanja

Maj-Britt slowly lowered the letter and felt for the first time in more than thirty years a need to pray to God. What Vanja had written was disgusting. May the Lord forgive her for the words she had just been tricked into reading.

9

The individual presentations had continued, taking up most of Thursday afternoon. Mattias had set the bar, and the rest of the participants had risen to the challenge. None of them wanted to be relegated to mediocrity by telling a boring story; they hadn't ended up in positions of authority for nothing. One fascinating account after another passed for review. Monika could only listen half-heartedly. It wasn't until she finally concluded her account and everyone's attention shifted to the person who was next that she realised fully how much energy it had taken. Any energy she had left was devoted to keeping herself upright in her chair. So much time had passed since she had confronted that memory; on the occasions when she had been forced to do so, she had merely passed over it quickly and left all the details in merciful shadow.

Unfamiliar voices followed, one after the other, separated only by the sound of applause. She participated in that as well, clapping her hands when necessary to avoid drawing attention to herself. And the whole time she was aware that he was sitting there. Right next to her sat someone who had the personality she so evidently lacked.

Someone who always made the right choice. Someone who had that trait so deeply engrained in his character that doubt never arose, not even in the presence of death when terror blinded reason.

She had turned her head to look at him once, wanting to know whether it was also visible in his face. Wanting to see how a person looked who was everything she had always dreamed of being, the person she could never be because what she had failed to do could never be made right. Her brother was dead forever, and she would always be the one who hadn't turned off the sauna and hadn't taken those two extra steps.

That night had revealed the deficiency in her character, and since then not a day had passed that she didn't feel it grating inside her. Her choice of profession, all her prestigious belongings, her way of driving herself relentlessly to obtain better results; all were a way of trying to compensate for the defect she carried inside her. To justify the fact that she was alive while he was dead. Through her struggle she had achieved much, but there was one fact she could never change: knowing that in the depths of her soul she was an egotistical and cowardly person. It was something you either were or you weren't. And after it was proven that that's what she was, she didn't deserve love either.

Even though she was still alive.

After the meeting she went to her room. The others had moved on to the bar, but she couldn't face it. Couldn't face the socialising and the small talk and pretending that everything was fine. She sat on her bed and weighed her mobile phone, still switched off, in her hand. She wanted so badly to hear his voice, but he would be able to tell that something was wrong and she wouldn't be able to explain. And the experience this afternoon had once again triggered all her doubts. He didn't know who she really was.

She was utterly alone; not even Thomas could share her shame.

The guilt. She had never allowed herself to mourn. Not deeply. Because how could she permit herself to do that? She had missed Lasse so terribly after she was left all alone with their mother. Missed him in a way she hadn't thought possible. He had always been there, and she had taken for granted that he would always continue to be there. There was nobody who could take his place. But her grief was so abject that it would desecrate his memory. She didn't have the right. Instead she did everything in her power to make her mother's loss more tolerable, tried to be happy and helpful, cheer her up as best she could. She envied her mother's right to indulge and wallow in sorrow without any obligations towards those who were still alive. Her sorrow was noble, genuine, not like Monika's, which served equally to hide the truth that was impossible to bear.

The betrayal. Horrified, she had realised that life outside their home would go on as if nothing had happened. Nothing was turned upside down or changed after the unthinkable happened. The same people were on the bus in the morning, the same programmes were on TV, and the neighbour was still adding an extension to his house. Everything continued without the rest of the world caring that he was gone, or even noticing. And her own life went on as well. The memory of him would one day lose its solid contours and fade; the emptiness would remain but the world would be changed so that the empty space he left would be less noticeable. The path he would have taken would grow narrower and narrower and finally vanish in obscurity, transformed into wondering about who he might have become and how his life might have turned out. And she could do nothing to prevent what had happened.

Nothing.

Success, admiration, status. Every day of her life she had been ready to trade all she had ever achieved for the opportunity to do it over.

Because what death demanded was unreasonable. What it demanded was that she should fully understand. And accept the inevitable truth. Never again.

Never again.

Never again, ever.

She ate in her room. Just before dinner she had called Åse and complained of a headache. Fifteen minutes later there was a knock at her door and there stood Åse with a tray full of food.

'I told the guru that you were eating in your room. Hope you feel better soon.'

She fell asleep the minute she lay down, and slept for almost nine hours. She slipped off into sleep to escape her guilty conscience at not ringing Thomas as she had promised. *Don't ever leave me alone with a silent phone again. I don't know if I could stand it.*

When she woke up she keyed in his number even though it was really too early.

'Hello?'

She could hear that he had just woken up.

'It's me . . . I'm sorry for not calling you yesterday.'

He didn't answer, and his silence scared her. She tried to think up an excuse but had none that was acceptable. And she didn't want to lie. Not to him. He had every reason in the world to say nothing. She knew far too well how she would feel if he was the one who went away on a course and didn't call.

I ask only one thing, and that's for you to be honest, that you tell me the truth so I'll understand what's happening.

She closed her eyes.

'Forgive me, Thomas. I had a tough day yesterday and afterwards I locked myself in my room; I couldn't even go to dinner.'

'Good grief. That sounds like a fun course. What was so tough about it?'

There was a hint of something in his voice, and she knew at once that what she had said was just making the whole thing worse. She had failed him by not calling and sharing her day with him, preferring to handle it on her own.

As usual.

She was going to wreck this too. Her cowardice would once again claim its due and rob her of what she wanted most of all. The only thing he required was honesty, and that was the one thing she was incapable of giving. Her secret would fester like a sore, keeping them apart. It was actually within reach, the dream that she had given up all hope of realising. No success in the world could measure up to the strength his love could give her. And yet it wasn't enough. She couldn't help the fact that she was not a heroic person, but at least she could muster the courage required to explain things to him.

As long as we're honest then neither of us has to be afraid. Don't you think?

How she had always wished for this, to stop being afraid.

She knew that she had to tell him, and what in the name of honesty did she have to lose? She would lose him in the end if she kept silent.

She had to take the risk.

But not now, not here on the phone. She wanted to be able to see his face.

'I'll tell you when I come home. And Thomas . . .'

In any case she had to confess to the one other thing that was so hard to say.

'. . . I love you.'

Friday and Saturday passed. Her decision to tell him was still firm and there was a sense of peace in having made up her mind. The intense pace of the course also helped to distract her. On Saturday evening, after too many lectures about visions and goals, effective delegation, and how to motivate your staff and create a positive work atmosphere, she sat down at one of the beautifully set tables in the dining room. Until then she had sat with Åse at every meal, and they had developed a real friendship. To say that Åse was a fresh breeze was an understatement; she was more like a hurricane that passed by each time you were near her. Monika liked her a lot, and she had already thought about inviting her and Börje to dinner sometime. She and Thomas. A couples' dinner.

If he stayed.

'Is this seat free?'

She turned round and there stood Mattias. Until

now they had only exchanged a few words; without thinking why she had chosen not to sit at his table at the previous meals.

'Of course.'

But she really wasn't happy about it.

'Your name is Monika, isn't it?'

She nodded and he pulled out the chair and sat down. On her right, where he had sat before.

On each plate was an intricately folded linen napkin, and Mattias studied the artistry for a moment before he demolished it and put it on his lap.

'That was a very strong presentation you gave. I haven't had a chance to tell you until now.'

Straight to the point. She had seen it before. People who had lived through great crises and been strengthened by their experience did not stoop to traditional polite nonsense. Wham!, right to the heart of the matter. Whether the people around them were ready or not.

'Thanks, yours was too.'

Åse came to her rescue. With her usual commotion she sat down in the chair across from Monika and immediately unfolded her napkin without so much as glancing at the artistic folds.

'God, I'm starving!'

With a scowl she read the little menu that decorated each bread plate.

'*Lax carpaccio*? You can starve to death eating that.'

Mattias laughed. Monika was uncomfortably aware of his presence. His entire existence was one big reminder.

Several other people sat down at their table, and soon all eight seats were taken. The mood became intimate. Forcing them all to reveal something about themselves during the introductions had been a brilliant move on the part of the course leader. After that, no concerns had seemed too private to share with one another. Monika already knew more about some of the participants than she knew about her co-workers. But they didn't know as much about her. And she wondered whether more people besides herself had altered the truth a bit when they had had the chance.

'How is your wife doing now, by the way?'

Åse was the one asking, and she directed her question to Mattias. She had long since wolfed down her *lax carpaccio* and was now spreading butter on a piece of crispbread while she waited for the entrée.

'Oh, she's doing quite well, actually. She'll never be completely the same, but enough so that everything functions. And she doesn't have pain anymore. If you met her and didn't know otherwise, you wouldn't be able to tell. It's more things like getting sore if she sits too long and stuff like that.'

'And your daughter, how old is she?'

Mattias lit up when she was mentioned.

'Daniella will be one in three weeks. It's strange, becoming a father. Being away from home for a few days has become really tough all of a sudden. A lot of things happen while you're gone.'

There was nodding and agreement all round the table, because everyone seemed to have small children who changed quite a bit in just a few days. Only Åse felt otherwise.

'I thought it was really great to get away from home for a while now and then when my kids were little. Just to be allowed to sleep through a whole night! But now that they're grown, I miss the sound of those little feet in the night.'

Åse had told Monika about her kids. A grown son and daughter who were the pride of her existence. The son had been born with no arms, and she had described her conflicting feelings after the delivery, and then her joy at the wonderful ability of children to adapt to any situation. Now that son had given her two grandchildren.

Monika took a gulp of wine and leaned back. She was missing Thomas. She shut off the noise around her and savoured the feeling. It was great to have a reason to feel this kind of longing. Her whole life she had hoped that someday she would have a chance to yearn like this. And now she finally did.

She suddenly realised that Mattias was talking to her.

'Excuse me, what did you say? I was somewhere else there.'

He smiled.

'I could see that. But it looked like it was a nice place, so don't let me disturb you.'

As if he hadn't disturbed her enough already. She felt instinctively that she didn't want to talk to him, but on the other hand she didn't want to seem uninteresting. If she were forced into a conversation now, it would have to be about something neutral.

'What kind of work do you do?'

There was almost a cloud of dust around that question, it was so boring, but Mattias wasn't about to be scared off.

'I've just started a new job as head of personnel for a large sporting goods store, not one of those big chains but an independent one. I've never been a boss before, so that's why they sent me to this course.'

He grinned.

'Not that I think it was actually necessary, since we only have six employees, but the owner of the store is a friend of mine, and he knows how bad our finances have been since Pernilla's accident. You know, the part I mentioned about not having any health insurance.'

She wanted to say something appropriate about how happy she was for his sake, but she wasn't going to lie anymore. Instead she said something about insurance companies in general, and he picked up on it right away and they were off on an interesting diversion. No matter how much she wanted to deny it, she had to admit that he was a very entertaining table companion, and for the next hour she had a great time, and she even laughed a few times. And how he talked about his wife! So full of love and loyalty – not ten minutes would pass during the conversation before he would mention her again. Quite naturally, she supposed, since she was part of his life. Monika wondered whether Thomas would ever talk about her in this way – whether she would ever be such a central part of his life, so natural and self-evident. Mattias told her about the difficult years after the accident, how it had brought them even closer together. With a laugh he told about how they tried to fill the emptiness left by their great passion for diving. How they tried one hobby after another, but since they couldn't afford to spend any money the choice was rather limited. He laughed the most when he described their brave attempts to take up birdwatching. How, after a day in a bush with only a magpie and two wagtails on their list, they were forced to admit that telling the anecdote would probably be more fun than ever doing it again. Later, in library books, Pernilla began reading about the history of Sweden, and after a while her interest in the topic became so intense that he began to think it was becoming obsessive. With a smile he confessed that she had also become a little too interested in Gustav II Adolf and the rest of those historical characters, but that it was probably all right because at least it didn't strain her back. And he told her how happy he was about his new job, which would finally make manageable the debts incurred during Pernilla's rehabilitation, not to mention the ongoing expense for all the chiropractors and masseuses that were necessary to alleviate her pain.

Someone clinking a glass brought all the conversations to a halt, and all eyes scanned the room for the source of the sound. The course leader had stood up.

'I just wanted to check that we're all gathered together. I have a question I'd like you to think about, and that is whether you might consider extending the day by two hours tomorrow so that we can squeeze in all the scheduled events. I'm afraid that, otherwise, we would have to cancel the stress management lecture.'

According to the programme the course was supposed to be over at lunchtime. She had promised to pick up her mother at three and drive her to the cemetery.

'All those who would consider staying please raise your hands.'

Almost everyone's hand went up. Åse's too. The only other person besides Monika at their table who didn't was Mattias. Åse noticed, remembered her responsibility as driver and lowered her hand.

'So you're in a hurry to get home?'

Monika didn't have a chance to reply before the course leader continued.

'It looks as though most of you don't mind staying, so that's what we'll do. As for now, I wish you a pleasant dinner.'

Åse had a frown on her face.

'Wait, I just have to check on something.'

She got up and left without further explanation. Mattias drank the last dregs from his glass.

'I'd like to skip the stress management and have a few free hours at home instead. I know the others I drove up here with are also in a hurry to get home.'

So he had shared a lift too. He must belong to the group that Åse had told her about when they first started their trip on Thursday morning. Monika decided that it was the first and last time she wouldn't bring her own car. If she ever drove to a course again, which under the present circumstances she strongly doubted, she would make sure she wasn't dependent on someone else. It was out of the question to call her mother and postpone the visit to the cemetery. She had already used up what little grace she had left.

Åse came back and sat down in her chair.

'No, it didn't work out, their car was already full. I thought you might be able to ride with the others from the city if you were in a hurry, because they're leaving early too. But it doesn't matter, I'll skip the stress management too.'

That part of the course was the reason Åse had come in the first place, and now it was Monika's fault that she would miss it. How she hated these eternal visits to the grave. She wished she could have told Åse that it didn't matter; that she would stay the extra two hours if it was important. But she knew what that would mean. Weeks of indignant silence as her mother managed to amplify Monika's guilty conscience, wordlessly accusing her of always thinking of herself first. And when her mother came so close to the truth, life was intolerable. Her only way out was to beg and cajole her to get things back to normal. She wouldn't be able to manage that now. Not now that she had decided to risk confessing everything to Thomas. It was either-or.

'I'd love to be able to say that I can stay, but I have to make a house call on a patient tomorrow afternoon.'

She felt herself blushing and pretended that she'd got something in her eye to have a chance to hide her face. She sat there on her chair, lying, and once more it was clear. She was incapable of making sacrifices, while Mattias never hesitated.

'If you're in such a rush to get home, you can take my place in the other car, so Åse can stay for the stress management. I can't imagine that Daniella will start talking precisely before four o'clock.'

It was hard to acknowledge the gratitude she felt.

'Are you sure?'

'Absolutely. I just wanted to go home, but it was nothing important. I'll stay and ride back with Åse.'

And so the decision was made.

Nothing had changed around them. Everything looked just as it had the moment before. Sometimes it's quite astounding how a crossroads that will change a person's life isn't noticed at the moment it appears.

10

She had stayed in bed for two days. Not for a second had she dared to sleep. The only times she managed to get up were to empty her bladder and open the balcony door for Saba. All her energy went into keeping the thoughts at bay. Like malicious insects they invaded her reality, and she flailed wildly to keep them off her. Vanja's memories and insinuations forced her again and again to the periphery of the world she had made her own. A flat of sixty-eight square metres or an illuminated circle of light with a sharply defined perimeter. A limited area formed by the interpretation of the truth that was tolerable. Out there everything was white. A white void where nothing existed. But now she found herself time after time standing at the very edge of the illuminated circle facing the whiteness, and suddenly she realised that something was moving out there, that there was more. In all that whiteness outside it was suddenly possible to discern shadows. Shadows of something that would not quite materialise but was coming closer and closer.

Vanja's letter was burned to ashes on the balcony. And yet it hadn't helped. Vanja was a mentally deranged woman who recounted events that had never happened, and distorted beyond recognition what might have occurred. All the other thoughts and speculations that had been recounted to Maj-Britt were so repulsive that she wished she had never read them. Even though her own relationship with God had been fairly strained, even non-existent, she definitely did not intend to blaspheme. And that was precisely what Vanja did! She blasphemed so terribly, and since Maj-Britt had read her words, she was guilty too. She had to get Vanja to stop sending those letters. Not even the consolation of stuffing something in her mouth remained as an escape for her. And during the past week that pain in her lower back had been so intense that it made her feel nauseous.

It was two days since she fell out of bed and Ellinor had rescued her. Today Ellinor would be coming back. Maj-Britt had decided during the night what she would do to be rid of her obligation and the hint of atonement that had resulted. She had already undressed. In only her underwear she now lay waiting for Ellinor to arrive. Once Ellinor saw her disgusting body she would back away in repugnance and lose her power. She would be ashamed of her reaction, which she would not be able to hide, and thus Maj-Britt would regain the advantage and her right to display her loathing.

Writing paper and a pen had been lying on the nightstand for twenty-four hours, right next to the note with Ellinor's mobile number, and no matter how much it went against the grain, she was forced to admit that it felt good to have that note lying there. If anything should happen again.

She detested that feeling.

The fact that Ellinor could offer her something that she didn't want.

Four crumpled-up attempts at letters lay on the floor. Saba had sniffed them curiously a couple of times before realising how pathetic they were and losing interest. Her hatred for Vanja was so strong that the words wouldn't come. What she had done was unforgivable. To crash into a world where she was not welcome and turn everything upside down. To lay claim to someone's time as if her warped opinions were worth any consideration whatsoever.

Maj-Britt reached once again for the pen and began to write:

Vanja,

I am writing this letter with a single purpose: to persuade you not to write letters to me!

That was good. That's how she should start. Actually, she also wanted to stop there, since that was the only thing she wanted to say.

Your speculations and thoughts do not interest me; on the contrary, I find them extremely repulsive.

She crossed out everything and wrote instead:

What you think and believe is your private business, but I would be grateful to be spared from sharing it. The fact that you presume the right to condemn my parents' faith, only then to surrender to something resembling a home-made heathen belief upsets me, to tell you the truth, and in view of . . .

*   *   *

'Hello!'

Maj-Britt quickly laid the pen and paper on the nightstand and pulled back the bed covers. She heard Ellinor hanging up her jacket on one of the hangers in the hall.

'It's only me!'

With great effort Saba managed to clamber over the edge of the basket to go and meet Ellinor. Maj-Britt heard the shopping bags being put down in the kitchen and Ellinor approaching the bedroom. Her heart beat faster, not from nervousness but from anticipation. For the first time in ages she felt calm, absolutely in a superior position. Her disgusting body was also her most powerful weapon. To expose it was to throw the viewer off balance.

Ellinor stopped short in the doorway. She seemed to want to say something but the words got stuck inside her lips. For a second Maj-Britt thought she had succeeded. For a second she managed to feel satisfied, but then Ellinor opened her mouth.

'Good Lord, you're a sight! We'll have to put some cream on that eczema right away.'

Maj-Britt hurriedly pulled up the covers to hide herself. The humiliation burned like fire. The feeling of nakedness overwhelmed her and she knew that she was blushing. It hadn't worked. The trick that always worked on the others had, as usual, not worked on Ellinor. Instead of gaining power and a safe distance, Maj-Britt had revealed her greatest shame, exposing herself and how wretched she was.

'Don't you have some lotion we can use? That must really, really hurt.'

Ellinor's agitation was unmistakable; Maj-Britt

swallowed and pulled the covers further up. She was defending herself from Ellinor's gaze, and felt just as vulnerable as she had that time when . . .

This vague sensation dissolved and vanished into whiteness. But something had approached and she was suddenly having a hard time breathing.

'Why didn't you say something? You must have had that for quite a while.'

Maj-Britt reached for the letter while trying to hide her naked arm as best she could under the covers.

'If we don't do something about this you're going to end up with open wounds. Please, Maj-Britt, let me take another look.'

This was unheard of. Not on her life! Never ever would she think of exposing herself to this person who didn't have the sense to keep her distance. Ellinor and Vanja. It seemed like the whole world had suddenly ganged up on her, had decided to break in and come after her at any cost.

'Get out of here and leave me in peace! I'm trying to write a letter and you're bothering me!'

Ellinor stood in silence for a while, looking at her. Maj-Britt kept her eyes fixed on the letter she was writing. Then she heard a little snort and, out of the corner of her eye, saw Ellinor back out of the room. Saba was still standing there but only for a moment; then she too turned her back on Maj-Britt and followed Ellinor.

Considering that you slaughtered your entire family and are sitting in prison for life, I don't really think I have any obligation to read your sick speculations! Your letters are disturbing and I say no thanks to any more letters from you. My family and I only want one thing – to be left in peace!!!!

Maj-Britt Pettersson

She wrote the address and without reading through what she had written she licked the envelope and sealed it. The sounds of Ellinor's movements in the flat were hard and angry, and it wasn't long before she appeared in the doorway again.

'I've put the food away in the fridge.'

She was clearly irritated.

'But I only bought meat, as you asked.'

Then she vanished again. Starting banging about with buckets and the vacuum cleaner, doing her duties. And Maj-Britt stayed in bed and realised that Ellinor had met her halfway yet again. Risking her job by ignoring all the regulations to please her. Maj-Britt covered her face with her hands. There was nowhere to flee to any longer. Her sanctuary had been invaded.

Suddenly, Ellinor was standing in the bedroom doorway. Maj-Britt had heard the front door open and, after a brief pause, close again. When the footsteps approached she had heart palpitations. Ellinor came over and sat down on the edge of the bed, down by Maj-Britt's feet where there was a little spot free. Saba left her basket and went up to her.

'My big brother was born with no arms. When we were little, I don't think it occurred to any of us that he was different, it was just natural because he had always been that way. Mamma and Pappa didn't make a big deal of it either. Obviously they were shocked when he was born, but they always made the best of the situation. He was the world's best big brother. Jesus, what games he could think up.'

Ellinor petted Saba on the head and smiled.

'It wasn't until he was a teenager that he understood how different he was. Like when he fell in love the first time and realised that he couldn't compete with boys who had arms and were like all the others. Who were "normal".'

Her fingers left Saba's neck and made a gesture in the air to indicate what she thought of the word 'normal'.

'My brother is one of those guys that all girls dream of meeting. Funny . . . smart . . . kind. He has a sense of humour and an imagination like no one I've ever met, arms or not. But then as a teenager there were no girls that even saw him, they just saw the space where his arms should have been, and eventually he did too.'

Maj-Britt pulled the covers up to her chin and hoped that this strange confession that Ellinor felt compelled to make would soon be over.

'And then when he realised that he would never become the man he dreamed of being, he became the opposite. Overnight he turned into an utter pig and nobody wanted to have anything to do with him. He was so awful that you didn't want to be anywhere near him. No one could work out why he was acting that way. Eventually he demanded that mother and father get him his own flat in a care home, but the staff could hardly cope with him there either. He was eighteen then. Eighteen years old and completely alone. He didn't want to see me or our mother and father, even though we were the only ones who really looked out for him. But I didn't care. I went there a couple of times a week and told him exactly what I thought. That he was a fucking self-pitying tosser who could go ahead and rot at that care home if that was what he wanted. He told me to piss off but I kept going to see him anyway. Sometimes he even refused to open the door. Then I would just shout through the keyhole.'

Good Lord, such language she was using! How was it possible to use so many swear words? Uneducated and vulgar, that's what she was!

Ellinor suddenly fell silent, and Maj-Britt presumed it was because she needed to catch her breath. Evidently not even she could keep up her inexhaustible torrent of words without oxygen. Too bad it didn't take long for her to catch her breath. Ellinor looked Maj-Britt right in the eye and continued.

'So, just keep sitting here, you fucking coward, and destroy your life. But don't think you're going to get rid of me. I'll be showing up here regularly to remind you what a fucking idiot you are.'

Maj-Britt clenched her jaw so tight it hurt.

'That was what I told my brother . . .'

Ellinor petted Saba's back one last time before she got up.

'Today he's married and he's got two kids, because in the end he couldn't stand my nagging. Is there anything special you'd like me to get next time?'

11

A new flame was flickering on the grave. She watched her mother's hands put back the burnt match in the box, for the umpteenth time. However many times it had been, she only knew it was far too many.

Her decision was final. She would tell Thomas the truth, for the first time in her life confess what had happened and what she had done. And not done. This time she wouldn't let the fear destroy everything. Not again.

The flat smelled stuffy and she was on her way over to the living-room window to open it when her mobile rang. She had just thought about calling him herself and would really have liked to first. Her mobile was in her handbag, and she went back out in the hall to retrieve it. An unfamiliar number showed on the display and it made her hesitate. He was the only one she wanted to talk to; she had absolutely no desire to get involved in a long conversation with someone else. But then she let her sense of duty take over.

'Hello, Monika here.'

At first she thought it was a wrong number, or someone trying to play a joke on her. A woman's voice she didn't know was shrieking from the phone, and it was impossible to understand what she was saying. She was just about to hang up when she suddenly realised it was Åse. Secure, matter-of-fact Åse who with her mere presence had helped her through the past few days. Åse belonged back at the course, and her voice sounded odd here in her airless flat.

'Åse, I can't hear what you're saying. What's happened?'

Suddenly she was able to catch a few words. Something about coming over, she was a doctor. She didn't have a chance to be scared. Not now. For a few seconds there was silence. She heard the sound of sirens approaching. Only then did she feel the first glimmer of trepidation. Nothing alarming, only a hint of heightened alertness.

'Åse, where are you? What's happening?'

The sound of panting. Shallow, rapid breathing, like a person in shock. Unknown voices in the background, a wordless wall of sound yielding no information. She made her decision unconsciously. Something about what was going on made Monika slip into her professional role.

'Åse, now listen to me. Tell me where you are.'

Maybe Åse could hear the change in her voice. Maybe that was just what she needed. Authority. Someone telling her what to do.

'I don't know, somewhere on the road . . . it just crashed, Monika . . . I didn't see it, I didn't even have a chance to hit the brakes.'

Her voice cracked. The secure, self-confident Åse started sobbing desperately. Monika's professional persona closed around her even tighter as she acknowledged

Åse's desperation. Like armour it slid into place, protecting her from becoming emotionally involved.

'I'm coming.'

It was as a doctor that she drove off. Her thoughts were running along an objective path that required only information; no emotional nonsense was allowed to penetrate. No hasty conclusions before verifying reliable facts. After every curve she expected to see an oncoming ambulance, but none appeared. Her phone rang once and she saw his name on the display. He didn't belong here right now, he would have to stand aside; right now she was a doctor on the way to an accident site.

She could see it a long way off. At the far end of a long row of flashing blue lights against a greyish-blue horizon. All the way up to the top of a hill. Emergency vehicles had parked every which way, and were now confined behind traffic cones and red-and-white plastic tape. A small queue of traffic had formed, and a policeman did his best to let it trickle past on the hard shoulder. Monika pulled over to the side and parked, her car's emergency lights flashing. It was a hundred metres to the cones and she jogged along-side the cars. All that existed was the accident site up ahead. It was the only thing that meant anything. Step by step she came closer. She was almost there but a fire engine was blocking her view. She slipped under-neath the red-and-white tape.

'Hey, this area's blocked off.'

'I'm a doctor and I know Åse.'

She didn't stop. Didn't even look at him. Just searched

the surroundings for data. The rear of the red van was sticking up from the ditch. BÖRJE'S CONSTRUCTION. Normal letters, perfectly legible. A cable from a tow-truck was fastened to a hook on the van and was slowly pulling the vehicle from its position.

Firemen, police, ambulance crew. But something was wrong. A disturbing calm prevailed in the midst of the visual chaos. No one but herself seemed to be in a hurry. A fireman was calmly and methodically packing up his tools. A paramedic in the front seat of the ambulance was filling out a report.

Then she caught sight of Åse. Leaning forward, her face in her hands, she was perched at the rear of the ambulance. Next to her sat a female police officer with an arm around her shoulders, and the expression on the woman's face took Monika's breath away. She stood motionless in the midst of it all. Someone came up and said something but she only saw a mouth moving. Only a few steps to go. More than two this time but just as difficult for her to take. What she wanted to know was concealed down there in the ditch, but the taut cable grew shorter and shorter and at any moment would reveal the full extent of the catastrophe. She put her hands in front of her eyes. In the darkness she heard that they had found the elk some distance away, in the woods. The engine noise from the tow-truck stopped, but she kept her hands where they were, not wanting to know.

She was back there again. Once again she stood there, very much alive, and it was all her fault. It was impossible to change a thing, to undo it; she had set the trap and Mattias would never get out.

She opened her eyes and something finally fell to

pieces inside her. Where the passenger side had been there was only crumpled sheet-metal and a piece of shattered window.

And then she saw the mangled body that was impossible to identify but should have been hers.

12

Hi, Majsan!

I suppose I should begin by thanking you for your letter even though I have to admit it didn't make me very happy. But that probably wasn't the point either. You can calm down, I won't continue our correspondence alone, but this letter seems necessary to send. It will be the last one.

I beg your pardon if I offended you with my speculations in my last letter, it was really not my intention. On the other hand, I don't intend to apologise for actually HAVING *the opinions that I have. If there's one thing I'm tired of it's people who think they're so perfect in their faith that they feel entitled to look down on that of others and condemn it. And in no way am I condemning your parents' faith as you said. I'm merely exercising my right to believe otherwise. I plan to keep thinking about things and see whether I can find some good new answers, because maybe we can agree that what we've had so far has not created a particularly pleasant world. As I read in a book the prison chaplain gave me: 'All great inventions and advances have been made based on a willingness to admit that no one has been correct so far, and then put all correctness aside and rethink things.'*

As far as my 'home-made heathen belief', the simplest

answer is that our beliefs are very different, but that's completely okay by me. The Bible says quite eloquently that only God has the right to judge. Most of us have thoughts about eternity now and then. I don't understand why we human beings, as soon as we find something to believe in, have to run out and try to convince everyone else that we're right, as if we don't dare believe anything by ourselves but have to do it in a group for it to count. Then it suddenly becomes important for everyone to believe the exact same thing, and how do we achieve that? Well, we set up laws and rules that fit into the framework we have erected, and to be included we have to adapt. We quite simply have to stop asking our own questions and hoping to find any answers, since the right ones have already been written down in the laws of the religion. That must be the purest coup de grâce *for all types of development, don't you think? Then it's merely a matter of power, isn't it? In any case, that's what religion is about for me, because no religion was created by any God but by us humans, and history has shown us what people think they can do in religion's name.*

As I read over what I've written I realise that I've probably offended you in this letter too. I just want you to know that I am also a believer, but my God is not as judgemental as yours. You wrote that considering the fact that I'm serving a life sentence, there is no reason to read my sick speculations. Well, that may be, but I still want to conclude by telling you my version of why I'm sitting here today.

Do you remember that I always dreamed of being a writer? In my childhood home that was just about like dreaming of becoming king, but our Swedish teacher (remember Sture Lundin?) encouraged my writing. After you and I lost contact I moved to Stockholm and there I studied to be a journalist. Not that any of my articles have become immortalised, but I made my living as a journalist for almost ten years. Then I met Örjan. If you only knew how much time I've spent trying to understand why I fell so crazily in love. Because looking back it's inconceivable that I closed my eyes to all the warning signs. And there were certainly more than enough of them. The strangest thing of all is that I felt safe with him, even though everything he said and did should have made me feel exactly the opposite. Even then he was drinking far too much, and he always had money without ever telling me where it came from. Now I realise that it was because he reminded me of my own father and that the 'security' came from recognising my own childhood. I felt at home with him and knew exactly how to act. I never fell in love with any of those 'kind, friendly' men I had run into over the years, because they made me feel insecure. I never knew how I should act with them. Örjan didn't like women to be too independent, and I didn't have to work because he could provide for us with his money. And fool that I was, I tried to adapt myself to his wishes, and about six months after we met I quit my job. Then it was my friends he didn't want me to see, and to avoid a fight I stopped communicating with them. Of course that made them stop calling me as well. In only a year I lost all contact with the outside world and had become more or less a slave. I won't tire you with the details, but Örjan was a sick person. He wasn't born that way, of course, but he had grown up in an abusive home and kept on living the way he had been taught. It began

almost imperceptibly. A nasty little comment now and then that gradually became so commonplace that I got used to it. Finally I ended up believing those things, and I began to think he had a right to say them. Then he started hitting me. There were days when I could hardly move, but it served me right, he said, because then he knew where he had me. But he knew that anyway, because I wasn't allowed to leave the house without asking his permission, which he never gave.

Now this is the hard part, telling you about my dear children. They are still in my thoughts, and so many times I've gone over and over all the 'if onlys'. But 17 years and 94 days ago, I saw no other solution than to take them with me into death, to save them from the hell we lived in, and it was MY *fault they were born into it. I could see no other solution. I was so bone-tired of always being afraid. Maybe only a person who has lived in constant fear for a long time can understand how it feels, and how powerless you become in the end. What happened to me was not important, but I could no longer stand watching my children suffer. I was so ashamed of myself and everything I had let happen that I didn't dare seek help. I was guilty too, after all! I hadn't stopped him in time! I had seen how he went after the children, and I hadn't dared stop him then either. I desired nothing more than death, but I couldn't leave my children with him. At that point my brain was so mixed up that there seemed no other way out. I saw it as our only salvation. I gave them sedatives and suffocated them in their beds. It was never my plan to kill Örjan, but he came home early unexpectedly, and found me in the children's bedroom. I've never been so scared in all my life. I managed to get out and run to the kitchen, and when he caught up with me I had a butcher's knife in my hand. Afterwards I emptied the petrol can that Örjan kept in the storeroom and lay down with the children and waited. What I remember most strongly about those hours was how I felt when I heard the flames crackling downstairs, slowly but surely destroying our prison. For the first time in my life I felt total peace.*

The worst moment I've ever had was when I woke up in the hospital a couple of weeks later. I'd survived, but my children were with him on the other side. I survived, but it means nothing to me that I got my life back.

I'm not trying to make excuses for what I did, but it's some solace to me to try to understand the reason why everything turned out the way it did. My punishment is not being locked up here. My punishment is a thousand times worse and will last the rest of my life. For every second that remains, it's seeing my children's eyes before me, remembering the looks they gave me when they saw what I was doing.

There is no hell after death to which your God can condemn us. We create our own hell here on earth by making the wrong choices. Life is not something that 'happens to us', it's something that we create and shape ourselves.

I will follow your wishes and stop writing to you. But I must write one more thing before our paths part once again. If it's true that you have pain somewhere, then I think you ought to have it examined, and for safety's sake you ought to do it as soon as possible.

You know I'm here if you need me.

Your friend,
Vanja

13

'Thanks for coming.'

Åse was sitting on the sofa in her cosy living room, and Börje had placed a blanket over her shoulders. Upset but exceedingly grateful, he now sat next to her with one rough fist holding her hand. He used the other hand to wipe his eyes from time to time.

Doctor Monika Lundvall had remained standing. Confident and professional on the surface, desperately holding herself together, she had made it through the past two hours despite her inner inferno. She spoke with the police and ambulance crew, asked the firemen what they were planning to do with the van, and, finally, full of information, drove Åse home and relayed all the essential facts to Börje. But there in the comfortable living room, Doctor Lundvall, for safety's sake, had chosen to remain standing. If she sat down in one of the inviting easy chairs and permitted herself to relax, she was afraid that Monika the young girl would manage to break out. Locked in behind her rational façade young Monika was wandering about amongst the wreckage, desperate and terrified. At any moment she might escape, and in that event Doctor Lundvall would have to leave. She was just about to begin her parting comments when she heard the front door open.

'Hello?'

It was Börje who answered. 'Hello, we're in here.' He looked at Doctor Lundvall and explained, 'It's our daughter Ellinor. I asked her to come over.'

She appeared in the doorway, a young blonde woman with a purposeful step. She had only one goal in sight, her parents there on the sofa. She didn't even see Doctor Lundvall as she passed her.

'How are you feeling?'

The daughter sat next to Åse and leaned her forehead on her shoulder. In Åse's lap all their hands met: mother, father, child. A close-knit family. They would stick together through thick and thin, all their lives.

'There's no danger, but she isn't quite able to talk about it yet. They gave her a sedative.' Börje's voice was calm and low but his tenderness radiated from his hands as they rearranged the blanket that had slipped down from Åse's shoulders. Then he stroked Ellinor's hair.

Monika was kicking and biting inside. Throwing herself again and again at the fragile shell that held her captive. Doctor Lundvall was having a hard time breathing, and things were starting to get urgent, very urgent.

'If it's all right with you I'll be leaving now.'

It was there in her voice. At any rate she could hear it herself. But maybe the people on the sofa were too immersed in their own gratitude to hear it. Börje got up and came over to her.

'I don't know what else to say but thank you. It's a bit hard to find the words right now.'

'You don't have to say a thing.'

She took his outstretched hand and pressed it

fleetingly, then turned to Åse, who was looking at her with a bottomless sorrow in her eyes.

'Goodbye Monika, thanks for coming.'

When she heard her name the façade cracked, but she managed to make it out to the car before the scream came.

The car knew the way better than she did. Incapable of making any decision at all, she suddenly found herself parked outside the cemetery. Her legs walked the familiar paths and the flame that had been lit in another time flickered in its holder. She sank to her knees. Rested her forehead against the cold stone and wept. For how long she didn't know. Darkness had fallen and the cemetery was empty; she and a headstone and a candle flame were all that were left. All the tears that had been stifled with such obedience and restraint over the years came welling up in a frenzy. But they gave her no comfort, they only drove her deeper into despair. There was nothing she could do. A woman had lost her beloved and a child had lost her father, and she just sat there, alive and of no use to any human being. Once again she was the one who had survived and had managed to kill someone who should have been allowed to live. If there was a God, his ways were truly inscrutable. Why take Mattias and let her go? Two people depended on him. His new job would have been their salvation. And Monika herself was expected to continue on as if nothing had happened. Just drive home to Thomas with all her opportunities in safe custody and begin to build her future. Return to her expensive possessions and her well-paid job and pretend she was caring for human lives, when the truth was quite the reverse.

She straightened up and read the words she had looked at thousands and thousands of times.

My beloved son.

So natural, always so present. And always so out of reach.

She placed her palms over his name on the cold stone, and in the depths of her heart she had only one desire.

That she once and for all might trade places.

14

Maj-Britt was sitting in her easy chair and the TV was on. Programme after programme rolled by; as soon as any thought managed to penetrate the images flickering past, she would click to another channel. The only thing she hadn't managed to do was escape the pain in her back. After she read Vanja's words it was more pronounced than ever.

Before she retreated to what the TV had to offer, she had managed to confirm the conspiracy. She hadn't said a word about her sore back, yet Ellinor had seen through her with her prying eyes. And she was the only one who could have told Vanja.

Everything would have returned to normal if it hadn't been for Ellinor. If Vanja sent any more letters, Maj-Britt could escape by refusing to read them, and what she had already been forced to read she could stifle with TV and food if she just made an effort. But then there was Ellinor. Pleasant little Ellinor, who in reality was in league with Vanja; it was no accident that they had both forced their way in at the same time and almost succeeded in overturning her world. Behind her back they had forged their evil plans; what they were after was incomprehensible. But hadn't life always been this way? Against her. And she had never understood why.

And then there was the shame. The fact that Vanja knew that she had lied about her life and knew that she was sitting there in the flat, dependent on home help for her continued existence. And the fact that through her lies Maj-Britt acknowledged what a failure she actually was.

She heard no word of greeting when the door opened and then shut. Saba raised her head and wagged her tail a little, but stayed lying there next to the balcony door. She wanted to go out, but Maj-Britt hadn't been able to get up.

She heard footsteps approaching, and when they stopped she knew that Ellinor was in the room, only a couple of metres behind her.

'Hi.'

Maj-Britt didn't reply, just turned up the volume with the remote. Ellinor appeared at the edge of her field of vision, on her way to Saba and the balcony door.

'Do you want to go out?'

Saba got up, wagged her tail, and squeezed her heavy body through the open door. Outside the wind was blowing, and when a gust tore the door wide open, Ellinor shut it again. Maj-Britt saw her standing there with her back to the room, gazing out through the glass door.

Something was different. Ellinor's usual chatter was gone, and there was an oppressive air about her that Maj-Britt found unpleasant. A confusing change that she had to handle in some way. Ellinor stood by the door for a long time, and when she suddenly started speaking it happened so unexpectedly that Maj-Britt gave a start.

'Do you know anyone in this building?'

'No.'

She answered even though she considered refraining. Ellinor's new behaviour scared her, especially since she now knew that the person behind the friendly façade was concealing her real intentions.

'There's a family living across the courtyard; the father died yesterday. In a traffic accident.'

Maj-Britt didn't want to know, but she could picture that father, the one who used to go out and push his daughter on the swing, and that mother who seemed to be in some kind of pain. As usual she was being informed of things that she didn't want to deal with, things she hadn't asked to be told. She changed the channel.

Ellinor opened the door to let Saba back in, and then Maj-Britt heard her go out to the kitchen. On the TV three people's faces were being transformed using plastic surgery and make-up, and Maj-Britt succeeded in keeping up her defences for a long time. But then Ellinor was back. Maj-Britt acted as if she didn't notice, but out of the corner of her eye she saw Ellinor come into the room with something in her hands and sit down on the sofa. She sat down with the self-confidence of someone who knows she can get back up from it at any time.

'I thought I'd mend this.'

Maj-Britt turned her head. Ellinor was sitting with her dress in her lap, one of the two she always wore. This one had started to come apart a bit at the seams. Maj-Britt wanted to object but knew it needed to be mended. The alternative was to take the trouble to have a new one made, and she shuddered at the memory of the last time she did that. Or sew it herself? Impossible. For some reason the thought had never crossed her mind, not even in the days when she could have managed it physically. She didn't even own a needle and thread. But to watch Ellinor's fingers moving over something that usually clung tight against her skin was repulsive.

Maj-Britt pressed her lips together and went back to watching TV. But then she reacted to a movement from the sofa. Ellinor had stretched her arm up over her head. Maj-Britt never had a chance to think. She never had a chance to figure out rationally what made her turn all her attention to Ellinor; at the same time she was filled with a terror so strong that she suddenly couldn't move. She stared at Ellinor. Between her hands was an arm's length of sewing thread, and Maj-Britt couldn't defend herself. As if bewitched she followed the thread down to the spool in Ellinor's left hand. And then it was too late. The memory forced its way in from the whiteness. Like a shade pulled down, with the spring stretched to the breaking point, and suddenly it rolls up with a snap. Maj-Britt sat as if paralysed and looked at what was taking shape before her. What had so long been repressed but which without warning had come back through all those years. And there was nothing she could do to protect herself.

Nothing.

She was sitting in the kitchen, but it wasn't her kitchen at home, it was the kitchen that belonged to the pastor and his family. She had been there for almost two weeks, sleeping in a cold room with two beds, and the pastor's wife had slept in the other bed. She had not been left alone for a minute, and she had not been allowed to leave the room for a second except to go to the bathroom, which she was allowed to do each morning and evening. But not alone; the door was always left ajar, with the pastor's wife waiting outside.

It was a big wooden house, and she didn't recognise the sounds that inhabited it. Particularly at night. The sounds would creep unexpectedly into the room through the dark floorboards, and then she was glad she wasn't alone. In the daytime she would have liked to be left in peace for a while. But that wasn't allowed. She was being punished and she knew it was necessary, knew that it was for her own good. It was meant to help her after the game they had played in the woodshed. It was supposed to help her drive out those thoughts that came over her and made her do things she didn't want to do.

Now she was sitting on a kitchen chair and watching the pastor's wife setting out cups and plates on a tray. She felt that she ought to help but didn't dare ask. In spite of the fact that they had spent every minute together the past few weeks, except for an hour now and then when the pastor himself had taken over, they didn't really know each other. Much of the time had passed in silence, and the rest they had devoted to prayers and the Holy Scriptures. Maj-Britt felt gratitude towards the woman who was willing to sacrifice so much of her time to help her, but she was also scared of her. It was quite clear that the pastor's wife didn't actually like her but was acting out of a sense of duty. It was something that had to be done.

Maj-Britt inhaled the sweet fragrance of newly

baked buns and glanced towards the window. It had grown dark outside. So many times she had stood on the other side, outside the fence down by the road, and looked towards the lovely house. Gazing at the illuminated windows and fantasising how it would feel to be allowed inside. In there on the other side, in the house that was so full of love that God Himself had chosen the man who lived there to preach His Word. And now she was sitting here in the kitchen. They had taken her in, opening their home and offering their time to help her and her parents to set everything right. She was filled with tremendous gratitude. They knew what she had done, and the first days she hadn't dared look any of them in the eye. She had done all she could to try and repress the memory, how she was standing in her knickers with her trousers pulled down in front of Vanja and Bosse when her father had discovered them. Bosse had been the doctor and Vanja the nurse, and they hadn't intended to do anything else, just pull down their pants one by one. The worst shame was admitting to herself that she had felt a tingling in her chest from excitement and curiosity. She hadn't even felt sick when Satan had seized hold of her, but she didn't dare admit to this. It would have to remain a secret that she would hide away forever, although it was impossible to keep any secrets from God. And maybe it was also impossible to keep any secrets from the pastor, because each night he had read to her: 'Though evil is sweet in his mouth, and he hides it under his tongue, though he spares it and does not forsake it, but still keeps it in his mouth, yet his food in his stomach turns sour; it becomes cobra venom within him. He swallows down riches and vomits them up again; God casts them out of his belly. He will suck the poison of cobras; the viper's tongue will slay him.'

And she had prayed all the more fervently that God might help her. For two weeks she had prayed to be chosen as the others in the Congregation had been chosen, that she too might be enfolded by His love and grace. She didn't ask to understand, she knew that His ways were inscrutable, but she wanted so much to be able to obey! For Him to force her into submission so that she might be cleansed.

Now she was sitting here in the kitchen and didn't know why, and since she didn't have anything else to do she began to pray, the way she had learned she should do the past two weeks. The Lord's grace must not be misused.

At regular intervals she heard the sound of china cups being returned to their saucers and the *pling* of the spoons as they slid beside the cups. The pastor's wife had gone into the dining room and it was from there the sounds were now finding their way back to the cupboards from which the cups had been taken. Everything felt homey and safe. The aroma of the buns and the sound of the table being set. She had been let out of her room, and that must mean she had fulfilled their expectations, that they had been successful in curing her and now trusted her to rejoin the rest of humanity.

'Maj-Britt, can you come here?'

She got up at once and went towards the dining room, from which the pastor's wife had called. She was standing behind a chair at the end of the table, resting her hands on the chair back. It was a beautiful room. A large brown table in the centre of the room with twelve chairs around it and then four more along two of the walls. The third wall was covered by a gigantic china cabinet which matched the rest of the furniture, and by the fourth wall stood Maj-Britt in the doorway to the kitchen.

'You can go and sit down there.'

She pointed to one of the chairs along the wall. Maj-Britt did as she was told. She wondered why the table was set with such lovely china and whom they were expecting for evening coffee. She almost felt a little thrill of anticipation, it had been so many days since she had seen anyone but the pastor and his wife. And she wondered whether Mamma and Pappa would come. Then she could show them that she had done penance and that their prayers had not been in vain. She could almost feel a hint of pride, nothing big or boastful, but more a slight sense of relief. She had managed to get rid of everything inside that had led her astray. Of course she had received help, but she was the one who had done it. Through her fervent prayers she had finally succeeded in taking control of the thoughts that were constantly slipping beyond the rules she had laid down for herself. God had finally listened and come to her aid. In His grace He had forgiven her and would not let her suffer anymore. Or her parents either, they would also be spared.

The pastor's wife went over to the china cabinet and pulled out the drawer beneath the centre door. With her back to Maj-Britt she rummaged around and there were sounds of small things being moved about. Then she turned round with a spool of thread in her hand. A wooden spool with pure white thread on it.

'Now take off your skirt and underwear.'

Maj-Britt didn't understand at first what she had said. For a fleeting moment there was still only the smell of freshly baked buns and hopeful trust. But then the terror came sneaking over her. Her clothes didn't need mending. What was the pastor's wife going to use the thread for? Maj-Britt inspected her skirt, looking for a seam that had split, but she couldn't find any.

'Just do as I say and then sit back down on the chair.'

Her voice was kind and friendly. It didn't match her words, and Maj-Britt didn't understand what she meant even though she understood what she said. Then the pastor's wife raised her arm above her head and pulled out an arm's length of thread. On the way down she glanced at her watch.

'You'll have to hurry so I have time to finish setting the table.'

Maj-Britt couldn't move. Take off her clothes, here in the pastor's dining room? She didn't understand, but she could see that the pastor's wife was beginning to get impatient and she didn't want to make her angry. With trembling hands she did as she was told and sat back down on the chair. The shame burned like fire. With her hands in her lap she tried to hide her secret place. Her clothes lay in a heap next to the chair, and it was hard to resist the urge to pick them up and run away.

The pastor's wife came over and knelt down by her side. Then she took the thin thread and tied it tight to her right leg; right below her knee she tied it with a simple knot before she tied the other end to the chair leg.

'We're doing this for your own good, Maj-Britt, so you will understand the seriousness of what you did.'

She took the pile of clothes and stood up.

'It's out of love for you that your parents and all of us in the Congregation are trying to help you find your way back to the true path.'

Maj-Britt was shaking. Her body was trembling with humiliation and fear. He had duped her, He had not forgiven her, only lulled her into false hope, biding His time.

'Out of love, Maj-Britt, even though it might not seem so now, but when you grow up you'll understand. We only want to teach you how you should have felt when you exposed yourself to that boy. And how you will feel for eternity if you don't change your behaviour.'

She folded up the clothes in a neat pile and went out to the kitchen. Maj-Britt sat utterly still. She was terrified that the thread would break if she moved.

Time passed. Totally white time, without seconds or minutes. Only moments that moved forward and grew more and more meaningless. There above the table hung a large crystal chandelier. The prisms blinked and shimmered. And the table was so beautifully set. Delicate white cups and two platters filled with the loveliest cinnamon buns. And it was good that she was tied to the chair, because otherwise she might have eaten all of them before the guests even arrived. But they seemed to be doing so now. She heard the doorbell and voices murmuring but not what was said, but it was surely none of her business. The draught from the front door made the prisms in the crystal chandelier glitter like gemstones. Imagine being able to sit and gaze at such a fantastic creation. And now all the guests were coming into the room, in pairs or one by one they sat down at the table; the Gustavssons and the Wedins, and there came Ingvar who led the choir. And the Gustavssons had their Gunnar with them, look how big he had grown. They were all wearing such fine clothes, suits and dresses, as if they were going to church on Sunday. Even Gunnar had a suit on, although he was only fourteen. It was dark blue and he was wearing a tie and looking so grown-up. And then Mamma and Pappa. It was so nice to see them because it had been quite a while, but they didn't have time for her now and she understood that. The pastor had begun to talk about things that had to do with the Congregation, and now the buns were passed around and coffee poured into the cups. But her mother looked so sad. Several times she wiped her eyes with a handkerchief and Maj-Britt would have liked to go over and comfort her, tell her that everything was all right, but she stayed in her chair and she knew that was what she had to do. They had done this for her sake, even though they were pretending she didn't exist. Only Gunnar stole a glance at her from time to time.

And suddenly everyone was leaving. They all got up and went out together to the hall and then all the voices stopped. Only a quiet murmuring which she had become accustomed to hearing from the pastor and his wife, and then time became divided into seconds again.

She was sitting on a chair in the pastor's dining room with no clothes on the lower part of her body, and now she understood how she should have felt.

And she had learned that she would never again do what she had done.

The next day she was allowed to go back home. They let her take the spool of thread as a reminder. It was put on the shelf in the kitchen so that she would never forget.

15

Some things were not meant to be kept by anyone. The sole purpose of some things was merely to pass by and remind certain people of what they would never be able to have. To make sure that they didn't neglect their hopeless longing, or simply forget about it. Or maybe even learn to live with it and feel a sense of contentment. No, when people didn't want to acknowledge their need it was time to remind them, give them a little taste, refresh their memory a bit.

Thomas had been that sort of person.

A reminder who had stopped by to tell her how life could have been. If she hadn't been someone who lived at the expense of others.

Someone who had squandered her right to life.

Everything was shattered. The dizzying feeling of hope had run out, dissolved in the limitless hopelessness that replaced it.

She was sitting on a chair by the living-room window. Her lovely living room where no price tag had hindered her, everything hand-picked, exquisite and meticulously arranged. A source of pride for the one who lived there and a challenge to those who came to visit.

Offering comparisons.
Making them want to have these things, too.
All her fine, expensive things.

All the lamps in the flat were turned off. A cold glow from outside painted a wide path on the parquet floor but stopped halfway up the bookshelf on the opposite wall. Just above the shelf with the glass sculpture, the sculpture that many of her fellow doctors also owned. Not quite identical but almost, which showed that they had both the means and the taste.

She had turned off the sound on her mobile phone. He called several times but she didn't answer. She just sat by the window in the living room, which was growing less and less important as the hours went by.

It had been easy to fill up the rest of her time. TV, gym, late nights at work. As a single person she was used to organising her time precisely, avoiding gaps when everything would come to a standstill and the worrying could take over. It was tough enough just to be alive. And when it got to be too much it was always possible to find consolation in a new jumper, an expensive bottle of wine, a pair of new shoes, or something to make her home even more perfect. And she could afford it.

All she was missing was a life.

And no fortune in the world could fix what had now been shattered.

The contours of the path of light at her feet grew vaguer and finally dissolved as dawn broke. A new day was approaching for her and for everyone else who was still here. But not for Mattias. And for Pernilla and their daughter the hopeless journey towards an acceptance of life's injustices and its unfathomable purpose was now starting.

The first day.

She closed her eyes.

For the first time in her life she wished she had some religious belief. Merely a tiny handle to hold on to; she would gladly exchange every object in the room for the ability, for a single second, to possess even a scrap of faith. A feeling that there was some meaning, some higher cause that she didn't understand, a divine plan to rely on. But there was none. Life had once and for all proven its total absurdity; no amount of effort had any effect at all. There was nothing she could believe in. No consolation to be had.

Her world was built on science. Everything she had learned, made use of, trusted in, had all been precisely weighed and measured and confirmed. She accepted only exact and rigorously worked experimental results whose validity could be proven. That was where security could be found. And here, in the perfect home. Things that could be seen and evaluated. That was how everything acquired worth. But now it no longer sufficed, not now that everything was toppling and shrieking for a purpose. It would be enough to have a sense of a tiny, tiny 'maybe' – the slightest hint, if only to enable her to set aside all logic and feel reassured.

The telephone rang. The usual four rings before the answering machine started.

'It's me again. I just wanted to say that I . . . I don't really know if I can handle things being this way . . .

I would be extremely grateful if you'd call me and explain what's happening, so I know. Surely that's not asking too much . . . or is it?'

She felt nothing when she heard his voice. He was calling from another life that no longer had anything to do with her. She had no right to it now. And she had no obligation to him; it was to others that she was indebted.

The telephone stood on the windowsill. She picked up the receiver and dialled his number, those familiar digits, for the last time and he answered immediately.

'Thomas.'

'This is Monika Lundvall. You left a message on my answering machine and asked for an explanation, so I just wanted to say that I don't want us to see each other anymore. Okay? Bye.'

She went out to the kitchen and poured water in the coffee-maker, pressed the button and stood there. It was twenty to seven. Somewhere not far away a little one-year-old would be waking up, and she no longer had a father. She went into her office, found the phone book and looked up his name. There was only one Mattias Andersson, but at least he was there. In the next issue he would be deleted. She wrote down the address and stored the number in her mobile. She went back to the kitchen. Steam was hissing out of the coffee-maker and she looked at the green button that showed the coffee was ready. She ignored it. Instead she went out to the hall and put on her coat.

It was a U-shaped block of flats, four storeys tall. On the lawn in the middle there was a little fenced playground with a bench, some swings and a sandbox.

The door with their number on it was on the left. She stopped for a moment and took in the atmosphere, searching for signs that indicated someone in the building had recently been struck by a tragedy. A sound made her turn her head. On the ground floor of the right wing a balcony door opened, and the fattest dog she had ever seen stuck its head out through an opening in the railing. It looked at her for a moment before it lost interest and contemplated the steps to the lawn.

Monika began walking towards the outside door she knew led to the Anderssons' stairwell. With each step she was conscious that she was walking in his footsteps, that it was his path she was taking. She put her hand on the black plastic doorknob. She closed her eyes and left her hand there. It was a strange thing about doorknobs. She never thought about them, but when she returned many years later to buildings she had lived in before, her hands always remembered the feel of the doorknob. They never forgot. Hands had their own ability to store memories and knowledge. This doorknob had been his. His hands had borne the memory of its shape, confidently pulling open the door each time he came home, and he had had no inkling on Thursday when he left that he would never do it again.

She opened the door and entered the stairwell. On the left wall, behind glass, was a list of the names of the residents, in white plastic capital letters on blue felt. The Anderssons' flat was on the third floor. Slowly, she started up the stairs. She let her hand glide up the banister and wondered if he also used to do that. The morning sounds seeped out of the doors she passed, muffled voices, someone running water. Further upstairs a door opened and was locked with a rattling bunch of keys. They met on the stairs between the second and third floors. An elderly man wearing a coat and carrying a briefcase said a polite 'hello'. Monika smiled and returned the greeting. Then he was gone and she took the stairs up to the third floor. There were three doors. The Anderssons lived behind the middle one. That's where they were.

A child's drawing was taped over the letter-box. Monika bent closer. Incomprehensible lines and curlicues drawn every which way with a green felt pen. Red arrows came out of the curlicues, and at the other end of them someone who could write had interpreted the artist's work: 'Daniella, Mamma Pernilla, Pappa Mattias.'

She moved her hand close to the door handle, letting it hover above without touching, wanting merely to experience the feeling of being really close. At the same moment Daniella started to cry inside, and she quickly pulled her hand back. The sound of another door being opened somewhere in the stairwell made her hurry back down the stairs and out to her car.

But now she knew where they were.

He was waiting outside her flat when she came home. Sitting in the deep window seat on the landing. She saw him before she took the last steps up the stairs, and her feet slowed down but didn't stop entirely. She walked straight past him and up to her door.

'I thought I made myself clear on the phone. I don't have anything else to say.'

She had her back to him, and her fingers were

searching for the right key. He didn't reply, but she felt his gaze on the back of her neck. She unlocked the door and turned round.

'What do you want?'

He looked tired, with dark circles under his eyes and stubble on his chin. She wanted nothing more than to throw herself into his arms.

'I just wanted to see you say it.'

Monika shifted impatiently from one foot to the other.

'Okay. I don't want us to see each other anymore.'

'You don't have any intention of telling me what happened?'

'Not a thing. I just realised that the two of us don't fit together. It was a mistake from the beginning.'

She took a step in towards her flat and started to close the door.

'Did you meet someone else?'

She stopped in the midst of her motion, thought for a second and realised that that was precisely what she had done.

'Yes.'

The noise he made sounded like a snort. Instinctively she had a need to defend herself; if a person snorted she had earned his contempt.

'I've met someone who really needs me.'

'And I suppose I don't, in your opinion.'

'Maybe you do, but not as much as he does.'

She shut the door and cut him out of her life. And she knew that every word she had said was true. She had met someone else; Thomas didn't have to know that he was now dead. Mattias's weighty responsibility lived on, and it was her duty to take over now.

That was the least she could do. It was impossible to undo things, so the only thing left was to try and set right as much as she could. By allowing herself a relationship with Thomas she had attempted to grab for herself the happiness to which she had no right. What had happened to Mattias was the final rebuke. The only thing left to do was subordinate herself. Her sacrifice was nothing compared to the devastation she had wrought.

She went into the bathroom and washed her hands. She heard the street door slam behind him out in the stairwell, and not until she saw her face in the mirror did she realise she was weeping.

Her fingers punched in the speed-dial number for the head of the clinic. For the first time in the eleven years she had worked there she called in sick. Since she didn't want to infect any of the others, they should probably count on her being off for the rest of the week. Then she went into the living room and let her index finger glide along the spines of the books. On the third shelf she found what she was looking for; she pulled out the book then, grabbing an apple from the fruit bowl on the table, went to lie down on the sofa, and turned to the first page of *The History of Sweden*.

16

She was standing in front of the mirror in her room, twisting and turning and trying to see how she looked from the back as well, but to see that view she had to contort her body in the most awkward way. The way she looked there in the mirror wouldn't be how she looked at all when she was facing straight ahead. And it was important how she looked from the back, because that was the direction he usually saw her from. But not today. Today it was going to be special.

She had been allowed to borrow Vanja's new blouse. Vanja, the only one who knew, the only one she had dared tell. It was so strange with Vanja. They had been friends for years but she really didn't understand why, they were such an improbable pair. Vanja was so brave; she didn't hesitate a second to say what she thought and she would stand up for her views in any situation. Maj-Britt knew that she had a tough time at home. Her father was a notorious figure in the community; everyone knew about him, and especially about his alcohol problem. But Vanja didn't let herself be dragged down by the gossip. If she so much as caught an inkling of any condescension she would strike back like lightning. She punched like a verbal boxer. And Maj-Britt would stand beside her and admire her, wishing that she could speak so frankly, and that, above all, she also dared stand up for her own point of view.

No God was mentioned in Vanja's home, but Satan was invoked frequently. Maj-Britt had a hard time deciding what she should think. She didn't like swear words, but in some strange way it was easier to breathe at Vanja's house. It was as though God had made a little refuge here on earth, and it was situated right in Vanja's home. Even when her father was drunk and sat muttering to himself at the kitchen table and Vanja was allowed to say the most awful things to him without being interrupted, even then it was easier to breathe there than it was at her own house. Because in her home God was ever-present. He noticed the slightest change in behaviour, He saw every thought and action, and later He would weigh them against any possible merits. No locked door, no lamps turned off, no solitude could shield her from His sight.

As long as Maj-Britt could remember, Vanja had been her porthole to the world outside. A little opening where fresh air streamed in from somewhere else. But she was careful not to show at home how much this connection really meant to her. Her parents would have preferred that she associate only with the young people in the Congregation, but while they hadn't done much to hide what they thought of Vanja, they hadn't expressly forbidden Maj-Britt to see her friend. Maj-Britt was deeply grateful. She didn't know how she would manage without Vanja. Who else could she turn to with her problems? She had tried asking Him, but He had never answered.

Vanja might not think that Maj-Britt had any real

problems, everything seemed perfectly normal, but Maj-Britt knew better. It was because of all those thoughts and the foul and loathsome things they led her to do that God didn't want her. She was terrified of going blind, or of hair growing on her palms. That's what happened to people who did what she'd been doing, but she'd never dared talk to Vanja about all that.

She heard her mother working in the kitchen. Dinner would soon be ready; after they ate, Maj-Britt was supposed to head off for choir practice. It was no longer the children's choir, which she had left when she turned fourteen. The past four years she had been singing in the church choir. Altos and sopranos and basses and tenors. She was a talented singer and had managed to convince her parents to let her sing in the parish choir, not just the one at her own Congregation. They'd agreed eventually on condition that she sing with the Congregation choir if there were ever a day when both choirs needed her.

He sang first tenor, and he did it with bravura. The choirmaster always chose him if the piece contained difficult passages.

'Göran, you take the high G. The rest of you can stay on the third if you can't reach that high.'

He had noticed her, she knew that, even though they had only exchanged a few words. She always sat with the other sopranos during the break, but sometimes their eyes found their way to each other amongst the altos and basses, just flicking over each other for a moment before shyly moving on. But this evening would be different. This evening there would be no choir to hide their glances, it would just be the two of them and the choirmaster, because they had been chosen as soloists for the Christmas concert. It was a tremendous feeling to have been selected. And especially with Göran.

As she approached the church she saw him from a distance. He was standing on the church steps reading his sheet music. Unconsciously, she slowed down because she didn't know if she could dare be alone with him. If the choirmaster was late they would be left standing there on the steps, and what would she say then? He raised his eyes and caught sight of her, and with her heart pounding she kept walking. He smiled as she approached.

'Hi.'

She greeted him quickly and then lowered her eyes. She felt as if she were burning when she looked directly at him, and her eyes kept flicking off in other directions.

There was a long silence, a little too long to be comfortable. They both stood there, leafing through their sheet music as if they had never seen it before. Maj-Britt realised in amazement that Göran, who otherwise was always used to being noticed and listened to, didn't seem to know what to say either.

'Have you had time to practise at all?'

She replied gratefully. 'Yes, a little bit. But I think it's quite hard without accompaniment.'

Göran nodded, and the next moment he said the strangest thing, which in the days to come she would keep repeating to herself.

'I'm almost more nervous about singing in front of just you than I am about the entire Christmas concert.'

He smiled shyly. And with the sound of the choirmaster's footsteps on the gravel path her eyes dared meet his for the first time.

'So we'll take it from the top without the introduction, and then you go directly to the second verse after the refrain.'

Maj-Britt had sat down on the edge of one of the pews. Although Göran had admitted how nervous he was, she felt thankful that she didn't have to go first. He wasn't the only one who was nervous. In a daze she sat there, astonished at his words. She watched him in front of her, following his slightest movement; he was so talented and so handsome. With his eyes closed he began to sing. His sonorous voice was jubilant, and she felt a chill run down her spine. Göran had laid his jacket on the pew next to her, and she secretively stuck her hand in it and touched the lining at the very spot that usually pressed against his heart. No man had ever been allowed to come near her, but now a little stray desire fluttered inside her chest. She wanted to be close to him, assure herself that she held his interest, because when he wasn't there he was still present inside her heart. It was inconceivable that a person who had never had anything to do with her life could suddenly fill her whole being.

When he was finished singing he opened his eyes and looked at her. In a moment of silent understanding they both knew.

Afterwards she told Vanja all about it. Again and again she told her what had happened and what he had said and in what tone of voice and how he had looked when he said it, and Vanja listened with patient interest and offered precisely the interpretations that Maj-Britt wanted to hear. In the evenings she lay in bed and counted the hours to the next choir practice when she would get to see him again. But nothing turned out the way she had hoped. Mixed in with the rest of the choir they were again like strangers to each other. Göran was the centre of attention as he always had been, and there was not a trace of the uncertainty he had revealed to her. The few times their eyes met they lost contact at once and drifted off amidst the choir.

Vanja had given her some good advice.

'But, Majsan, you have to talk to him, you know that, don't you?'

But what was she going to say?

'Well, think up something you know will spark his interest. What else does he do besides sing in the choir? There must be something else he's interested in. Or drop something right in front of him so you have a reason to start talking. You must have some sheet music or something that you could drop . . .'

It was easy for Vanja; she was so brave. But Maj-Britt's sheet music was almost glued to her hands, and to make it flutter all the way over to the tenors would take a miracle. But He who performed such things was very clearly not interested. And Vanja was not satisfied. After each choir practice she rang to hear all the details.

Finally, Vanja herself solved the problem. Through shrewd detective work amongst her friends, she ascertained that Göran was interested too. So, when pressuring Maj-Britt didn't work, she took the matter into her own hands. One evening she rang Maj-Britt and asked her to come down to the kiosk. Maj-Britt didn't want to, and for the first time Vanja got angry and called her a bore. Maj-Britt didn't want to be a bore, especially not in Vanja's eyes, so in spite of her parents' surprise she put on her jacket and headed off. She wasn't allowed to use make-up, but she usually borrowed some from Vanja, carefully wiping it off before she got home. She hadn't even brushed her hair before she set off, and she fretted about it as she neared the kiosk. Because there he stood. Right next to the ice-cream sign by the bicycle stand. He smiled and said hi and she did too and then they just stood there, shy and embarrassed, and it felt just like it did the time they had stood on the church steps. Vanja never showed up. Or Bosse, the boy that Göran was waiting for. Maj-Britt kept glancing at her watch to assure him that she really was waiting for someone, and Göran did his best to keep the conversation going. They talked exclusively about the two people who hadn't shown up yet. And why they hadn't. It took them twenty minutes before they clicked. Bosse was Vanja's cousin, and as the seconds ticked by Maj-Britt realised that Vanja probably had no intention of appearing at the kiosk that evening either. She had decided to give fate a little push. Göran was the first to figure it out.

'If Bosse doesn't come and Vanja doesn't either, what do you think we should do?'

Maj-Britt had no idea. What do you do on a Tuesday evening when you're eighteen and have just realised that your secret love is no longer secret, and that he is standing on the other side of the bicycle stand and has also just been revealed? At that precise moment it began to rain, and neither of them really wanted to leave. It wasn't a little drizzle, it was a cloudburst that came out of nowhere. The kiosk owner had started to close and was winding in the awning that would have protected them.

It was Göran who first started to laugh. He tried to hold it back, but then the rain came down so hard that there was no resisting it any longer. Maj-Britt began to laugh too. Liberated, she let him take her hand and they ran off together under the cover of his jacket.

'We could go over to my house for a while if you want.'

'Can we do that?'

They had stopped on the other side of the road where they normally would have parted. He seemed surprised by the question.

'Why not?'

She didn't answer, only smiled uncertainly. Some things were so simple for other people.

'I have my own entrance so you don't even have to meet my mother and father if you don't want to.'

She hesitated a tiny, tiny bit, but then nodded and let herself be drawn into all the wondrous things that were about to happen.

As he had described, he had his own entrance. A door at the end of the house and behind it a stairway to the second floor. He even had a little cooker with two burners and an oven, almost like his own flat. And why shouldn't he? He was twenty years old, after all, and could have moved away if he'd wanted to. She could have moved out too, for that matter. Yet, the idea was inconceivable.

He opened a cupboard in the hallway and gave her a fluffy towel to dry off the worst of the rain. He hung her soaked jacket on the back of a chair and moved it in front of the heater. He had only a small hallway and one room with a dark-brown bookcase, an unmade bed and a desk with a chair. The sound of a TV in his parents' part of the house revealed that you could hear every sound in the house.

'I wasn't sure if you would come.'

He went over to the unmade bed and tossed the spread over it.

'Would you like some tea?'

'Yes, please.'

He picked up a saucepan from the cooker, which stood on the low bookshelf.

'Sit down if you like.'

He disappeared into the hall, going to what she assumed was a bathroom, as she heard water running and the clink of china. She looked around to find somewhere to sit. It was either the chair with the wet jacket on it by the heater, or the unmade bed. She stood where she was. But after he had made tea and she held one of the mismatched cups in her hands and he asked whether she wouldn't like to sit next to him, she complied. They drank their tea and he did most of the talking. He told her about his future plans. He wanted to move away and maybe apply to the music college in Stockholm or Gothenburg. He was tired of this provincial town. Hadn't she, who sang so well, ever thought about doing something with her voice? She let herself be swept along by his dreams, amazed at all the possibilities he suddenly conjured up. Even though she was eighteen and an adult, the thought had never entered her mind that there were alternatives to those the Congregation regarded as acceptable. She had never realised that being an adult meant that she was a grown-up with the right to make her own decisions about her life. There was only one thing she knew for sure at that moment: she didn't want to be anywhere else than where she was right now. In Göran's room with an empty teacup in her hand. Everything else was unimportant.

And after that evening everything was as it should be. Months went by and outwardly everything looked the same. But inside a change was stirring. A reckless curiosity was emerging which began to question all limitations.

No God in the world could have anything against what she finally was able to experience. Not even her parents' God.

But for safety's sake it was best that her parents didn't find out a thing.

17

Seven days after the accident Åse called. The only time Monika had left her flat was when she drove her mother to the cemetery and then stopped by the bookshop to buy more books. She was almost up to the nineteenth century, and no detail of Swedish history had been too insignificant to memorise. Learning facts had never been a problem for Monika.

'I'm sorry I haven't called before now, but I haven't really felt like doing anything. I just wanted to thank you for coming, Monika. I didn't dare call Börje at home because he's already had a minor heart attack and I didn't know whether he could handle a phone call like that.'

Åse's voice sounded tired and flat. It was hard to believe it was the same person.

'I was happy to do it.'

There was a pause. Monika kept reading about the crop failures of 1771.

'I drove out there yesterday.'

'To the scene of the accident?'

She turned a page.

'No, to see her. Pernilla.'

Monika stopped reading and sat up on the sofa.

'You drove out there?'

'I just had to, I never could have lived with myself

otherwise. I had to look her in the eye and tell her how sorry I am.'

Monika put down her book.

'So how was she?'

There was a long sigh.

'It's all so ghastly.'

Monika wanted to know more. Get every detail out of Åse that might be useful.

'But how was she?'

'Well, what can I say? Sad. But composed, more or less. I think she's been taking sedatives to get through the first few days. But that little girl . . .'

Her voice broke.

'She was crawling around on the floor and laughing and it was so . . . it's so awful what I've done.'

'It wasn't your fault, Åse. When an elk appears like that you don't have a chance.'

'But I shouldn't have been driving so fast. I knew that there weren't any wildlife fences on that part of the road.'

Monika hesitated. None of it was Åse's fault. It had all been fate. Except that the wrong person was sitting in the passenger seat.

There was a silence and Åse collected herself. She sniffled a few times but stopped crying.

'Mattias's parents were there for a couple of days, but they live in Spain so now they've gone back. Pernilla's father is alive but apparently suffers from dementia and is in some home somewhere, and her mother died ten years ago, but she was getting help from the Council. Some volunteer crisis group that comes over and takes care of her daughter so she can get some sleep.'

Monika listened with interest. A volunteer crisis group?

'Which crisis group was it, do you know?'

'No.'

She wrote down CRISIS GROUP???? under her notes about Jacob Magnus Sprengporten and underlined the words several times.

'I was so afraid that she'd be angry or something but she wasn't. She even thanked me for being brave enough to come over. Börje and Ellinor came along, I didn't dare go alone. She was so grateful to find out all the details about how it happened; she said it helped to know.'

Monika could feel her body stiffen.

'What sort of details?'

'About the accident itself. How it was at the accident site. And how he had been during the course. I said that he had talked a lot about her and Daniella.'

Monika needed to know more about those details that Pernilla had been told, but it was a hard question to ask. Åse left her no choice. She did her best to try to make the question sound natural.

'Not that it makes any difference, but . . . did you say anything about me?'

There was a brief pause. Monika was on tenterhooks. What if Åse had managed to ruin everything?

'No . . .'

She was staring into space. Then she got up and walked towards the computer in her office; she was halfway there when Åse asked the question.

'But how are *you* feeling now?'

She stopped. Her eyes fixed on the wall above the computer screen. Åse had broached the question so cautiously, almost timidly, as if she scarcely dared utter it.

'How do you mean?'

She sounded sharper than she intended.

'Well, I just mean that I thought you might have known that . . . or maybe you had thought that . . . but there really isn't any reason for . . .'

For about half a minute Åse did her best to try and erase her question in a long ramble about unrelated trivia. Monika stood quite still. Her guilt belonged to her; it was nobody else's business. But the question made her see that Åse had also recognised it and that it was absolutely essential to keep Åse away from Pernilla. She couldn't risk having Åse running over there and sooner or later revealing that everything was actually Monika's fault.

'Are you still there?'

Monika replied at once.

'Yes, I'm here. I was just thinking.'

'I don't know quite what to do. I'd like so much to help her in some way.'

Monika sat down at the computer and logged on to the Internet, going to the Council's home page. She typed 'crisis group' in the search box and got a hit at once. She scanned the screen quickly. The hibiscus on the windowsill needed water. She went over and pressed her finger into the dry soil.

'The fact is, Åse, that I think the best thing you can do for her is leave her alone. There's nothing you can do. I'm telling you this as a doctor because I have experience with these matters. You have to try to distinguish between what's good for her and what's really only for your own sake.'

Åse was silent and Monika waited. She wanted to have Pernilla to herself. She was her responsibility and no one else's.

Åse sounded almost bewildered when she continued.

'Do you really think so?'

'Yes. I've been through this before in similar cases.'

Silence again. She pinched off a dry leaf and headed for the kitchen.

'Try to get hold of yourself, Åse, your family needs you. What happened can't be undone, and the best thing you can do is to try and get on with your own life and realise that nothing was your fault.'

She went over to the worktop and opened the cupboard concealing the rubbish bag. She crumbled the dry leaf in her hand and let the pieces fall amongst the rest of the rubbish.

'I'll call you in a few days and see how you're doing.'

And then they hung up.

But Monika never would call. It would be Åse who rang next time.

Monika was in a bad mood after their conversation. Things were happening there in Pernilla's flat that were beyond her control. It was time to make the next move. Time to step into her new role in earnest. She went out into the hall and put on her coat and boots.

In the car she felt relieved, now that she was on her way. The thing was always to pick the direction that was most difficult; after she had chosen a goal the rest was merely a matter of taking action. And she was good at that. Her task had pushed out the hopelessness inside her, and now she was filled with resolve. Everything had taken on meaning again.

She didn't hesitate when she went in the main door this time, just checked the doorknob's shape with her hand and knew that it would soon feel like an old acquaintance. She continued past their door and halfway up to the fourth floor, pausing only briefly, with her ear against the door panel when she went by. Everything was quiet inside. She sat down on the stairs, folding her coat in half under her for protection from the cold stone. An hour passed. Every time she heard someone coming she stood up and pretended she was on her way up or down, whichever seemed the most natural. One time the same man came back who had left an hour earlier and they agreed with a smile that they had to stop seeing each other like this. Monika had just folded up her coat to sit down again when the door finally opened.

She was completely out of sight and saw only the feet of the person who came out. Women's shoes. The door was closed without anything being said, and the stranger's feet headed for the stairs. Monika followed. The woman was in late middle age with her hair up and wearing a beige coat. When she reached the main door Monika had caught up, and she smiled when the woman held the door open for her. She thanked her and walked to her car.

She had already saved the number on her mobile; copied from the Council's home page.

'I'm calling about Pernilla Andersson, whom you've been helping the past few days.'

'Ah, yes, of course . . . yes, that's right.'

'She asked me to ring and thank you so much for the assistance and tell you that you don't have to come anymore. She has friends who are taking over now.'

The man in the crisis group was glad that they had been of use and asked her to tell Pernilla not to hesitate to call again if she needed any further support or help. Monika didn't think it would be necessary, but thanked him politely for the offer.

It was important that it be done correctly.

Really important.

She sat in her car for half an hour before she returned to their door. She stood there for a minute, breathing quietly, then scrupulously assumed her professional role, although leaving her top button undone. She was there as a friend, not as a doctor. It was as both Monika and Doctor Lundvall that she had to fulfil this task, but she needed her professional demeanour. Because what she was now about to do required more than her private persona.

She knocked lightly on the door, not wanting to wake anyone who might be sleeping. When nothing happened and a long time had passed, she knocked a bit harder, and then she heard footsteps approaching.

Just listen. Don't try to comfort her, just listen and be there.

She had attended several courses about how to deal with people suffering from grief.

The door opened. Monika smiled.

'Pernilla?'

'Yes.'

She didn't look the way Monika had imagined. She was short and slim with short dark hair. She was dressed in grey jogging trousers and a knit jersey that was much too big.

'My name is Monika, and I'm from the crisis group.'

'Ah, I didn't think anyone was coming today. They said they were short-staffed.'

Monika smiled even more broadly.

'We worked it out.'

Pernilla left the door open and went into the flat. Monika took the first step over the threshold. She could feel it at once. Feel the relief. It was as if something was suddenly released, and for a second she was worried that it would make her weak again. Just to see Pernilla with her own eyes, form her own picture of her face and be allowed into her presence made everything easier to bear. She could accomplish something here. Make everything less unforgivable. But she had to proceed cautiously, couldn't be in too much of a hurry; Pernilla had to be given the chance to understand that she could be trusted. That Monika was here to help her, and solve all her problems.

She hung up her coat and left her boots by the door. There were several pairs of men's shoes there. Gym shoes and Oxfords that were much too large to fit Pernilla's tiny feet. Left behind, never again to be needed. She passed a bathroom door with a little red ceramic heart on it and continued into the flat. The kitchen was to the right, and at the other end of the hall was an entrance towards what seemed to be the living room. She looked around carefully, not wanting to miss a single detail in her effort to get to know the woman who lived here. Her taste, her values, the sort of qualities she preferred in a friend. She would take as much time as was needed; the only hurry was to sort out the most dangerous traps. If Pernilla rejected her she would be lost.

Pernilla was sitting on the sofa, leafing through a newspaper, seemingly without interest. Daniella was nowhere to be seen. On an old chest of drawers with a stripped finish stood a burning candle in a brass candlestick, and the glow fell over his broad smile. The photograph had been enlarged and put in a glossy gold frame. Monika looked down at the floor when he met her gaze, wanting to get out of his field of vision, but his accusing eyes had a view of the whole room. There was no escape. She could feel him watching her suspiciously and questioning her presence, but she would show him; over time he would learn that she was his ally and that he could trust her. That she wouldn't deceive him again.

Pernilla put down the newspaper on the chest of drawers and looked at her.

'Seriously, I think we can manage by ourselves this evening. I mean if you're short-staffed.'

'No, there's no danger of that. Absolutely none.'

Monika wondered uneasily what was expected of her, what the others from the crisis group had done to make themselves useful. But she couldn't think of anything before Pernilla went on.

'I don't want to seem ungrateful, but, to be quite honest, it's beginning to be a bit tiresome always having strangers here in the flat. Nothing personal, of course.'

Pernilla gave a little smile, as if to minimise her words, but the smile never reached her eyes.

'I really think I need to be alone for a while.'

Monika smiled back to conceal her desperation. Not now, not when she was so close.

Then Pernilla threw out the lifeline that Monika so urgently needed.

'But if you could just help me take down something in the kitchen before you go.'

Monika felt the fear subside; all she needed was a way in, a little opening to be able to demonstrate the value of her presence. She gratefully accepted the assignment.

'Of course, no problem, what is it?'

Pernilla got up from the sofa and Monika noticed the grimace she made when her back straightened. Saw her twist her right shoulder forward in an attempt to be rid of the pain.

'It's the smoke alarm in the ceiling. The battery is going dead, so it keeps beeping.'

Monika followed Pernilla into the kitchen. Quickly looked around to learn some more. Mostly things from Ikea, lots of pictures and notes on the refrigerator, some ceramic objects that looked home-made, three historical portraits in simple frames over the kitchen table. She resisted the temptation to go over to the refrigerator and read the notes. That would have to come later.

Pernilla pulled out a chair and set it underneath the smoke alarm.

'I have a problem with my back, and raising my arm above my head is simply impossible.'

Monika climbed up on the chair.

'What sort of problem do you have with your back?'

An attempt to break the ice. They didn't know each other. Starting now Monika would forget everything she already knew.

'I was in an accident five years ago. A diving accident.'

Monika twisted the alarm box off the holder.

'That sounds serious.'

'Yes, it was, but I'm better now.'

Pernilla fell silent. Monika handed her the alarm. Pernilla picked out the battery and went over to the counter. When she opened the cupboard Monika glimpsed cleaning supplies and a pull-out recycling bin.

Pernilla turned round and Monika realised that she was expecting her to leave now that she had finished her task. But she hadn't finished. Not by a long shot. Monika turned to the portraits on the wall.

'What a lovely portrait of Sofia Magdalena. It was Carl Gustav Pilo who painted it, wasn't it?'

She could see that Pernilla was surprised.

'Yes, it could be. I'm not really sure.'

Pernilla went over to the portrait to check whether there was a signature, but apparently couldn't find one. She turned to Monika again.

'Are you interested in art?'

Monika smiled.

'No, not in art particularly, but in history. Especially the history of Sweden. You pick up a few artists' names in the process. I go through periods when I get almost fanatical about reading history books.'

Pernilla gave a little smile, and this time her eyes began to sparkle a bit.

'How strange. I'm really interested in history too. Mattias often used that very word. That I was almost fanatical.'

Monika stood silently, relinquishing the initiative. Pernilla looked at the portrait again.

'There's something consoling about history. Reading

about all these destinies that have come and gone. At any rate it's helped me gain a little perspective on my own problems, I mean all the trouble with my back after the accident and all.'

Monika nodded with interest, as if she were actually following along. Following along intently. Pernilla looked down at her hands.

'But now I don't know.'

She paused for a moment.

'How there could be any consolation in history, I mean. Other than that he's dead like all the rest.'

Just listen. Don't try to comfort her, just listen and be there.

Silence. Not only because of what she had learned in her courses, but because she couldn't think of anything to say. She glanced furtively at the jumble on the refrigerator door. She wanted so badly to have a closer look. Try to find more ways into Pernilla's life.

'He had to choose between this and what he had on when he died. When he was packing, I mean.'

Pernilla stroked the big woollen jumper she was wearing. Pulled up the collar and pressed it against her cheek.

'I did a big load of laundry the day before he died. Emptied the whole laundry basket. So now I don't even have the smell of him left.'

Just listen. But they hadn't said much at those courses about how to act to be able to withstand everything you heard.

It was Daniella who rescued her. A newly awakened discontent was audible from the room next to the kitchen. Pernilla let go of the collar and left. Monika took three steps over to the refrigerator and quickly began looking through the collage. Family photos. Coupons from a pizzeria. A strip of pictures of Mattias and Pernilla from a photo booth. Several incomprehensible drawings by a child. Some clippings from a newspaper. She had barely managed to read the headline of one of them before Pernilla returned.

'This is Daniella.'

The child hid her face against her mother's neck.

'She's just woken up but she'll be wide awake soon.'

Monika went over to them and put her hand on Daniella's back.

Daniella pressed her face even harder into her hiding place.

'We'll have to say hello later after you've had time to wake up.'

Pernilla pulled out a kitchen chair and sat down with Daniella on her lap. Once again the feeling that she expected Monika to leave, as she had asked her to do. But Monika wanted to stay a bit longer. Stay here where it was possible for her to breathe.

'What an elegant ceramic bowl.'

She pointed to a bowl on the windowsill.

'Oh, that. I made it myself.'

'Really?'

Monika went over and took a closer look. Blue and thrown a little askew.

'Really very fine. I once took a pottery course too, but I haven't had a chance the past few years. My job takes up too much time.'

That wasn't even a lie. She had taken ceramics as an option in high school.

'That one is really crooked. I only saved it as a

reminder that I had to stop ceramics when I injured my back. I just couldn't sit still very long anymore.'

Pernilla sat looking at the bowl.

'Mattias liked that one too. He said it reminded him of me. I wanted to throw it out but he absolutely insisted we keep it.'

Each time his name was spoken Monika could feel her own heartbeat. How her pulse quickened, signalling danger. Daniella had come out of her hiding place and sat looking at her. Monika smiled.

'I could take her outside for a bit if you like, so you can have a little peace and quiet. I notice there's a playground.'

Pernilla leaned her cheek against her daughter's head.

'Would you like that, sweetie? Do you want to go outside and swing a little?'

Daniella raised her head and nodded. Monika felt the panic subside. Her heart calmed down and fell back into its normal rhythm. She had passed the first test.

Now all she had to manage was the rest.

18

There was blood in the toilet when she peed. She had discovered it several days before, but it may have been going on for longer than that. It was a long time since her periods had stopped, so she knew it meant that something was wrong. But she couldn't deal with it. Not that too. She tried to drive it into all the whiteness, but the boundaries were no longer there. Everything that had been kept outside at a safe distance had returned and taken shape in a sharp cone of light, and it left Maj-Britt with a sadness that was too much to bear. So a little blood in her urine didn't matter much. Everything was still intolerable.

Vanja was right. The images in her memory had neither been invented nor distorted, and her black words on white paper had forced all of Maj-Britt's emotional memories to return. She was back in the midst of the terror. She had partially sensed it when it was actually happening, but she couldn't fully understand it.

Because you don't do that to your child.

Not if you love her.

That would have been easier to forget.

She stood by the balcony door and looked out across the lawn. A woman she had never seen before was pushing a child on a swing. She recognised the child. It was the girl who used to be there with her father and sometimes also with her mother, who always seemed in some sort of pain. She wondered if that was the family Ellinor had told her about, the family with the father who had died in a car crash a little while ago. She looked towards the window where she had seen the mother standing, but it was empty.

A week had passed since everything that no longer existed had suddenly reappeared. She knew that it had happened because of Vanja. And because of Ellinor. For seven days Maj-Britt had tried giving her the silent treatment. She had come and gone but Maj-Britt hadn't said a word. She had done her chores but Maj-Britt had pretended she didn't exist. But she needed to know. The questions were growing stronger with each day that passed, and now she couldn't stand living in uncertainty any longer. The terror was still strong enough, and the threat she felt from both of them was more than she could handle. How did they know each other? Why had they suddenly decided on a concerted attack? She needed to know what their plan was so that she would have a chance to defend herself. But what was it she was supposed to defend? The only thing they had achieved by forcing Maj-Britt to remember was to rob her of all incentive.

To defend something.

But she had to find out what that something was.

She heard the key in the door and then Ellinor's greeting as she hung up her jacket. Saba appeared in the bedroom doorway and went to meet her. Maj-Britt heard them greeting each other and then the sound of Saba's paws on the parquet floor when the dog went back in and lay down. Maj-Britt stood there by the window and pretended not to notice that Ellinor looked at her on her way to the kitchen. She heard her put down the shopping on the kitchen table, and at that moment she made up her mind. This time she wasn't going to get away. Maj-Britt went out in the hall, felt Ellinor's jacket to make sure that her phone was in one of the pockets. She mustn't have it on her. Because now Maj-Britt was going to find out everything that was going on.

She stood there and waited. Ellinor came out of the kitchen with a bucket in her hand and stopped when she saw her.

'Hi.'

Maj-Britt didn't reply.

'How are things?'

Ellinor waited a few seconds before she sighed and answered herself.

'Fine, thanks, how are things with you?'

She had adopted this annoying habit during the past week. Creating her own conversations instead of putting up with Maj-Britt's silence. And it was astonishing how many words that skinny girl's body could contain. Not to mention the answers she supplied on Maj-Britt's behalf. Astonishing was the word. She walked around in her deceitfulness with no shame in her body. But now there would be an end to that.

Ellinor opened the bathroom door and disappeared from view. Maj-Britt heard the bucket being filled with water. It was only three steps. Three steps and then Maj-Britt slammed the door.

'What are you doing?'

Maj-Britt leaned her whole weight against the door and watched the door handle being pressed down. But the door couldn't be budged. At least not by such a tiny creature as Ellinor, when a mountain was standing on the other side and holding it shut.

'Maj-Britt, stop it! What do you think you're doing?'

'How do you know Vanja?'

There was silence for a few seconds.

'Vanja who?'

Maj-Britt shook her head crossly.

'You can do better than that.'

'What do you mean? Vanja who? I don't know any Vanja.'

Maj-Britt stood silent. Sooner or later she would have to confess. Otherwise she'd have to stay there in the bathroom.

'Maj-Britt, open this door. What the hell are you up to?'

'Don't swear.'

'Why not? You've locked me in the goddamn bathroom!'

So far she was only angry. But when she understood that Maj-Britt was serious, an uneasiness would come creeping in. Then she would find out what it felt like. How it was to find yourself in the midst of a piercing, paralysing fear.

And to be utterly at someone else's mercy.

'Oh . . . you mean that Vanja Tyrén?'

There now.

'Exactly. You're a clever idiot.'

'I don't know her, you're the one who does. Open the door now, Maj-Britt.'

'You're not getting out of there until you tell me how you know her.'

The stabbing pain in her lower back almost made her black out. Maj-Britt leaned forward in an attempt to relieve the pain. Sharp as an an icepick, it dug through layer after layer. She was breathing fast through her nose, in and out, in and out, but it refused to relent.

'But I don't know Vanja Tyrén. How would I know her? She's in prison.'

She needed a chair. Maybe it would get a little better if she could only sit down.

'What's this all about? Did she say we know each other, or what? If she did, she's lying.'

The closest chair was in the kitchen, but then she'd have to leave the door, and she couldn't do that.

'Come on, Maj-Britt, let me out and then we can talk about this, otherwise I'll call security.'

Maj-Britt swallowed. It was hard to speak when it hurt so much.

'Go ahead. Can you reach your jacket out in the hall?'

It was silent on the other side of the door.

Maj-Britt could feel her eyes filling with tears, and she pressed her hand against the point where the pain had gathered. She needed to empty her bladder. Nothing ever went the way she wanted. Everything was always against her. This wasn't such a great idea after all. She realised it now, but there was nothing to be done about it. Ellinor was locked in the bathroom and if Maj-Britt didn't find out now then she never would. The probability that Ellinor would come back after this was nil. Maj-Britt would be left not knowing, and some other repulsive little person would show up with her buckets and contemptuous looks.

All these choices. Some made so quickly that it was impossible to comprehend that their results could be so crucial. But afterwards they sat there like big red blots. As clearly as road-signs they marked the route through the past. *Here's where you turned off. Here's where it all began, everything that came afterwards.*

But it never worked to go back the same way. That was the problem. It was a one-way path.

He stood there with his hoe and the woven basket next to him, trimming the garden path. It didn't look like it really needed it, but that had never made any difference. It was the joy of doing the task that was the goal. Maj-Britt knew that because they had told her. But she also knew that it was important for the garden to be perfect, and that wasn't something they needed to say. It was important to be exacting about everything that was visible. Everything that was seen outwardly. You were responsible for the unseen yourself, and there the Lord was the absolute judge.

Her father stopped hoeing when she opened the gate. She took off her cap and brushed back her hair from her high forehead.

'How did the practice go?'

She had been to choir practice. In any case that was what they believed. For a year there had often been extra choir practice at the oddest times, but now her double life had become a strain. Continuing to hide the truth began to feel impossible. To keep sneaking around with the love she felt. She was nineteen and had made her decision. For months she had been gathering her courage, with Göran supporting her. Today they would lay all their cards on the table, but until that moment he stood out of sight a short distance away.

She looked around the garden and then caught sight of her mother. She was down on her hands and knees by the flowerbed outside the kitchen window.

'Father, there's something I need to discuss with you. You and Mother.'

Instantly, her father got a worried furrow between his eyebrows. This had never happened before. That she took the initiative for a conversation.

'Nothing's happened, I hope?'

'Nothing dangerous that you have to worry about, but I have to tell you something. Could we go inside for a bit?'

Her father looked at the gravel path at his feet. He wasn't really finished yet, and he hated to interrupt a task before it was completed. She knew that. She also knew that this wasn't the best situation for the conversation that was to come, but Göran was standing out there on the road and she had promised. Promised to give them finally the opportunity to create a life together. A real life.

'Go on inside. I just have to get someone I want you to meet.'

Her father looked at once through the gate. She saw it in his eyes. Would have known it even if her eyes had been closed.

'Do you have guests with you now? Because we're busy . . .'

He looked down at his work clothes and ran his hands over them hastily as if that would make them cleaner. And she was already regretting it. Bringing home guests without letting her parents prepare themselves was against the unwritten rules of their home. This had turned out all wrong. She had let herself be talked into something that was bound to fail. Göran had such a hard time understanding how it was. Everything was so different in his own family.

'Inga, Maj-Britt has a guest with her.'

Her mother stopped weeding the flowerbed at once and stood up.

'A guest? What sort of guest?'

Maj-Britt smiled and tried to radiate a calm that she didn't feel.

'If you just go on in we'll be there in . . . Is fifteen minutes all right? And you don't have to make coffee or anything, I just want to introduce . . .'

She had intended to say 'him' but wanted to wait with that. Things were bad enough already. Her mother didn't reply. Just brushed off the worst of the dirt from her trouser legs and hurried in through the kitchen door. Her father picked up the basket and hoe to put them back in the shed. It was obvious. He was already annoyed at being interrupted. He looked around when he crossed the lawn to make sure that nothing else was lying outside making a mess.

'You could bring in Mother's tools over there.'

It was not merely a suggestion, and she did as he said.

They stopped on the steps for a minute and held hands. Göran's hand was damp, which was unusual.

'Everything will be fine. By the way, I promised my mother we'd ask if they'd like to come over for coffee someday so that they can finally meet. Remind me, so I don't forget to say it.'

Everything was so easy for Göran. And soon it would be for her too.

She put her hand on the doorknob and knew that now was the time. It was now or never.

She had made up her mind.

No one met them in the hall. They hung up their jackets and heard the water running in the kitchen and then the slapping sound of someone wearing thin-soled shoes approaching. Her mother appeared in the doorway. She was wearing her flowered dress and her black shoes that she only wore on special occasions. And for a moment Maj-Britt thought they might understand what a solemn occasion this was. That they were doing it for her sake.

Her mother smiled and held out her hand to Göran.

'Welcome.'

'This is my mother, Inga, and this is Göran.'

They shook hands and her mother's smile grew wider.

'It's nice of Maj-Britt to bring one of her friends home, but you really must excuse us for not preparing anything. I had to fix something from what we have.'

'But that's not necessary. Really.' Göran smiled back. 'I just wanted to come by and say hello.'

'Nonsense, of course we have to offer you something. Maj-Britt's father is waiting in the living room, so you can go on in and I'll be there in a moment with coffee. Maj-Britt, please help me in the kitchen.'

Her mother left and for a moment they looked at each other. Squeezed each other's hands hard and nodded. We'll get through this. Maj-Britt pointed towards the living room and Göran took a deep breath. Then he silently mouthed the three words that filled her with new courage. She smiled and pointed first to herself and then to him and nodded. Because she really did.

Her mother was standing with her back to her, pouring boiling water into the coffee filter. They had taken out the fine china and the elegant porcelain coffee-pot with the blue flowers on it. She suddenly had a guilty conscience. She should have warned them that they were having company instead of subjecting them to this. She saw that her mother's hand was shaking. She seemed suddenly in such a hurry.

'You didn't have to go to all this trouble.'

Her mother said nothing, only let a little more water run over the side of the saucepan and mix with the black sludge in the coffee filter. Maj-Britt wanted to go into the living room. She didn't want to leave him alone in there with her father. They had decided that they would do this together. As they would everything else from now on.

She looked around.

'What can I do?'

'So he sings in the choir?'

'Yes. First tenor.'

Not a sound was heard from the living room. Not even the slightest murmur.

'Should I take this in?'

Maj-Britt pointed at the little tray with the sugar bowl and jug. The same pattern as the coffee-pot. They had really made an effort.

'Fill it with cream first.'

Maj-Britt took cream out of the refrigerator; by the time she had filled the jug, the coffee had finally run through the filter. Her mother stood with the coffee-pot in one hand and with the other she straightened her hair.

'Shall we go in then?'

Maj-Britt nodded.

Her father was sitting at the table in the living room, wearing his best black suit. The sharp ironed pleats on the white tablecloth stuck up from the tabletop but were held down by the blue-flowered china cups and the plate with eight types of little cakes. Göran stood up when they entered the room.

'What a feast. I didn't intend for you to go to all this trouble.'

Her mother smiled.

'Nonsense, it was no trouble at all. I just put together some things we had in the house. A little coffee?'

Maj-Britt sat quite still. There was something unreal about the whole situation. Göran and Mother and Father in the same room. Two worlds, so utterly different from each other but suddenly in the same field of vision. All the people she loved most gathered in the same place at the same time. And Göran here in her home, where God constantly watched over everything that went on. They were here together. All together. And everything was permitted. They even offered him coffee from the fine china. Wearing their Sunday best.

They all sat with their coffee and the cakes they

had chosen on their side plates. Fleeting smiles were exchanged across the table but nothing was said, nothing important, nothing beyond the polite chit-chat about excellent pastry and well-made coffee. Göran did the best he could, and she felt the seconds ticking away, the situation becoming more and more intolerable. The feeling of standing before an abyss. Enjoying the last seconds in safety before the leap into the unknown.

'So you met each other in the choir?'

It was her father asking. He stirred his coffee with his spoon and let it drip before he placed it on the saucer.

'Yes.'

Maj-Britt wanted to say something else but nothing came out.

'We saw you at the Christmas concert last year, when you sang the solo. You have a beautiful voice, really fine. Was it "O Holy Night" you sang?'

'Yes it was, and then I sang "Advent" as well, but it's probably "O Holy Night" that's best known, I would think.'

Then silence returned. Her father started stirring once again, and the sound seemed somehow comforting. Only the ticking of the wall clock and the rhythmic sound of the spoon in his cup. Nothing to be worried about. Everything was as it should be. They were sitting here together and perhaps they ought to talk a little more but nobody asked any questions and no opportunity for conversation was offered. Göran sought out her eyes. She gave him a swift glance and then looked down at the floor.

She didn't dare.

Göran set down his cup.

'There is one thing that Majsan and I would like to tell you.'

The spoon in the cup stopped. Maj-Britt held her breath. She was still standing on the edge but suddenly it gave way even though she had not taken the step voluntarily.

'Yes?'

Her father let his gaze flit between them, from Göran to Maj-Britt and back again. A curious smile played on his face, as if he had just received an unexpected present. And Maj-Britt understood at once. What they were going to say was so unthinkable that it hadn't even crossed her father's mind.

'I'm thinking of applying to Björkliden Music College and will be moving away from here and I've asked Maj-Britt to come with me and she has said yes.'

She had never before experienced in reality what happened next, though she had seen it on TV a few times. The way the picture suddenly froze and everything stopped. She couldn't even tell whether the ticking from the wall clock could still be heard. Then everything started to move again, but a little more slowly now. As if the paralysis still lingered and had to be softened up before everything could be restored. Her father's smile was not exactly erased, rather it happened through a gradual change in the expression on his face. His features dissolved and when they finally coalesced again Maj-Britt could read utter despair in his face.

'But . . .'

'And of course we will get married since we intend to live together.'

She could hear the desperation in Göran's voice. She looked at her mother. She was sitting with her head bowed and her hands clasped in her lap. Her right thumb was rubbing her left hand, swiftly moving back and forth.

Then Maj-Britt met her father's eyes, and what she saw she would spend the rest of her life trying to forget. She saw sorrow, but something else that was much more familiar. Contempt. Her lies had been revealed and she had betrayed her parents. The ones who had done everything for her, done everything to help her. Now she had turned her back on them and the Congregation by choosing a man outside their circle, and she hadn't even asked for their approval. She had simply come here and forced them into their fine clothes and delivered her message.

She couldn't identify the colour of her father's face.

'I'd like to speak with Maj-Britt in private.'

Göran didn't budge from his chair.

'No. I'm staying here. From now on you will have to regard us as a couple, and what concerns Majsan also concerns me.'

Yes, the clock was indeed ticking. She could hear it now. She was resting in the regular rhythm, tick, tock, tick, tock.

'I think I still have the right to talk to my own daughter in private!'

'She is my future wife. From now on we do everything together.'

'All right, stay if you want. You may as well hear it. It was decided long ago whom Maj-Britt would marry, and you're not the one, I can assure you of that. His name is Gunnar Gustavsson. A young man in the Congregation, and both Maj-Britt's mother and I have great confidence in him. I don't know what sort of belief you have, but since I have never seen you at any of our meetings I strongly doubt that you are of the same faith as Maj-Britt, and therefore marriage is out of the question.'

Maj-Britt stared at her father. Gunnar Gustavsson? The boy who had sat in his best suit at the pastor's home and watched her be humiliated? Her father looked at her and his voice dripped with disgust.

'Don't look so confused. You know very well that it was arranged long ago. But we and Gunnar have decided to wait until God regards you as ready since you have had such problems with . . .'

He broke off and his lower lip quivered when he pressed his lips together. Two pink strips with nothing but white around them. Her mother was rocking back and forth and a low moaning was heard. In her lap her fingers were twisting round each other over and over.

'What sort of problems?'

It was Göran who asked. Only Göran wondered what sort of problems she had had. She was back in the pastor's dining room. Sitting there naked and bound and maybe it was all her fault. They had done everything to save her but she refused to let herself be saved. And since she wouldn't obey she had damned herself for all eternity, which was one thing; but she had also dragged them down with her in the fall. Because they had conceived her in sin, and their God wouldn't have anything to do with her. Because in the end she gave up and was no longer willing to renounce everything to please Him. And now Göran wondered what sort of problems she had had, and if there was the slightest chance of undoing everything she had done then she must do it now.

'I asked what sort of problems Majsan has had.'

There was irritation in his voice, and Maj-Britt was astonished at how it was possible for him actually to dare take such a tone here and now and in this house. Everything she had learned and realised in the past year drained out of her. The certainty that the love she and Göran shared was pure and beautiful, that it had made her grow as a human being. The conviction that because it made them so happy it was meant to be and could not be a sin. Not even to their God. Now suddenly nothing felt certain any longer.

'Why don't you say something, Maj-Britt? Have you completely lost your voice?'

It was her father speaking to her.

'Why don't you tell him about your problems?'

Maj-Britt swallowed. Shame burned in her body.

'Maj-Britt has had problems with paying attention to her relationship with God, and the fact that you are here can be regarded as one result of that. If someone is pure in soul, those types of perversions cannot intrude, for a true Christian refrains from the damnation of sexuality, and does so with joy and gratitude! We have done everything to help her but now she has obviously let herself be led astray in earnest.'

Göran stared at him. Her father continued. Each syllable was like the crack of a whip.

'You wondered what sort of problems she has had. Self-abuse, that's what it's called!'

Jesus Christ, let me get out of this. Lord forgive me for all I have done. Help me, please, help me!

How could they know?

'Fornication, Maj-Britt, that's what you've been devoting yourself to. What you're doing is sinful and is considered apostasy from the true path.'

Göran looked bewildered. As if the words he heard were spoken in a language that was foreign to him. When her father spoke again she flinched from the power in his voice.

'Maj-Britt, I want you to look me in the eye and answer my question. Is it true as he says that you intend to leave here with him? Is that what you came here to tell us?'

Maj-Britt's mother broke into tears and rocked back and forth with her face hidden in her hands.

'You know that Christ died on the cross for our sins. He died for your sake, Maj-Britt, for your sake! And now you do this to Him. You will be eternally damned, shut out forever from God's kingdom.'

Göran stood up.

'What kind of nonsense is this?'

Her father stood up, too. Like two fighting cocks they stood face to face, measuring each other across the ironed tablecloth. Saliva sprayed out of her father's mouth when he answered the blasphemous outburst.

'You emissary of Satan! The Lord will punish you for this, because you have enticed her into depravity. You will come to regret this, mark my words.'

Göran went over to Maj-Britt's chair and held out his hand.

'Come, Majsan, we don't have to stay and listen to this.'

Maj-Britt couldn't move. Her leg was still tied to the chair.

'If you leave now, Maj-Britt, then you won't be welcome in this house again.'

'Come on, Majsan!'

'Do you hear that, Maj-Britt? If you choose to go with this man then you will have to face the consequences. A poisonous root must be severed from the others so as not to spread its infection. If you go now you will renounce your Congregation and your right to God's mercy, and you are no longer our daughter.'

Göran took her hand.

'Come now, Majsan, we're going.'

The clock on the wall struck five times, flinging out the exact time into the room. And just at that moment she did not know that a big red blot was taking shape in the calendar.

Maj-Britt stood up. She let Göran's hand lead her out to the hall and then, after he helped her on with her jacket, out the door. Not a sound was heard from the living room. Not even the moaning of her mother. Only a withering silence that would never end.

Göran pulled her with him down the garden walk and out through the gate, but there he stopped and took her in his arms. Her arms hung at her sides.

'They'll come around. You just have to give them a little time.'

Everything was empty. There was no joy, no relief that the lies were over, no anticipation of the opportunities that awaited. She couldn't even share Göran's anger. Only a huge black sorrow at all the ineptitude. Her own and her parents'. At Göran's, who could not understand what he had caused in there. And at the Lord's, who had created them all with free will, but who still damned those who did not do His will. Who was always intent on punishing her.

She had longed so much for them to be able to sleep together a whole night, and now they would finally be able to do it, but everything had been ruined. She wanted Vanja to come, and Göran borrowed his parents' car and drove over to get her. During the trip he told Vanja in detail about the visit to Maj-Britt's home, and Vanja was fuming with anger when she came in the door.

'Damn it, Majsan. Don't you let them destroy this, too! You've got to show them instead.'

Göran made one pot of tea after another, and as the night wore on Maj-Britt listened to Vanja's increasingly fantastic interpretations of the problem. She even managed to make Maj-Britt laugh a few times. But it was at the end of a long persuasive tirade that she suddenly said the words that truly startled Maj-Britt.

'You have to dare to let go of the old if you want to make room for the new, don't you think? Nothing can start to grow if there isn't any room.'

Vanja fell silent as if she herself were pondering what she had said.

'Jesus, that was really good.'

And she asked Göran for a pen and quickly jotted down her words on a piece of paper. She read them silently to herself and then let out a big laugh.

'Ha! If I ever write that book I'm going to put those words in it.'

Maj-Britt smiled. Vanja and her dreams of being a writer. With her whole heart Maj-Britt wished her all the luck in the world.

Vanja looked at her watch.

'Just because I came up with such a good point, I have now made up my mind and I take this decision at twenty minutes to four on the fifteenth of June, nineteen hundred and sixty-nine. I'm moving to Stockholm. Then we can move at the same time, Majsan, even if it's not to the same city, and without me you certainly don't want to stay here in this hole of a town, do you?'

Both Göran and Maj-Britt laughed.

And when dawn came her confidence had returned. She had chosen correctly and they weren't going to be allowed to take this away from her. Her wonderful Vanja. Like a stone statue she was always there when Maj-Britt needed her. What would she have done if she hadn't been there?

Vanja.

And Ellinor.

Maj-Britt listened at the bathroom door. It was quiet in there. The pain in her back had subsided. Only a bearable ache remained. And an urgent need to go to the toilet.

'I swear to God I don't know that Vanja.'

Maj-Britt snorted. Go ahead and swear. It doesn't matter to me. And probably not to Him either.

'They're going to be calling for me soon, I was supposed to be with the next client more than half an hour ago.'

It didn't make any sense. She was never going to get the truth out of her. And soon she was going to wet herself. Maj-Britt sighed, turned round and opened the door. Ellinor was sitting on the toilet seat with the lid down.

'Get out. I have to go to the toilet.'

Ellinor looked up at her and slowly shook her head.

'You're crazy. What the hell are you up to?'

'I have to pee, I said. Get out.'

But Ellinor stayed where she was.

'I'm not moving until you tell me why you think I know her.'

Ellinor calmly leaned back and crossed her arms over her chest, sitting there comfortably with her legs crossed. Maj-Britt gritted her teeth. If only she didn't feel such revulsion at the thought of touching her she would have slapped her. A hard slap across the face.

'Then I'll pee on the floor. And you know who gets to clean it up.'

'Go ahead and do it.'

Ellinor brushed something off her trouser leg. Soon Maj-Britt wouldn't be able to hold it any longer, but never in her life would she humiliate herself like this, not in front of that loathsome little creature who always managed to get the upper hand. And she definitely couldn't risk Ellinor discovering blood in her urine, then the little traitor would press the big alarm button. There was only one thing to do, no matter how much she hated the thought.

'It was just something she wrote in a letter.'

'In a letter? What did she write?'

'It has nothing to do with you, can you move now?'

Ellinor stayed where she was. Maj-Britt was getting more and more desperate. She felt a few drops ooze out.

'I must have misunderstood and I apologise for locking you in here. Okay, will you go now?'

Finally, Ellinor got up, took her bucket and with a

sour look went out the door. Maj-Britt hurried to lock it and sat down on the toilet as fast as she could, feeling the relief as her bladder was finally allowed to release the pressure.

She heard the front door close. Bye, Ellinor. We won't be seeing each other again.

Suddenly, utterly without warning, she felt a hard lump in her throat. No matter how she tried to swallow it, she couldn't. Tears came too; quite without cause they welled up over her eyelids, and to her horror she felt that she couldn't stop them. It was as if something were breaking inside her, and she hid her face in her hands.

A sorrow too heavy to bear.

Finally defeated, she was forced to acknowledge how foolish her longing was. No matter how much she wished that there was someone, just one person, who would voluntarily stay with her for a little while without having to be paid to do it, it would never happen.

19

She had called her work to take five days of the leave she was due. She had lost track of how much she had accumulated, because until now it had never interested her. Five weeks' holiday per year was more than she ever wanted, and over the years the unused days had piled up. They hadn't asked why she wanted to take the time off, and she knew that she had the confidence of management. A conscientious department head like herself would never stay away from her job so long unless there was a serious reason for it.

In the days that followed she went to see Pernilla every afternoon. She had told her that she would be the only one coming from the crisis group in future, and Pernilla took the news without displaying a hint of either joy or dislike. Monika took it as a good sign. For the time being she was content merely to be accepted.

She spent the greater part of her time outdoors with Daniella. The playground soon became a bore, so their walks grew longer. Slowly but surely she managed to win Daniella's trust, and she knew that it was a good route to take, to reach the mother through the child's approval. Because it was Pernilla who held the power. Monika was aware of this every second of the day.

There was an ever-present risk of being suddenly banished; Pernilla might think they could get along better without her help. The mere thought of someday no longer being welcome made Monika realise to what lengths she was prepared to go to avoid being sent away. She had so much more to put right.

Once a friend of Pernilla's came by, and Monika had mixed feelings when she had to go away and leave them alone. Of course she should have been glad for Pernilla's sake, but at the same time she wanted to be part of what was happening, wanted to know what they talked about, whether Pernilla had any plans for the future that Monika didn't know about. But most often Pernilla would just take a nap while Monika and Daniella set off on their excursions. Monika tried to stay in the flat when they returned, to show how well she and Daniella were getting along. Most of the time Pernilla would retreat to the bedroom, and they didn't talk much with each other, but Monika enjoyed every second she was allowed to be there. Only Mattias's eyes made her feel ill at ease. They watched her from the chest of drawers when she sat on the floor and played with Daniella. But maybe he was beginning to understand that she was there for a good purpose, now that she returned faithfully every day to assume her responsibilities.

Although Pernilla didn't say much, Monika felt that she was making a contribution just by being in the flat, and each time she left, her sense of calm remained for a couple of hours. The feeling that she had succeeded in the first stage of an honourable undertaking.

That she had earned a moment's respite. And she also realised how meaningless everything else had become. As if all the trivialities were peeled away and only a single purpose for her existence was left. But after a few hours the heart palpitations came back. She knew her science, knew exactly what sort of automatic changes were taking place in her body. That its sole purpose was to maximise her chances of survival. Fear directed her blood to the large muscles and her liver released its supply of glucose to give them fuel to work with; the pounding in her ears was her heart working to raise her blood pressure. Her spleen contracted to squirt out more red blood cells and raise the blood's capacity for oxygen uptake, while adrenaline and nor-adrenaline streamed through her body. But this time it did no good that she had received the highest marks in all her exams. What they had forgotten to teach her was how to handle the reaction. Her whole body was working to help her to flee, but what did you do when it wasn't possible to flee? In the daytime she felt like she was inside a glass bubble, shielded from everything happening outside, as if it no longer concerned her. In the evenings she drove to the gym to exhaust herself with a hard workout, but she couldn't fall asleep when she finally went to bed. When she turned off the light the fear came creeping in. And the confusion. The thoughts she had managed to fend off in the daytime by staying in continuous motion demanded attention in the dark, but that was out of the question. She suspected that her thoughts might make her doubt what she was doing, and for that reason she had every right to keep them at a distance. Since nothing ever conformed to reason or fairness, she was fully justified in planning her own strategy to bring order to the system. The forces that ruled life and death lacked all logic and discrimination. No acceptance was possible. She had to find an opportunity to make amends.

When she finally got to sleep, other dangers were lurking. Thomas would appear in her dreams. He came and went at will and awakened a longing in her that left everything reeling. What she had purposely forced her brain to forget remained as a memory in her body, and her hands refused to ward it off.

She wrote herself a prescription for sleeping pills as a means of defence.

After that she was left in peace.

On the third day she gathered her courage and suggested that she stay and fix dinner for them that evening. Yes, and go out to run errands first, of course. She added that she didn't mind at all. Pernilla hesitated only briefly, but then admitted that it would really be appreciated. Her back had grown worse since she was alone, and she hadn't been to her chiropractor in over three weeks. Monika knew that she didn't have the money, but she needed to hear it from Pernilla and above all she needed more details. She hoped to find out more during dinner.

She stood in the hall putting on her coat, having decided to make beef Wellington with pommes au gratin. She was wondering whether to buy a bottle of wine when Pernilla came out to the hallway.

'By the way, I'm a vegetarian. I don't think I told you, did I?'

Monika smiled.

'What luck. I didn't want to say that I was because I thought you might want to have meat. How long have you been a vegetarian?'

'Since I was eighteen.'

Monika fastened the last button on her coat.

'Is there anything you particularly feel like having?'

Pernilla sighed.

'No. To be honest, I'm not even very hungry.'

'You ought to try and eat. I'll find something at the grocer's. Would you like a glass of wine, by the way? I can stop at the off-licence and buy a bottle if you like.'

Pernilla thought for a bit.

'Someone else from the crisis group who was here said I should be careful with alcohol for the time being. It's apparently quite common to start consoling yourself with a couple of glasses of wine in the evening when you're in my situation.'

Monika didn't reply, but wondered briefly if she had been rebuked. But then Pernilla went on.

'But there's not much risk of that, because I can't afford to buy any. I would very much like to have a glass of wine.'

Monika spent a long time choosing vegetables. She didn't know any vegetarian recipes, and finally she asked one of the staff for help. Oh yes, there were various recipe suggestions on a stand over there by the dairy counter, and she picked one with chanterelles that looked rather luxurious and that she thought she could manage to prepare. She was feeling almost excited when she went back to her car with bags filled with food. Pernilla's trust in her seemed to have grown, and the threat of being sent away seemed less imminent. And tonight they would eat dinner together. They would have a chance to get to know each other a little better and she didn't intend to disappoint Pernilla. She had just put down the bags to take out her car keys when she saw it. She didn't see where it came from, but suddenly it was standing there on the pavement, right next to one of the bags. A silver-grey pigeon with iridescent purple wings. Monika dropped her car keys. With tiny black eyes it was staring accusingly at Monika, and she was suddenly afraid that the pigeon would do her harm. Without taking her eyes off it, she bent down and picked up her keys, unlocked the car and opened the door. Not until she picked up the bags did it flutter off in alarm above the parking lot, and she loaded the shopping into the car as quickly as she could. She locked the doors before she drove off.

When she parked outside Pernilla's building she sat in the car for a while to collect herself. She saw that fat dog again. Only a few metres from the balcony where it lived the dog was doing its business, but as soon as it was done it wanted to go back inside. Somebody opened the balcony door, but it was dark in the flat so she couldn't make out whether it was a woman or a man.

Pernilla was sitting on the sofa watching TV. She had put on Mattias's big pullover again, and Monika saw that she had been crying. In front of her on the table lay a stack of opened envelopes. Monika put down the bags. The hope that she would feel better again as soon as she got back inside the flat had been satisfied, and she felt all her resolve returning. She sat down next to Pernilla on the sofa. It was time to take the next step.

'How's it going?'

Pernilla didn't answer. She closed her eyes and hid her face in her hands. Monika stole a look at the envelopes on the table. Most of them were addressed to Mattias, and they all looked like bills. This was a golden opportunity that mustn't be wasted.

'I realise it must be tough to open all his letters.'

Pernilla took her hands away and sniffled a little. Pulled up her legs and wrapped her arms around them.

'I haven't been able to open the mail for a while, but I did it while you were out shopping.'

Monika got up and went into the kitchen to get some paper towels, which she handed to Pernilla when she returned. Pernilla blew her nose and crumpled up the paper into a ball.

'We won't be able to afford to stay here. I always knew that, but I just couldn't think about it.'

Monika sat in silence for a while. It was this information she had waited for Pernilla to confide in her.

'Forgive me for asking, but were you covered by insurance? I mean, accident insurance?'

Pernilla sighed. And then the whole story came out. The one Mattias had told and which it was now all right for her to know about. This time the account was more detailed. Monika memorised every detail, every number, noted precisely all the particulars in her well-trained memory, and when Pernilla had finished talking Monika was familiar with the whole problem.

The loan they had been forced to take to pay their bills after Pernilla's accident had not been a normal bank loan, but a Finax loan with an interest rate of 32 percent. And since they had not been able to afford any amortisation, the principal amount increased each month and was now up to 718,000 kronor. Pernilla's only income was her disability pension, and even if it were possible to obtain a housing allowance, she wouldn't be able to make ends meet.

'Mattias had just started a new job and we were so happy about it. We would have had some tough years but at least we could begin to pay off this bloody loan.'

Monika had already thought out what she would say when this occasion arose, and now the time was finally here.

'You know, I was just sitting here thinking about something. I can't promise anything, of course, but I know that there's a programme that you can apply to when something like this happens.'

'What sort of programme?'

'I'm not quite sure, but I was helping someone else after a death in her family, on behalf of the crisis group, and she got help from that programme. I promise I'll look it up tomorrow morning.'

Pernilla shifted position and turned towards her. For that moment she had Pernilla's full attention.

'Well, if you have time and feel like doing it, that would be very kind.'

Her heart was beating in a nice, steady rhythm.

'Of course I can arrange it. But I'd need documentation. Loans, insurance, your living expenses, that sort of thing. How much your rehabilitation costs.

Chiropractors, massage. Do you think you could get all that together?'

Pernilla nodded.

And while Monika stood in the kitchen sautéeing chanterelles, Daniella playing at her feet, and Pernilla coming in now and then to ask about some papers she wondered whether Monika would need, she felt for the first time in ages a strange feeling of serenity.

20

For three days no one from the home help agency had called. Neither Ellinor nor anyone else. She had enough food to last, there was no danger of that, but she began to wonder a little. Maybe Ellinor had been so angry that she hadn't even arranged for a replacement, thought she'd leave the problem to Maj-Britt to solve as best she could. That would be just like her.

But at least there was food. After three days, with no replenishment needed. She hadn't called the pizza delivery in weeks. Something had changed, and she suspected that it had to do with the pain she was feeling. And the blood in her urine. It just wasn't possible to eat like she did before; her desire for food had vanished like everything else. Her dress that she had been afraid she would outgrow had suddenly become roomier, and sometimes she even imagined that it was a little easier to get up out of the arm chair. But despite all that she was sadder than ever, and she had lost all her incentive.

She stood at the living-room window and looked out over the courtyard. That woman she didn't know was out there at the swings with the child again. With endless patience she pushed the swing, over and over. Maj-Britt looked at the child but couldn't focus on the image. So many years had passed. The memory had lain untouched so long, yet it had not lost any of its sharpness. Everything had been much simpler when the details hovered within reach. What good were memories that were impossible to endure?

'Is it really true?'

She wondered at once how she ever could have doubted. How in her wildest imagination she could have believed that he might not be happy. She had worried that he might think it was interrupting his plans for a musical education, that he thought it would be all right to wait a bit. But now he stood there beaming with joy and was simply happy that he would soon be a father. She was already in her fourth month. Anyone who wanted to could quickly figure out that it had happened before the wedding, but that didn't matter anymore. She had chosen sides and did not regret it.

Things had turned out just as her father had predicted that day. Her parents hadn't even come to the wedding, even though it was held in the church only a few hundred metres from their home. Maj-Britt wondered what they were thinking when they heard the church bells ring. She found it so peculiar. That the same God who in her home had damned Göran's and her love, only a few hundred metres away would bless their marriage.

The bridegroom's side of the church was full, but on the bride's side sat only Vanja. In the middle of the front pew.

She loved Göran and he loved her. She refused to accept that there could be any sin in it. But sometimes doubt would come over her when she thought about the folks at home who no longer wanted to have anything to do with her. Then it was hard to stand firm and hold fast to her conviction that she had done the right thing. Because everyone was gone. They had purged her like a weed from their lives and their community. She had been a part of the Congregation since the day she was born, and when everyone disappeared they took the greater part of her childhood with them. Nobody was left who shared her memories. She would miss the fellowship, being included, being able to take part in the strong community. Everything she was used to, knew about, felt at home with, everything was gone and she was no longer welcome. There was nothing to go back to, should it be necessary one day. Or to visit, if she was struck by homesickness.

Even though the anger was still strong, she sometimes felt a lump in her throat when she thought about Mother and Father. But then she began to think the way Vanja had said: Don't let them destroy this too. Show them instead!

Sometimes she woke up at night and it was always the same dream. She was standing alone on a rock in a stormy sea and all the others had climbed aboard a ship. They all stood there on the deck, but no matter how she screamed and waved they pretended not to see her. When the ship vanished in the distance and she realised that they intended to leave her to her fate, she would wake up with terror like a noose around her neck. She tried to explain to Göran how she felt, but he didn't even try to understand. He just called them crazy people and in that way he became just as condemning as her father had been. As if that were any better.

The only one she had left was Vanja, but they lived so far apart. And it was already getting harder to think of anything to talk about on the phone or in letters, now that they lived such completely different lives. Vanja's life in Stockholm seemed so exciting and adventurous, while nothing much happened at Maj-Britt's house. She pottered about in the little house they had rented just outside town and tried to make the days pass while Göran was at school. They would only be living there temporarily. There was neither a bath nor a toilet, and when the temperature dropped below freezing it was hard to get any real heat in the house. For the time being they were making do with an outhouse, since it was just the two of them. When the baby was born things would get worse.

But then there was the other difficulty. It was something that gave her great pleasure, although it was hard to admit that she actually liked it. She had hoped that it would get a bit easier after they were married, but it hadn't. There was still something in her that said they didn't have the right to devote themselves to such things. Not merely as pure enjoyment. Not unless it had some purpose.

She was strict about having the lights out. She still covered herself if Göran ever happened to see her naked. At first he had laughed at her, not unkindly but lovingly, but lately she thought she could sense a touch of annoyance in his voice. He used to say how beautiful she was and how much he liked seeing her naked and that it made him feel aroused. Maj-Britt didn't want to listen to that, she really didn't; it was one thing to do it in the dark but quite another matter to talk about it. His habit of putting words to what they did embarrassed her, and she always asked him to stop. It was as if the words in themselves made the whole thing indecent. Just as if they had been doing it with the lights on, so it was all visible. It wasn't that she didn't want to. She loved it when he touched her. It was as if their unity grew even stronger when they were so close to each other, as if they shared a great secret. But afterwards the guilt feelings always followed. More and more often she would doubt whether what they were doing was actually right and proper. Whether it was really possible to justify all the pleasure she permitted herself. And sometimes she imagined that someone was standing there peeking at her, shocked at her loose ways and meticulously jotting down everything in a notebook.

They had agreed that Göran should finish his year at the local college. They paid so little rent that they could get by well enough on his school loan. But when the baby came he would have to get a job, anything at all he said, just so it paid enough. She sensed what he was feeling deep inside, that his dreams of the music college could not be curbed quite so easily as he would have her believe. Sometimes his mother would ring. Maj-Britt wanted so much to hear whether she had seen her parents, but she never asked. No one mentioned them anymore; they were obliterated, as if they had never existed. Just as they and the Congregation had done with her.

Days came and went and it grew harder and harder to fill the hours. She knew nobody but Göran and some of his classmates in that town, but the few times she went along and joined them she felt even more lonely. They all had their training in common, and they had developed a special jargon that she couldn't follow. Göran was the oldest student at the school, and she thought he acted childishly when they were with his classmates. They drank whisky and soda and listened to music, and it was all so far removed from what she was used to and how things had been before they moved. Back then the two of them had had the choir in common, and in the evenings they preferred to spend time with each other. Reading books, talking, making love. She always felt inferior to the others in the group, especially the women. She would sit there with her growing belly, silent and bored because she never had anything to talk about, and Göran didn't seem to understand that she got tired early and that most of all she wanted to go home. She longed for Vanja, who would have understood how Maj-Britt felt and taken her side. Vanja would have said all the things she was unable to say herself. She especially didn't like Harriet; there was something about the way she looked at Göran that bothered her. Silently she imagined what Vanja would have done if she had seen those looks. Then things felt a little easier.

One Friday evening she came home and she could smell that he had been drinking. She couldn't tell by the way he was acting, but she was standing at the sink in the kitchen and he came and stood behind her and put his hands on her shoulders and then she could smell it on his breath. She kept washing dishes. His hands fumbled along her sides and found their way underneath her jumper, and when he pressed against her she could feel he was aroused. She closed her eyes, trying to control her breathing. She was not going to give in, not this time. She would show him that she could control her desire and that she wasn't a slave to lust.

'Stop it.'

Göran kept on caressing her.

'Göran, please stop it.'

His hands disappeared. And she heard the front door slam.

It took her almost an hour to get over the desire he had awakened.

Her belly kept growing. Signs of life from Vanja came less and less often, and Göran's days at school never seemed to end. Sometimes he didn't come home before eight in the evening. There were extra rehearsals and choir practice and all sorts of things that kept him at school and were obligatory for all students. Her belly was big and heavy and she convinced herself that that was why they never touched each other anymore.

That it was the reason she had pulled away.

Over time he had stopped even trying.

She had plenty of time to worry in her solitude. Her thoughts raced around wildly in circles and never met any counter-arguments since they were never spoken. She had thought that everything would be so much easier once she got away from all those watching eyes. That she would finally feel complete after she freed herself from all the pressure and was able to take part in the world that had been revealed to her only in glimpses over the years, partly through Vanja, but above all through Göran. She had thought it would be much better if she had to take responsibility for her own life and her own decisions, instead of merely accommodating

Him, who still never answered or showed what He thought. But that's not the way it had turned out. Instead she now understood how uncomplicated her old life had been, when she could simply surrender to the Congregation's common outlook and guidelines. How simple it had been when she didn't have to think for herself. Out here she stood utterly alone.

A poisonous root that was banished so it wouldn't spread its infection.

And she had chosen it of her own free will.

She had been so sure that their love and everything it implied was natural and healthy. That it was her father and mother and the Congregation who had been wrong. Now she realised how selfishly she had behaved. She had only been thinking of herself and her own satisfaction. Now that the anger had subsided and the sorrow caught up, she realised in what despair she must have left her parents, what shame they must have felt. There was no compassion in what she had done, only a huge, detestable egotism. She had believed that she could trade her fear of God for the love she felt for Göran, that it would heal her; she had accused them of forcing her to choose. But now the suspicion had arisen that she might simply have given in, that her choice was really only based on her inability to keep her desire in check. The pastor's words haunted her.

The purpose of sexuality is children, just as the biological purpose of eating is to nourish the body. If we ate whenever we felt like it and ate as much as we wanted, some of us would inevitably eat too much. Virtue demands control of the body and virtue brings light. There is no conflict between God and nature, but if we mean by nature our natural desire, then we must learn to keep it in check, if we do not want to destroy our lives.

And he quoted from Romans: *For I know that in me (that is, in my flesh) nothing good dwells.*

With each day that she wandered around in those closed circles she began to be more and more convinced that he had been correct. Because what they had done wasn't right, she could sense that now. They had conceived a child almost within the bonds of marriage and that was fine, but to continue to do it was indefensible. It wasn't because of her parents' attitude that she had changed, but because she herself had come to a realisation. She had suddenly begun to feel dirty. Impure. And because she knew that it came from what they were doing, then it couldn't be right, since it caused her so much anguish.

Impure.

The nature of the flesh is enmity towards God.

It was hard to wash herself clean enough at the kitchen sink, but buses passed by on the main road twice a day, and from the bus station in town it was only a few hundred metres to the bathhouse. She began going there daily but never said anything about it to Göran. She was always back by the time he came home. They would eat dinner and exchange a few words, but the conversations became more and more trivial and her thoughts more and more suffocating. She thought that surely everything would improve when the baby arrived and he left school so that it would just be them again. Then maybe they could start working on another baby. Then they could be together again without it being wrong.

She had found the phone number of the College's office and had memorised it. The appointed day was approaching, and if she went into labour while Göran was at school she was supposed to call. He had already arranged to borrow a car so she didn't have to worry. That's what he said.

She was standing in the shower at the bathhouse when her waters broke. Utterly without warning she felt that something was happening, and when she turned off the shower the water kept running down her legs. There was an older woman in the stall facing hers and Maj-Britt had turned her back – it was unpleasant to expose her nakedness to other women in the shower-room as well. She grabbed her towel and went out and sat down on the bench in the changing room. The first pains came just as she got her underwear on. She managed to put on the rest of her clothes, and when she was dressed she asked the woman from the shower-room to find out where there was a telephone.

They grew closer to each other again during the delivery. He held her hand and wiped her brow and was so eager to do all he could to help her through the labour pains. Everything would be good again, she knew that now. She would talk to him about all the things she'd been thinking that were slowly but surely breaking her apart, try to get him to understand. She did her utmost to endure the pains that were tearing her body to bits and wondered why God was so cruel that He punished women so much for the sin that Eve had committed. The words from Scripture echoed in her head: *Behold, I was brought forth in iniquity, and in sin my mother conceived me.*

Time passed. The pains lashed her for hours but her body refused to open and release what it had created. It greedily kept its grip on the child that was struggling inside to emerge into life, and the midwife seemed more and more concerned. Twenty hours had passed when they were forced to give up. The decision was made and Maj-Britt was led away to the operating room to deliver the child by Caesarean section.

Behold, I was brought forth in iniquity, and in sin my mother conceived me.

'Majsan.'

She heard the voice but it was coming from far away. She was someplace other than where the voice originated. A faint shimmer of light penetrated at intervals through the mists of her vision, and the voice she heard echoed as if down a long tunnel.

'Majsan, can you hear me?'

She managed to open her eyes. Vague contours of what was close by took shape, and her eyes reluctantly adjusted their focus and then lost it again.

'It's a little girl.'

And then she suddenly saw. The anaesthesia was slowly releasing its grip and she could see that he was standing there with a newborn baby in his arms. Göran was still there, he hadn't abandoned her. And the baby in his arms must be their baby, the one her body had been unable to give birth to on its own. The child in his arms was wearing white clothes, she could see that too. It was perfect and clear and washed and pure and was wearing white clothes.

'Darling, it's a little girl.'

He placed the little creature on her arm and her eyes desperately tried to adjust their focus to the new distance. A little girl.

The door opened and a nurse rolled in a pay phone.

'You probably want to call and tell everyone the happy news.'

And Göran called his parents. And Vanja. Maj-Britt only managed to say a few words, but Vanja shrieked with delight on the other end.

But they never called anyone else.

Things didn't turn out quite the way Göran had said. Instead of taking a job he asked his parents for financial help so he could finish his second year at the school. And the flat that he had promised they would move to would also have to wait for a while. But he had talked with the Council and it shouldn't be any problem when they were ready. Or so they said.

Maj-Britt continued to keep her thoughts to herself but at least now she had something to distract her. They decided to name the girl Susanna; they would have her christened in the church back home, by the same pastor who had married them. She wrote a letter to her parents and told them that they now had a grandchild and about the date of the christening, but she never received a reply.

There was something wrong with the girl, Maj-Britt could feel it. It wasn't that she didn't like her, but she felt it was necessary to maintain a certain distance. The baby needed so much, and it was important for her to learn from the start to control her needs. Raising a child was also about setting limits, and no responsible parent would let her child's will subvert the authority of an adult. That would be doing them a disservice. She breast-fed every four hours as she had been advised to do, and let the child cry herself to sleep if she was hungry in between. At seven o'clock every evening she had to go to sleep; that was the proper time, as they had told her at the child care centre. It could take a few hours for the baby to fall asleep; eventually she couldn't hear her shrieks any longer. But Göran had a hard time accepting this. The nights he came home before the baby went to sleep he would pace up and down, questioning more and more strongly the child-rearing methods that allowed a small girl to lie in bed alone and cry herself to sleep.

She was four months old when it was confirmed. Maj-Britt had known that something wasn't right but she had refused to let her suspicions become fact. By means of various excuses she had succeeded in avoiding the latest check-ups at the child care centre, but finally they had called and threatened to pay a home visit if Maj-Britt didn't bring the child in. Göran hadn't been privy to her suspicions; she had borne them alone. Nor did he know that she was skipping the required check-ups. She didn't want to go, didn't want to sit there and get the news and pretend that she didn't already know what was going on. Or the reason why it had turned out this way.

Self-abuse is what it's called.

And it was as she had suspected. She received the news the same way she would have listened to road directions. She merely asked a few supplementary questions for clarification. In the evening she passed on the news to Göran in the same way.

'She's blind. They confirmed it at the check-up today. We have to go back in two weeks.'

From that day everything began to crumble. The last desperate remnants of their attempt to break away finally disappeared, and all that remained were shame, remorse and dread. The regret and the guilt ate through her body like acid, the body she hated more than anything on earth, and that never did her anything but harm. The same body on which the palpable proof of her sin was now dependent every four hours. *An evil tree bears evil fruit. For the sake of sin each human being stands with real guilt before God and is threatened by His wrath and punishing justice. The overwhelming, dark desire for evil is propagated and is passed down from generation to generation, and this inherited sin is the cause of all other sins in thought, word and deed.*

In her pride she had rebelled against God, and the punishment was more loathsome than she ever could have imagined. He had kept silent and ignored her, and He had turned His wrath on her offspring instead. He would let the next generation bear the punishment that she herself should have borne.

And then came the letter from her parents. They had heard it through the grapevine. They had not forgiven her, but the whole Congregation would offer prayers for her child who had been struck by God's righteous retribution.

A few months passed. Göran grew more and more taciturn during the hours he was home. He didn't even talk about the new flat anymore, the one they were supposed to move to in early summer. Two rooms and a kitchen on the ground floor, 68 square metres with a balcony. And a bathroom. Finally, they would get a bathroom so she could wash herself properly.

She had already started to pack because she needed something to do; it had become harder and harder to sit still. She had just opened the linen cupboard in the hall above the stairs and was reaching for a stack of sheets. They had got them from Göran's parents, his initials were primly embroidered on them in blue. She saw that the girl was crawling across the threshold from the bedroom, that she bumped her head on the doorjamb and just sat there. There was no gate to protect her from the stairs. Maj-Britt walked past her and went over to the packing carton that was set up on the bed and placed the sheets inside. When she turned round she hit her shin on the bedstead. The pain was brief and explosive and only lasted a second, but it was as if the physical sensation swept away a barrier inside her. Everything turned white. The scream came first. She screamed until her throat hurt, but it didn't help. The girl was scared by her wailing, and Maj-Britt saw out of the corner of her eye that she was sobbing and crawling farther out in the hall. Closer to the stairs. But her rage could not be quelled; it grew ever stronger, and she grabbed hold of the carton in front of her with both hands and hurled it with all her might at the wall.

'I hate You! Hate You, do You hear that? You know that I was ready to sacrifice everything but it was never enough!'

She clenched her fists and shook them at the ceiling.

'Do You hear me? Do You? Can't You answer just once when someone speaks to You?'

All her pent-up fury exploded and gushed out like a tidal wave. She felt it throbbing in her temples and she tore the sheets off the bed and heaved them across the room. A picture on the wall was caught in their sweep and there was no gate on the stairs out in the hall, and now her blind daughter could no longer be seen, she had disappeared beyond the door frame. But something could no longer be stopped, something had once and for all shattered inside her, and now it had to get out or she would explode.

'You think You can win, don't You? That I'm going to pray and beg Your forgiveness now that it's all too late, now that You've made her take the punishment I was supposed to have. Is that what You think, is it?'

There was nothing left to throw, so she picked up the carton and threw it one more time. She stood in the bedroom and threw a carton even though there was no gate in front of the stairs out there in the hall.

'I can get along without You from now on, do You hear me?'

And afterwards she remembered that just at that moment she had to go out in the hall because there was no gate in front of the stairs and her blind daughter was alone out there on the floor, but she never made it that far.

She didn't scream when she fell.

There were only a couple of thuds and then everything was quiet.

21

There was something special about the nights. To be awake while others were sleeping. When everything had quieted down, when the thoughts of all people were gathered up and sorted into various dream states, leaving the air free. It was as if it became easier to think then, as if her musings had an easier time emerging when they didn't have to make way for all the rushing traffic. During her student days she had often turned night into day, and whenever possible she preferred to study for her exams at night. When the air was free.

Now the night had become associated with danger, for precisely the same reason. The fewer distractions and disturbing elements there were, the more often the field was clear. Something in there was protesting and seeking contact with her, and the quieter the night got, the harder it was to avoid hearing. Something in there blamed her, despite her brave attempts to bring about order and justice, and she had to watch out that she was not dragged down into the depths. She could only imagine what it would feel like to end up there; the slightest intimation of such a state was enough to scare her out of her wits. For twenty-three years she had managed to keep a distance from the darkness that was growing ever denser, but now it had grown so vast that it had almost reached the surface. The only way to maintain the slight distance that was still left was to stay in motion at all times. Because there was an urgency, a real urgency. She could feel in her whole body how much urgency there was. If only she made a decent effort, it would be possible to make everything right.

She had turned on the radio to drown out the worst of the silence. Pernilla's papers were spread out on the big oak kitchen table that was specially built to stand right where it stood. With room for ten people. There was no tiredness in her body, it was almost 3:30 in the morning and she was into her third glass of a 1979 Glen Mhor. She had bought the whisky during a trip abroad to supplement the exclusive contents of her bar cabinet, and it had made a good impression on some well-chosen guests. But it functioned equally well as an anaesthetic.

She punched in Pernilla's income on her calculator and totalled it up again, but it didn't help. The situation was really as bad as Pernilla had said. Daniella would get a child's stipend, but it was based on Mattias's general supplementary pension and wouldn't be very much. She had searched online and found out how to calculate it. Before the diving accident they had lived hand to mouth, working a bit here and there, saving enough to take a trip once in a while. After the accident Mattias had worked a little, but the jobs hadn't been particularly well-paid. Pernilla had been right. They would be forced to move if they didn't get some help.

Not until she heard the morning paper land on the hall floor did she get up and go into the bedroom.

The box of sleeping pills lay on her nightstand and she pressed a pill out of the foil pack and swallowed it with the dregs from a glass of water that had stood there since the night before. She wasn't tired in the least, but she had to start work again and she had to get a few hours' sleep. If she took the pill now and stayed up for half an hour she would fall asleep as soon as she lay down.

Not one thought would manage to take shape.

Dinner.

She followed the unfamiliar chanterelle recipe meticulously and the whole thing turned out quite well, even though she would have preferred a piece of meat on the plate next to all those vegetables. Pernilla sat in silence. Monika filled her wine glass when needed but refrained from drinking any herself. She wanted to stay sharp, and, besides, she had to drive. She sat enjoying the thought that she would get to take Pernilla's papers with her when she drove home. She was looking forward to familiarising herself fully with the situation. The papers were not merely an information source, they were also a guarantee, a temporary breathing space where she didn't have to worry. With them in her hands she was certain to be allowed to return, at least one more time. She looked at the stack of papers lying on the kitchen worktop and noticed how soothing it felt.

She wiped up the last food on her plate with a piece of bread and got ready for what she had to say. That they would be forced to make a slight change in what they might almost call 'their routines'. She liked that expression, *their* routines. But now they would have to be altered a bit. She couldn't jeopardise her job. Then they would both lose. So she sat and prepared for what had to be said.

'My leave of absence is up tomorrow, so I'll have to go back to work.'

There was no reaction from across the table.

'But I'd like to continue to drop by in the evenings if that would be any help.'

Pernilla said nothing, only nodded a little, but she didn't really seem to be listening. Her lack of interest made Monika uneasy. She hadn't been able to make herself indispensable, and each time she was reminded of any lack of control the darkness pressed in closer and closer.

'I thought I might be able to come by tomorrow evening and tell you about that programme and how my talk with them has gone; I'm planning to ring them first thing in the morning.'

Pernilla sat jabbing her fork at a chanterelle that was left on her plate. She hadn't eaten much, even though she had said the food was good.

'Sure, if you feel like it, otherwise we can do it on the phone.'

She didn't take her eyes off the chanterelle, and with the help of the fork it made its way through the sauce, drawing an irregular trail between a lettuce leaf and a leftover wedge of potato.

'It's better if I come by, it's no problem, and I have to give you your papers back anyway.'

Pernilla nodded, put down her fork and took a gulp of wine. There was a very long pause. Monika glanced at Sofia Magdalena, wondering how she could bring the conversation round to some historical topic that might lighten the mood a little and make Pernilla realise how much they had in common, when Pernilla beat her to it. Except that the part of the story she wanted to talk about was the part that Monika wanted to avoid at all costs. The words hit her like a punch in the stomach.

'It's his birthday tomorrow.'

Monika swallowed. She looked at Pernilla and realised her mistake. Until now Pernilla had almost never mentioned his name, and Monika had begun to relax, believing that it would continue that way as she hurried past his gaze in the living room whenever she had to walk by. But now Pernilla was starting to be affected by the wine. Monika in her foolishness had bought the wine and kept refilling her glass. The effect could be seen in Pernilla's listless movements, and when she blinked it took longer than usual for her eyelids to close and then open again. Monika saw the tears streaming down Pernilla's cheeks; they were running in a different way than they had the other times she had wept. On those occasions Pernilla had retreated with her grief, trying to hide. Now she sat there exposed on her chair, making no attempt to conceal her despair. The alcohol had dissolved all her barriers and Monika cursed her stupidity. She should have known better. But now she would have to atone for her mistake, as she was forced to endure every word.

'He would have been thirty. We were supposed to go out to eat for once, I arranged for a babysitter months ago, it was going to be a surprise.'

Monika clenched her fists and pressed her nails into her palms. It was a relief when it hurt somewhere she could pinpoint.

Pernilla picked up her fork again and let it return to the chanterelle.

'They rang from the funeral home this morning; he was cremated yesterday. Well, what they managed to scrape up of him, although they didn't say that. So now he isn't merely dead, now he's been annihilated as well, only a little ash in an urn down there at the funeral home waiting to be picked up.'

Monika wondered how hot the oven should be for the blueberry pie she had bought for dessert. She had forgotten to check before she threw out the package. Two hundred degrees Celsius should do it. If she put a little foil on top it wouldn't burn.

'I picked a white one. They had a whole catalogue with caskets and urns in different colours and shapes and price ranges, but I took the one that was cheapest because I knew he'd think it was crazy to waste money on an expensive urn.'

And she had to whip the vanilla sauce too, she'd forgotten about that. She wondered whether they had an electric mixer, because she hadn't seen one when she'd made dinner, but maybe there was one in a cupboard she hadn't looked in.

'I'm not going to have a burial. I know he wouldn't want to be buried somewhere, he'll be scattered at sea, he loved the sea. I know how much he missed diving and that in his heart he wanted to start again, it was only because of me that he didn't.'

Imagine, Sofia Magdalena was engaged to Gustav III when she was just five years old. It said in the books that she had led a melancholy life, she had been shy and withdrawn and subjected to a strict upbringing. She came to Sweden at nineteen and had a hard time adjusting to life at the Swedish court.

'Why couldn't he have lived long enough to dive one more time? Just one more time!'

How loud she was talking. She was going to wake Daniella if she didn't pipe down soon.

'Why wasn't he allowed to do it? Why? Just one last time!'

Monika gave a start when Pernilla suddenly stood up and went into the bedroom. It was clear that the wine had affected her legs too. Monika searched the kitchen for the whisk she needed but found none. Then Pernilla reappeared and now she had Mattias's woollen jumper in her arms, holding it close to her as if in an embrace. She sank down on the chair and her face was contorted with anguish and now she was shrieking more than talking.

'I want him to be here! Here with me! Why can't he be here with me?'

Keep moving. Keeping herself in constant motion made it possible to stay out of all this. It was when she stopped that everything hurt.

Doctor Monika Lundvall stood up. Mattias Andersson's widow sat across the table and was sobbing so hard she was shaking. The poor woman wrapped her arms round herself and rocked back and forth. Doctor Lundvall had seen this so many times. Loved ones had died and the relatives were left behind in inconsolable despair. And they could never be comforted. People in the midst of grief were in a world of their own. No matter how many years a person studied medicine or stood right next to them, they were still in a different place. There was nothing you could say to cheer them up, nothing you could do to make them feel better. All you could do was to be there and listen to their unbearable sorrow. Endure it even though their distress raged all around them that everything was meaningless, that life was so ruthless it was no use even trying. You might as well give up at once. What was the point when it could all end an hour from now? Why make an effort when everything was steadily moving towards the same inexorable end? And it was impossible to avoid. People in grief were one big reminder. Why try at all? Why?

'Pernilla, come, let's put you to bed. Come on now.'

Doctor Lundvall went round the table and put a hand on her shoulder.

The woman kept on rocking back and forth.

'Come on.'

Doctor Lundvall took hold of Pernilla's shoulders and helped her up from the chair. With an arm round her shoulders she led the woman into the bedroom. Like a child Pernilla let herself be led and did as she was told, lying down obediently in the bed. Doctor Lundvall pulled up the covers from the empty side of the double bed and tucked them around her. Then she sat down on the edge of the bed and stroked Pernilla's forehead. Gentle, calm movements that made her breathe more easily. She stayed there. The red numbers on the clock radio changed and returned in new combinations. Pernilla was now sound asleep, and Doctor Lundvall went back to the subject of her leave of absence.

Now only Monika was left.

'Forgive me.'

One big reminder.

'Forgive me. Forgive me because I wasn't braver.'

She stroked away a lock of hair from her brow.

'I would do anything to make him come back to life.'

Pernilla took in a shuddery breath. And Monika felt that she wanted to say it out loud. Even if Pernilla didn't hear. To confess.

'It was my fault, I was the one who betrayed him. I left him there even though I could have saved him. Forgive me, Pernilla, for not being braver. I would do anything at all, anything, if only I could give you Lasse back again.'

22

'Why didn't you say something?'

Four days had passed since the bathroom incident, and nobody from the agency had shown up. Now Ellinor was suddenly standing in the hall, and she flung out the question before she even managed to close the front door. The words echoed from the stairwell. Maj-Britt was standing near the living-room window and was so surprised by her own reaction that she didn't even register that she had just been asked a question.

How she had detested that voice. It had plagued her like an ingenious torture instrument with its inexhaustible flow of words, but now she had a feeling of gratitude. She had come back. In spite of what had happened last time.

Ellinor had come back.

Maj-Britt remained by the living-room window. What she felt was so unfamiliar that she completely lost her bearings, she no longer remembered how you were supposed to act in situations like this, when you actually experienced something that might easily be mistaken for a mild form of happiness.

She didn't have much chance to think about it because the next moment Ellinor came storming into the room, and it was quite obvious that she wasn't expecting to be welcomed with delight. Because she was furious. Really fuming. She stared at Maj-Britt and completely ignored Saba, who stood wagging her tail obsequiously at her feet.

'You have pain in your back, don't you, where you usually put your hand? Admit it!'

The question was so unexpected that Maj-Britt totally forgot her gratitude and retreated at once to her usual defensive position. She saw that Ellinor had a folded piece of paper in her hand. A piece of lined paper torn from a notebook.

'What do you mean?'

'Why didn't you say something?'

'Are you aware that it's been four days since the last time you were here? I could have starved to death.'

'That's right. Or you could have gone out to the shop.'

Her voice was just as fierce as her gaze, and Maj-Britt realised that something had happened during those four days Ellinor had stayed away. Maj-Britt sensed that it had to do with that piece of paper she was holding. It was so similar to other pieces of paper which had intruded into her flat a while back, and which she was sorry she had ever read. Ellinor must have seen her expression, because now she unfolded the sheet of paper and held it out to her.

'This was why you thought I knew Vanja Tyrén, right? Because she wrote that you had pain somewhere, so you thought I was the one who told her, right?'

Maj-Britt felt her ears flame red. Since the past had come back she had been almost anaesthetised, it was as if a peculiar gap had formed between all her emotions and what she had suddenly remembered. She sensed that the reprieve was temporary, and now that she saw the paper being held out to her the gap was reduced to nothing more than a thin little membrane. Nothing in the world could make her take it. Nothing.

'Since you refused to tell me, I wrote to her myself and asked what actually happened, what it was that made you believe she and I knew each other. Today I got her answer.'

Maj-Britt didn't want to know. No, she didn't, she didn't. She had been unmasked. With Ellinor's letter Vanja had learned that Maj-Britt had actually lied; she now knew what a pitiful failure of a human being Maj-Britt had turned into. But naturally Ellinor did not intend to let her escape. Not this time either. Her voice lashed out the words when she started to read.

'*Dear Ellinor, Thanks for your letter. I'm glad there are people like you out there with a genuine empathy for your fellow human beings. It gives me hope for the future. Most people who are locked in the bathroom by their clients would probably have left the whole thing behind like an unpleasant memory and chosen not to go back there again. I'm glad for Majsan's sake that she has you, and do try to forgive her. I don't think she meant as much harm as it may have seemed and the fault is actually mine. I wrote something in a letter that no doubt scared her, and to be honest that was my intention, because I think it might be urgent. I wrote that if Majsan has pain somewhere then she has to seek medical help. I had hoped that she would have already done something about it before she got my letter, but apparently she chose not to, and the choice is naturally her own and no one else's.'*

Ellinor raised her eyes and glared at Maj-Britt, who turned her back and looked out the window. Ellinor continued reading.

'Now I realise that you probably wonder how in the world I could know this, and I sense that you have already decided to write another letter to ask me. To save you some time I'm answering you now. The only person I'm willing to tell it to is Majsan, and I don't intend to do so either by letter or telephone. Best of luck, Ellinor. My warmest regards, Vanja Tyrén.'

It was finally quiet. Maj-Britt felt that disgusting lump in her throat. She tried to swallow but it wouldn't budge, and even grew bigger, forcing tears to her eyes. She was thankful that she had her back to Ellinor so she wouldn't see. Her weakness would be used against her, she knew that, that's how it had always been. It was when you dropped your guard that you made yourself most vulnerable.

'Dear Maj-Britt. Let me ring and make an appointment with a doctor.'

'No!'

'But I'll go with you, I promise.'

Ellinor sounded different now. Not as angry, but concerned instead. She had been easier to deal with when she was angry, when Maj-Britt was fully justified in defending herself.

'Why should I listen to someone doing life in prison who has some peculiar notion about me?'

'Because that particular notion is right. Isn't it? You *do* have pain in your back. Admit it.'

She hadn't even sounded angry in the letter. Even though Maj-Britt had lied to her. Vanja still cared about her welfare despite her nasty reply. She felt herself blushing, the colour of shame creeping across her cheeks when she thought about what she had written to Vanja.

Vanja.

Maybe the only person who had really cared about her. Ever.

'Can't you at least find out what she knows?'

Maj-Britt swallowed in an attempt to get control of her voice.

'How? She didn't want to say, either in a letter or on the phone. And she can't come here.'

'No, but you can go to see her.'

Maj-Britt snorted. That was impossible, of course, and Ellinor knew it as well as she did, although she felt she had to suggest it. Just to have an opportunity to emphasise Maj-Britt's disadvantage. She leaned on the windowsill. She was so tired. So dead tired of having to force herself to keep breathing. The pain had been so constant lately that she had almost grown used to it, accepted it as a natural condition. Sometimes she even experienced it as pleasant, since it took her mind off what hurt even more. Until it got so intense that it was almost unbearable.

Maj-Britt's knees began to give way and she turned round. The lump in her throat had become manageable and no longer threatened to expose her feelings. She went over to the easy chair and tried to hide the grimace prompted by the pain when she sat down.

'How long have you been in pain?'

Ellinor sat on the sofa. On the way there she put

Vanja's letter on the table. Maj-Britt looked at it and knew that she would read it again, see the words with her own eyes, the words that Vanja had written. How could she have known? Vanja was no enemy, never had been. She had merely done as Maj-Britt had asked and stopped sending her letters. Not out of anger but out of consideration.

But how could she have known?

'How long have you been in pain?'

She couldn't lie anymore. Couldn't keep it up any longer. Because there was really nothing to defend.

'I don't know.'

'Well, about how long?'

'It crept up on me. It didn't hurt all the time at first, just now and then.'

'But now it hurts all the time?'

Maj-Britt made one last brave attempt to defend herself by not answering. That was all she could do. She already knew it was futile.

'Maj-Britt, does it hurt all the time?'

It had lasted five seconds. Maj-Britt nodded.

Ellinor gave a heavy sigh.

'I only want to help you, don't you see that?'

'Well, you are getting paid for it, after all.'

It was unfair and she knew it, but sometimes she said things out of habit. The words were so much a part of her life in the flat that they didn't even have to be consciously thought before they spilled out. She was actually aware that Ellinor had done a lot more for her than she was really paid to do. A lot more. But for the life of her Maj-Britt couldn't understand why. And of course Ellinor reacted.

'Why do you always have to make things so hard?

I understand that you have probably had a hell of a lot of trouble in your life, but do you have to make the whole world suffer for it? Can't you try to make a distinction between those you should hate and those who don't deserve it?'

Maj-Britt turned to look at the window. Hate. She tasted the word. Who actually deserved her hate? Whose fault had it all been?

Were her parents to blame?

The Congregation?

Göran?

He had understood what happened. He didn't accuse her straight out, but she remembered the look on his face. Göran's contempt had soon developed to open hatred. When it was time to move to the flat they had been hoping to get for so long, she had to move alone. And here she had stayed. Hadn't contacted anyone or given out her new address, not even to Vanja. She had no idea where Göran went after the papers were signed and the divorce granted, and after a couple of years she wasn't even interested in knowing.

Ellinor sounded rather dejected when she went on; her voice had lost its fire and she started by taking a deep breath.

'But Vanja's right, of course. You make your own choices.'

Maj-Britt started at the words.

'What do you mean by that?'

'It's your life, isn't it? You're the one who decides. I can't force you to go to the doctor.'

Maj-Britt fell silent. She couldn't face thinking it

all the way through. That it might be life-threatening. That whatever was hurting inside her body might be the beginning of the end. The end of something that had been so totally meaningless, yet she had taken for granted that it would go on.

'Is it because you don't want to leave the flat that you won't go to the doctor?'

Maj-Britt considered this. Yes. That was definitely one reason. The thought of forcing herself out of the flat was terrifying. But it was only one of the reasons; the other was more crucial.

They would have to touch her. She would have to take off her clothes and she would be forced to let them touch her disgusting body.

Suddenly Ellinor straightened up and looked like she had just had an idea.

'What if a doctor came here?'

Maj-Britt got palpitations from the mere suggestion. Ellinor's attempt to find a simple solution was backing her into a corner. It would be so much easier just to admit that it was impossible, so that she could renounce all responsibility and not even have to consider making a decision.

'What sort of doctor?'

Ellinor's enthusiasm was back, now that she obviously thought she had found a solution.

'My mother knows a doctor I can call. I'm sure I can get her to come here.'

Her. Then maybe that would be possible to endure. At least maybe.

'Dear Maj-Britt. Please let me ring and ask her, at any rate. All right?'

Maj-Britt didn't reply, and Ellinor got more excited.

'Then I'll ring her, okay? Just call and see what she says.'

And so apparently some sort of decision was made. Maj-Britt had neither agreed nor objected. She still had the chance to blame everything on Ellinor if things went wrong.

That would make it so much easier to endure.

If there were always someone else to blame.

23

The clock radio woke her at seven thirty and she didn't feel the least bit tired. Her whole system was revving up even before she opened her eyes. She had fallen asleep as soon as her head hit the pillow and then slept dreamlessly for three hours. That was enough. The sleeping pills had not failed her, they effectively blocked all entry and prevented him from getting in. Then she was spared the piercing emptiness in her chest when she awoke and he was gone again.

She left the radio on while she got ready and ate breakfast. In passing she was informed about all the murders, rapes and executions that had occurred in the world in the past day, and the information settled into some remote convolution of her brain as she put her coffee cup in the dishwasher. Pernilla's papers were already packed into her briefcase. She had decided to call the clinic and say she wouldn't be in before lunch.

She was out much too early. It turned out that the bank wouldn't open for another thirty minutes. Now to her annoyance she suddenly had an extra half hour, and to stand and wait outside the door was not a viable alternative. She had to do something in the meantime. In future she would plan a little better. See to it that she didn't have this sort of unwelcome surprise that upset her planning. She headed down the street and scanned some display windows without seeing anything that interested her. She passed the news-stand, 7-YEAR-OLD BOY IN RITUAL MURDER and WOMAN (93) RAPED BY BURGLAR, saw that Hemtex was having a sale on curtain material, but didn't notice the car that honked angrily as she crossed the street right in front of it.

She was the first customer in the bank this morning, and she nodded at a woman she recognised. The woman waved and Monika took a number for 'other matters'. Her finger hadn't even left the button before a beep told her it was her turn. She went up to the window indicated. The man on the other side was wearing a tie and dark suit and couldn't be older than his twenties.

She placed her driver's licence on the counter.

'I'd like to check the balance in my account.'

The man took her driver's licence and started typing on his computer.

'Let's see. Is it just a savings account or do you want to know about your interest-bearing cheque account?'

'The savings account and my money market funds.'

Money had never really interested her. Not since she began making so much that she never had to worry. She had a high salary and worked a good deal, and she had no major expenses. Four years ago she had allowed herself to buy an apartment in one of the city's newly renovated historic buildings, and her mother had expressed her utter dismay. Monika had never told her what it cost, but her mother managed to figure it out from the local paper, an article in which the reporter was shocked at the scandalous property prices. And her mother had leisurely inspected the apartment and found more defects than a professional surveyor.

'Let's take a look. You have two hundred and eighty-seven thousand in your savings account, and then you have a money market fund that at today's rates is worth ninety-eight thousand kronor.'

Monika wrote down the figures. Investing money had never interested her, but at some point she had followed the bank's advice and put a little of her money into various funds. But it actually made her rather uncomfortable. In a bank account she knew what the interest was and wouldn't be hit by any unpleasant surprises. The yield from a mutual fund was more uncertain, and she didn't like taking risks.

'Okay, what about the Asia fund then?'

He typed in some more numbers.

'Sixty-eight thousand five hundred.'

Monika shifted her feet.

'I'd like to cash in all of them and withdraw what I have in the savings account.'

He gave her a quick look before his hand went back to the keyboard.

'Would you like a cashier's cheque or would you like the money transferred to an account?'

She thought it over. Once more she was surprised at her lack of planning. It wasn't like her to ignore details. In future she should think things through a little better.

'If you put the funds into my cheque account, can I make transfers by phone to someone else's account later? I mean even a large amount?'

He suddenly looked unsure. Hesitated a bit with his answer.

'Yes, technically you can transfer the money, but it depends on what you want to do with it, whether it's legal with regard to taxes, I mean. If there's something you want to buy, then a cashier's cheque is preferable.'

'No, I'm not buying anything.'

He hesitated again. Looked around as if he wanted some colleague to come and help him.

'This will be quite a considerable sum that is being transferred, so . . .'

He typed again.

'Four hundred and fifty-three thousand five hundred and twenty-three kronor. I just want you to know that such a large transfer might interest the tax authorities.'

Monika suddenly noticed that her vague irritation was growing stronger and that it would soon become apparent to the man on the other side of the counter. This wasn't like her, either. Not caring what that officious man thought of her. That for once she might be viewed as annoying with all her demands. But she would have to take it a little easy. She wasn't finished yet, she had more matters to take care of, and it would be more difficult if she lost his goodwill.

'Then I'll take a cashier's cheque.'

He nodded and was about to pull out a drawer when she continued.

'And then I'd like to take out a loan.'

He began digging in the drawer and found the paper with the survey of her apartment. It was nine months old, but the building was known all over the city.

Everyone knew how attractive the flats were. For those who could afford them.

He gently closed the drawer, looking at her a bit longer this time, and then began reading the paper. She didn't take her eyes off him as he scanned the document. She already had a mortgage on the apartment even though she could have made a large cash downpayment. Someone had told her that for tax reasons it was better to have the loan outstanding instead of paying it off with the money she had in the bank.

When he finished reading he looked at her again.

'How much did you have in mind?'

'How much could I borrow?'

He stood quite still. Then his hand went to his throat and tugged a little on the perfect knot of his necktie. He pulled out the drawer again and took out a form.

'Please fill this out while I do some calculations.'

She read the paper lying on the counter. Income, length of employment, marital status, number of children to support.

She took a pen and started filling in the information.

Her gaze settled on the hand holding the pen, and suddenly she didn't recognise it. She recognised the ring she had bought for herself and saw that her fingers were making the motions she was telling them to do, but the hand seemed somehow separate, as if it belonged to someone else's body.

'You can borrow three hundred thousand more on the equity in your property.'

He had gone over the completed form and familiarised himself with what else he needed to know, and now he placed a loan proposal on the counter in front of her. She had seen him talking with one of his colleagues. Noticed that during the conversation they had looked at her a few times, but she didn't care. It was strange how unmoved it all left her. But three hundred thousand wasn't enough. She needed more, and she slid his proposal back across the counter.

'How much can I borrow beyond this amount?'

She could see that he hesitated. She sensed his anxiety and was perfectly aware that she was the cause of it, but it didn't faze her. She had a mission to fulfil and he had nothing to do with it.

And what should she do with her money if she didn't even have the right to be alive?

'It's easier if we know what you will be using the money for. I mean, if, for example, you want to buy a house or a car, it would be much easier for us to grant a loan.'

'But that's not what I'm going to do. I'm quite pleased with my BMW.'

Her hand again. It looked different. And the words she heard herself saying were unfamiliar too.

'I can see here that you have an excellent income and . . . you're a doctor . . . and your ability to repay the loan is undeniably excellent. And only one child to support.'

He hesitated.

'Wait just a moment, I'll consult my colleague.'

He strode through the bank. She looked at the paper she had filled out.

She had at least been honest, obviously, and put down her obligation to support Daniella.

But *only* one child to support.

He was an idiot.

He was conferring with the woman she had said hello to when she came in. That was good. She presumably knew all about Monika's spotless past. There were no payment problems; in all those years she had never paid a bill late. She had always been a conscientious citizen, no one could complain on that score. It wasn't actually possible to accuse her of that defect any longer, the one that sat inside her but couldn't be seen, because she had once and for all decided to atone for it. She would sacrifice everything she had ever wanted and subjugate herself. What more could she be expected to do? In order to get back the right to exist.

She didn't notice that he had returned until she heard him speaking to her.

'We can issue an unsecured loan for another two hundred thousand in view of the amount you usually save.'

He picked up his pen and calculated quickly. Nine hundred and fifty-three thousand, five hundred. It wasn't really enough but apparently it was all she could manage at present. It would have to do. Pernilla would at least be able to pay off her loan. And Monika herself could continue to help with whatever she could.

'Okay. I'll take it in the same cashier's check.'

'In what name?'

She thought for a moment. The tax authorities might be interested.

'Put it in mine.'

* * *

Her agitation increased with each step as she approached. With each intersection the accelerator seemed harder to press down. She had to force herself to drive in through the gates to the clinic grounds and further to the parking lot. Someone had had the audacity to take her parking space, and she angrily jotted down the licence number on a parking receipt. She would find out who the owner of that car was and personally ring and tell him off. Or her. She realised that it might even feel good. To be able to take it out on someone. Someone who had done wrong. To be able to say what a bloody idiot he or she was and be fully justified in taking the upper hand.

She parked her car in the next space and hurried towards the entrance. The red brick façade loomed before her. This had been her refuge, giving purpose to her life, but now she felt nothing. Everything associated with this building now stood in the way of what she needed to devote herself to. She had to drive to Pernilla's and see how she was doing today. Whether she was feeling bad after all the wine she drank. Find out whether there was anything she could do. The distaste increased with each step she took towards the entrance, and by the time she managed to place her hand on the handle of the entry door she realised that it would be impossible. That familiar shape. The hand that instantly felt at home and tried to send impulses to the Monika who was usually there but who was no longer accessible.

You have sworn upon your honour that you in your work as a physician shall strive to serve your fellow man with humanity and respect for life as a guiding principle. Your goal shall be to preserve and promote health, to prevent illness, and to cure the sick and alleviate their suffering.

Only two people had the right to demand that of her. Only those two to whom she was indebted. They were the only ones.

Suddenly she felt ill. She backed up a few steps and then turned and ran back to her car. Behind locked doors she let her gaze sweep across the façade to make sure that no one had seen her from any of the windows. Without checking behind her properly she backed out of the parking space and almost collided with the ticket machine. Then she continued out the gates going much too fast, but when she had gone some distance she pulled over to the kerb and stopped. She took out her mobile and punched in the letters.

'Taking one more week's leave of absence. Best wishes, Monika L.'

Message sent.

It took only a minute before the phone rang. She recognised the head of the clinic's number on the display but stuffed the mobile back in her handbag. A minute later the beeps sounded, telling her he had left a message.

Pernilla and Daniella were out in the playground when she parked outside their building. She could see them from the car, and she sat there, watching them. It felt good to sit there in secret and still be able to keep them under supervision. For once to have control even when Pernilla was nearby. To be spared subjecting herself to her moods and having to watch each word carefully in fear of being sent away. She sat there for a long time. Watching Daniella swing back and forth, back and forth. Pernilla was pushing her, but with her gaze turned in another direction, out into empty nothingness.

Dinner yesterday. All the intolerable things Pernilla had said. If they could meet somewhere else it would certainly be easier. Somewhere Mattias's presence was not so obvious. Where Pernilla and Monika could have the chance to be in peace with their tentative friendship. And then she decided. It would be better for them to meet at her place instead. Where there was no admittance to Mattias.

She started the car and drove back into town.

She drove past Olsson's antiquarian bookshop. She had seen them that morning but hadn't really registered what they were until she suddenly remembered now. They were hanging in the display window, two historical pictures in simple gold frames. One of them was a map from Sweden's glory days and the other was a lithograph of Karl XIV Johan's coronation. She bought them for twelve hundred kronor and then continued on to the Emmaus Secondhand Shop. They had several ceramic objects that looked home-made, and none of the ones she picked would make Pernilla feel inferior.

She left all her purchases in the hall, went into her study and called before she even took off her coat. It rang several times but nobody answered. Maybe they were still out in the playground; if so, they had certainly been there a long time. She saw by the clock that it had been over an hour since she had seen them there, and it made her uneasy that they weren't back yet. She hung up and went to take off her coat. The uneasiness refused to let her go. She kept calling every five minutes for the next hour, and when Pernilla finally answered she was practically beside herself with worry.

'Yes, hi, it's Monika, where have you two been?'

Pernilla didn't answer at once, and Monika realised that her question had been overhasty. At least phrasing it in that tone of voice. And she could hear that Pernilla thought so too.

'Out. Why do you ask?'

Monika swallowed.

'Oh, I was just wondering, I didn't mean anything by it.'

Did she dare ask? Now that things had got off on the wrong foot? She wasn't sure that she would be able to handle a rejection. But she had to meet with her. She had all her papers, she had to have a chance to give them back, and of course she had some good news!

'I thought I'd ask if you'd like to come here and have dinner tonight.'

Pernilla didn't reply, and Monika could feel the adrenaline forcing her heart to speed up. At the same time she could feel how unfair it was, when she had such good intentions. Pernilla should really be meeting her halfway.

'I thought we could eat a bit early so that Daniella could come along too. Maybe at four or five or so, if that would work.'

Pernilla still didn't reply, and Monika was feeling more and more stressed. She hadn't intended to bring it up in advance but Pernilla's hesitation forced her to say something. In any case she had to give her a little hint.

'I have some good news for you.'

This constant desire for control. It was going to drive her crazy. Always demeaning herself, playing the underdog. Being forced to ask everything twice.

'What would that be?'

No. She didn't intend to say any more. She had the right to be there in person when she gave her the news. To be there and share in the joy for once. She deserved it, as a matter of fact.

'Did you ring that programme?'

'I'll tell you when you come. I can pick you up if you like.'

Pernilla had given in. Agreed to come over. But she hadn't sounded particularly happy. Monika still felt the irritation that had been triggered at the bank. Even Pernilla was exasperating her. No one did what she wanted and nothing was ever the way she had imagined. Nothing Monika did was ever good enough.

She picked them up at four and not much was said during the drive. It was obvious that Pernilla didn't want to talk about yesterday's dinner, and Monika wasn't very interested in doing so either. Pernilla sat in the back seat with Daniella on her lap. Since they didn't have a car, they had no child's seat, and it occurred to Monika that she should buy one. For the future. Considering all the things they would be doing together.

For the moment she felt quite secure, and she had almost managed to put herself in an anticipatory mood when Pernilla suddenly asked, 'Would you mind stopping right up ahead? I just have to run in and do a quick errand.'

Monika pulled into a space between two cars and

turned off the engine. Pernilla climbed out with Daniella in her arms, and Monika opened her door and stretched out her arms to take her. Then Pernilla went down a lane and Monika and Daniella stayed in the car and sang 'Itsy Bitsy Spider'. Over and over again. Monika looked more and more nervously at the clock and started to wonder how the root vegetable casserole at home in the oven was faring. When Itsy Bitsy had climbed up the tree seven more times, the passenger door was suddenly opened. Pernilla put a large white box on the floor in front of the passenger seat and stretched out her arms for Daniella. And then they drove off again. Monika stole a glance at the carton. As big as a six-pack of beer it stood there on the floor and kept drawing her eyes over and over again. White and anonymous, without a word on it as a clue. Today she had acted far too curious once already, and she knew it was risky, but finally she couldn't contain herself any longer.

'What's in the box?'

She could see Pernilla in the rear-view mirror. She sat looking out the side window and didn't change her expression when she replied.

'It's just Mattias.'

A shock went through the car. First it hit Monika but her hands transmitted it to the car, which swerved violently. Pernilla instinctively threw out her arm and grabbed the handle above the back door, and with the other she took a tighter grip on Daniella.

'Sorry, a cat ran in front of the car.'

Monika tried to control her breathing. The white box stood like a reproach on the floor, and even though she tried to keep her eyes on the road, the box managed time after time to tear them away. And each time it looked bigger. As if it were growing each time she looked away.

This is how much is left of me. Hope you have a nice dinner.

Only a few hundred metres to go. She had to get out of the car.

It was all your fault. It doesn't matter what you do now.

It was impossible to breathe. She had to get out.

Monika was standing utterly still next to the door on the driver's side. She had discovered that the air was hard to breathe even outside the car. The air was hard to breathe wherever she was, each time she tried to take a breath.

'Is this where you live? How elegant.'

Pernilla had climbed out on the other side with Daniella in her arms. She had fallen asleep on the way and her head was resting against Pernilla's shoulder.

'You take the urn. I don't want to leave it in the car.'

It had sounded more like an order than a question, and either way it left Monika with no choice. She looked at the white box through the window.

Come on. I can't walk myself, as you well know.

'Which door is it? Daniella's getting a little heavy for my back.'

Monika slowly went round the car and opened the passenger door.

'It's number four over there.'

Pernilla started walking.

Monika's hands shook as she reached for the box.

She lifted it carefully and locked the car with a button on her key. She followed Pernilla with the box held out in front of her, as far from her as she could without looking too strange. But when she had to go through the door and also hold it open for Pernilla, she was forced to hold it with one arm, tight to her body, almost in an embrace. The little resistance that was left inside her was sucked towards the box as if into a black hole. She felt a pressure across her chest. She could hardly breathe. She shouldn't have invited them over; she had to do something to get out of this, anything at all.

'What a lovely flat.'

Monika was standing inside the front door and didn't know where to put him. The hall floor didn't seem suitable, but she had to put him down somewhere so she could breathe again. She hurried into the living room and looked around. First she went over to the bookshelf but changed her mind and continued to the table instead. Her hands released their grip and she sat him next to the pile of history books and the new ceramic fruit bowl.

She saw that Pernilla had followed her and was laying Daniella on the sofa. She grimaced when she straightened up and tried to stretch out her back.

'What a great place.'

Monika tried to smile and went back out to the hall. Exhausted, she took off her jacket and then went out to the kitchen, leaning her hands on the kitchen worktop. She closed her eyes and tried to get control of the nausea she felt. Everything was spinning inside, and she felt dangerously close to the boundary that she had so successfully managed to avoid. The one that prevented her from breaking into bits completely. With an effort of will she managed to take out the casserole and turn off the oven.

She saw through the doorway into her study that Pernilla was examining the old map she had bought that afternoon, which had now replaced what usually hung on the same nail. She went over to the refrigerator and took out the big plastic water bottle and the salad she had prepared. Then she sank onto one of the chairs at the table.

She couldn't utter a word. Not even announce that dinner was ready. But Pernilla appeared of her own accord after looking round the flat and went to sit at the other side of the table. She felt Pernilla looking at her, felt the terror of not being good enough in her eyes.

'How are you feeling?'

She nodded and tried to smile again. But Pernilla didn't give up.

'You look a little pale.'

'I didn't sleep well last night. Actually I'm feeling a little sick.'

The white box was like a magnet in the living room. With each breath she was aware of its presence.

I want to eat dinner too! Can you hear me out there? I want to be included!

'What was it you wanted to tell me?'

Pernilla had begun to serve herself from the casserole. Monika tried to remember the answer to her question. Her head was spinning. She gripped the chair cushion she was sitting on in an attempt to make it stop.

'Did you call the programme?'

Pernilla poured water into Monika's glass.

'Have some water. You're really pale. You're not going to faint, are you?'

Monika shook her head.

'There's no danger of that, I just felt a bit tired all of a sudden.'

She was so close to the boundary now. So dangerously close. She had to see to it that Pernilla got out of here. She couldn't show herself as weak. How could she be of any help, if Pernilla was the one who had to take care of her? Pernilla would reject her, no longer have any use for her.

She swallowed.

'They said they wanted to help you, so I tried to pressure them and asked them to give us some money since it was so urgent. I drove over there with all your papers so they could see for themselves, told them about your accident and all the trouble with the insurance that didn't cover it.'

She took a sip of water. She had thought that this would be a solemn moment. A great stride forward in their friendship. Now she just wanted to get it over with so that she could take a couple of sleeping pills and escape.

'So are they going to come up with any money?'

Monika nodded and took another swallow of water. Just a little one, the risk was great that it would come right back up.

'You're going to get nine hundred and fifty-three thousand.'

Pernilla dropped her fork.

'Kronor?'

Monika did her best to smile but was unsure of the result.

'Is that true?'

She nodded again.

The reaction she had so longed for bloomed on Pernilla's face. For the first time she saw genuine joy and gratitude. Words came tumbling out of her mouth as fast as the impact of the news sank in.

Monika felt nothing.

'But that's utterly fantastic. Are you sure they were serious? That means we can stay in the flat and I can pay off the loan. Are you really sure they meant it, seriously? Well, I don't know how I can ever thank you for this.'

Do you know, Monika? Do you know how she could thank you for this? Considering everything you've done for her?

Monika got up.

'Excuse me, I have to go to the bathroom.'

She braced herself against chair backs and door frames on her way to the bathroom, and with the door locked she just stood there. Leaning against the sink she looked at her own face until the reflection dissolved and turned into that of a monster. She was so close now. So dangerously close. The darkness lay just below the surface, vibrating. Pressing against the thin membrane and finding small holes. She had to confess. She had to go out to Pernilla and confess her guilt. That it was all her fault. If she didn't do it now she would never be able to do it. Then her lies would have to go on forever. And she would always have to live with the terror of being unmasked.

At that moment the telephone rang. Monika stood

there and let it ring. But then there was a tentative knock on the bathroom door.

'Monika. There's a call for you. She didn't say her name.'

Monika took a deep breath and opened the door to take the cordless phone that Pernilla handed to her. She wasn't sure her voice would hold.

'Yes, this is Monika.'

'Hi, it's Åse. I don't want to bother you if you have company, but I just have a brief question.'

In a flash the membrane was intact again and what had leaked out was in safe custody on the other side. Her first impulse was to pull the door shut behind her, but the need to see Pernilla's face took precedence. To see whether she reacted, recognised the voice of the woman who with her deep guilt had visited her flat. Pernilla had sat down at the table again, and all Monika could see was her back.

'That's all right, it's a good friend who came over for dinner.'

At any rate she had resumed eating. Monika desperately tried to tell herself that was a good sign.

'Well, the fact is, my daughter Ellinor is working as a home help and she needs your help. As a doctor. I know she wouldn't ask if it weren't important. I just wonder if it's okay if I give her your number so she can ring you. She needs to get in touch with a doctor who might consider making a house call to one of her clients.'

All Monika wanted was to end the conversation, find out what Pernilla had understood or not understood, and return to her seat at the dinner table so that she could see her face. To put to rest the uncertainty, she was willing to go along with anything.

'Of course, no problem. Please ask her to call a bit later this evening so we can arrange a time.'

And that was the end of the conversation. Monika remained standing, totally still. She looked at Pernilla's mute back there at the kitchen table, every detail suddenly rendered with such sharpness that it made her eyes burn. She felt the dread of taking the few steps that would give her the opportunity to interpret Pernilla's expression, show her whether she had been unmasked or not, whether the time had come when she would be forced to confess. Her legs wouldn't obey her. As long as she stood where she was, she was allowed to put things off.

Then Pernilla turned round, and it seemed to take an eternity before Monika could see her face.

'God, this thing about the money is unbelievable. Thank you, Monika, thank you so much.'

The dizziness and nausea were gone, along with her indecision. The deep fright she had felt at the risk of being unmasked had convinced her. It was already too late to turn back.

She had reached the point of no return.

To subjugate herself and take responsibility for Mattias was her only means of escape.

24

Maj-Britt demanded that Ellinor report every word that was said during the phone conversation with the doctor, and Ellinor did the best she could. Maj-Britt wanted to know every syllable, every nuance, the least little tone of voice with which she had been delivered up. She could hardly feel the pain any longer, all her attention was circling round the forthcoming doctor's visit. And she was afraid; her fear had reached heights it had never even approached before. Soon the front door would open and a strange person would enter her stronghold, and she herself had participated in inviting that person in. And that put her at a disadvantage that was almost impossible to bear.

'I just told her the truth, that you had pain in your lower back.'

'And how did you explain that it was necessary for her to come here?'

'I said that you would rather not leave your flat.'

'What else did you say?'

'I didn't say much more than that.'

Maj-Britt had a hunch that Ellinor must have said something else but didn't want to tell her. She must have described her repulsive body, her unwillingness to co-operate and her disagreeable behaviour. Filth had been said about her, and now she had to let the person who had heard those words come here and touch her.

Touch her!

She deeply regretted letting herself be talked into this.

Ellinor claimed that she had a free day and that was why she could stay at the flat so long, but Maj-Britt refused to be invaded once again by Ellinor's goodwill. There must be a reason. Why would she do all this if there wasn't some underlying reason?

It was a quarter to eleven; only fifteen minutes to go. Fifteen unbearable minutes before the torture would begin.

Maj-Britt paced up and down the flat, ignoring the pain in her knees. It was a greater torment to sit still.

'How do you know this doctor?'

Ellinor was sitting cross-legged on the sofa.

'I don't, my mother does. They met at a course a few weeks ago.'

Ellinor got up, went over to the window and looked at the façade of the building across the courtyard.

'Do you remember that I mentioned something about a car crash?'

Maj-Britt was just about to reply but never got that far, because the doorbell rang at that very instant. Two short signals that marked the end of her respite.

Ellinor looked at her, then took the few steps necessary to stand right in front of her.

'It will be fine, Maj-Britt. I'll stay here the whole time.'

And then she reached out her hand in an attempt to place it on Maj-Britt's arm. Maj-Britt managed to defend herself by taking a quick step back. Their eyes met briefly and then Ellinor vanished out to the hall.

Maj-Britt heard the door open. Heard their voices taking turns, but her mind refused to interpret the words, refused to realise that there was no longer any chance of escape. The lump in her throat cut into her flesh and she didn't want to. Didn't want to! Didn't want to be forced to take off her clothes and expose herself to foreign eyes.

Not again.

And then they were suddenly standing in the living-room doorway. Ellinor and the doctor she had called, who in her mercy had taken the trouble to come. Maj-Britt didn't recognise her at first. But it was the woman she had seen out there in the playground, with the fatherless child. Who with endless patience had tirelessly pushed the girl on the swing. Now she was standing there in Maj-Britt's living room, smiling and reaching out her hand to her.

'Hello, Maj-Britt. My name is Monika Lundvall.'

Maj-Britt looked at the hand that was extended towards her. In desperation she tried to swallow the lump in her throat that was cutting into her flesh, but it didn't work. She could feel the tears welling up and knew that she didn't want to be here. Not at all.

'Maj-Britt?'

Someone was saying her name. There was no possibility of escape. She was surrounded in her own home.

'Maj-Britt. You two can go into the bedroom if you like, and I'll wait out here.'

It was Ellinor. Maj-Britt saw her walk over to the bedroom door and call Saba to her.

Maj-Britt forced herself to walk towards the bedroom. She felt that the doctor was on her heels and she heard the door closing behind them. Now it was only the two of them in the room. She and the person who quite soon would force herself on her. She no longer remembered why she had voluntarily gone along with this. What could she possibly have wished to achieve?

'Would you begin by showing me where the pain is?'

Maj-Britt turned her back and did as she was told. The tears were running down her cheeks but she didn't dare wipe them off out of fear of being exposed. The next moment the hands were on her. Her body stiffened and she squeezed her eyes shut in an attempt to retreat back into the darkness but in there she was only more conscious of them. The way they groped and squeezed the spot she had pointed out. Imagine that she just stood there and let it happen. She was waiting for the terrible part. To be asked to take off her clothes.

'Is this where it hurts?'

Maj-Britt nodded quickly.

'Have you had any other symptoms?'

She couldn't answer.

'I'm thinking of fever, weight loss. You haven't seen any blood in your urine, have you?'

And that was when she first realised what she had got herself into. In her stupidity she had thought that if she went along with the examination, then everything would go back to normal. She would put a stop to Ellinor's eternal nagging and maybe even get some medicine prescribed, but she hadn't thought any further than that. She had been so afraid of the examination itself that she hadn't even considered what the results might be. Now she realised that the doctor, behind her back, suspected the reason for her pain, and she was suddenly unsure that she wanted to know. Because what could it lead to but more outrages?

She had let herself be duped.

The hands went away.

'I need to feel your back better. You only need to pull up your dress.'

Maj-Britt couldn't move. She felt the hands return and fumble along her sides. When her dress was pulled up, the disgust she felt was so strong that she wanted to throw up. The fingers groped over her skin and in between her rolls of fat, pressing and squeezing and finally she could no longer hold back. Her body convulsed. She felt to her relief that the hands went away and her dress fell back and again covered her legs.

'Ellinor! Ellinor, do you have a bucket?'

She heard the door open and their voices out there in the flat and in the next moment Ellinor was next to her with the green bucket. A dishrag lay like a dried shell in the bottom but Ellinor let it lie there, holding up the bucket in front of Maj-Britt, but nothing came out. She hadn't eaten anything since the day before, so her stomach was empty. Slowly the terror retreated into its crevices and left the field free for the anger to which she was entitled. She shoved away the bucket and glowered at Ellinor who had tricked her into this, and Ellinor knew it as well as she did. Maj-Britt could see it in her eyes. That Ellinor only now understood what she had subjected her to.

'Out!'

'Does it feel better now?'

'Get out of here!'

And then she was alone with the doctor again. But she was no longer afraid. From now on she intended to decide what they would be allowed to do with her.

'So. What's the diagnosis?'

She felt that her voice had regained its strength, and she looked the doctor straight in the eye.

'It's too soon to tell. I want to do a few tests as well.'

And Maj-Britt complied. She sat there obediently on the chair while she was stuck in the inside of her arm and watched her blood being collected in various vials. They would not be allowed to do anything to her unless she gave permission. Not a thing. It was still her body, even if there was a disease in it. The doctor did her best to take her blood pressure, and Maj-Britt felt relatively calm again. Now that she had regained control.

'I've seen you out in the playground a few times. With that child who lives across the way.'

She had intended it as a polite thing to say, an ordinary attempt at some sort of conversation. She knew of course that chit-chat wasn't her forte, but she never would have suspected her words would have such an effect. The change was palpable through the entire room. An invisible shift in power had occurred. Maj-Britt noticed the woman's movements suddenly stop and then resume at a faster pace, but at first she didn't understand what had happened. All she knew was that the doctor who had just taken her blood pressure had reacted to her words. All the little unwelcome people who had come and gone in her flat in the past twenty-five years had chiselled out a unique ability in her to sniff out people's weaknesses. It had been a matter of pure instinct for self-preservation, her only possibility of retaining something of her dignity in the face of their contempt. To quickly assure herself of their weak points and make use of the knowledge when it was needed. If for no other reason than to get rid of them. Ellinor had been her first failure.

The doctor rolled up the blood-pressure cuff and stuffed it back in her bag.

'No, it must have been someone else you saw.'

And to her surprise Maj-Britt realised that she had sniffed correctly. The doctor was lying to her. Lying right to her face. And one other thing she knew clearly, and that was the satisfaction of suddenly having regained her equilibrium. The invisible power shift meant that she could now demand respect. She was no longer subject to that woman's hands and well-educated supposition about a possible illness. Thin, successful and superior, in her great mercy she had agreed to see Maj-Britt despite her minuscule importance. Made the effort to come here since she wasn't in any shape to leave her flat. An inferior being.

Without a clue to how it had actually happened, she had become aware of a possible tiny advantage. That was always good to have if the person should prove to be too pushy and it became necessary to get rid of her. And people did have a tendency to become that way.

Pushy.

25

She should never have gone there. As soon as she heard the address she should have realised the danger and pulled out of it, but by then she had already promised. And she didn't want any sort of conflict with Åse. Why not, she had no idea; she only felt an indefinable need to stay on good terms with her. With everyone who might know the true story. No one could accuse her of being someone who failed to come through in an emergency, who refused to take her share of responsibility. At least she had *that* remaining on the plus side, and she wouldn't let anyone take it away from her.

She could still sense the irrational fear she had felt during the conversation with Åse. With astounding clarity it was hovering just beneath the surface, as if waiting for the right opportunity to reappear at the slightest reminder. The threat that she would have to confront Pernilla, be forced to confess. In a lucid moment she had realised to her dismay that the guilt had only grown greater. Her sacrifices were being annihilated in the shadow of her lies, and becoming mixed in with everything she had done that was already unforgivable. If Pernilla ever found out the truth, her contempt would eliminate every way out but one, and that was to vanish from the face of the earth.

But Monika owed it to Mattias to stay put.

And she owed Lasse some justification for her life.

Ellinor had given scanty information over the phone. She said only that one of her clients had severe lower back pain and needed medical attention but was refusing to leave her flat. When Monika finally had a chance to see the patient there in the living room, she was astonished that Ellinor hadn't told her more. Or perhaps given her a little warning. Monika couldn't remember ever having seen such a morbidly obese woman before, except perhaps in photographs when she was in medical school, and the sight of her immense size at first made her nearly speechless. She was quite certain that she had been able to conceal her surprise, though her somewhat delayed words of greeting may have revealed her reaction. But she thought that her professional demeanour had served her well. Then there was the patient's behaviour. Monika had treated others who were afraid of being touched, but never anyone so markedly filled with anxiety as this woman. It was like an invisible shell all around her that had to be broken through before she could be reached. And when Monika's hands touched the huge body, it shook as if with spasms. Since it was scarcely possible to feel anything through all those layers of fat, she had let the woman be and concentrated on taking samples instead.

She felt schizoid stepping into her professional role again. Her insides were divided into two feuding camps, one of them satisfied at the objectivity of the examination she was performing, while the other noticed with annoyance that minutes which could have been put to better use were ticking away to no advantage. But at least there was still a hint of a longed-for calm. The tricks of the trade that she knew so well. Resting in her own competence. For a short while she could be in total control and know exactly what had to be done. For the first time in weeks she could leave behind her subordinate position and be treated with respect.

It was just at that moment that the woman opened her mouth and confirmed all the misgivings she had felt ever since Ellinor had given her the address. That someone might have seen her. Before the woman even finished her sentence Monika was wrenched back to her self-imposed inferno, and no tricks in the world could protect her from the threat she faced. Faster than she thought possible she beat a retreat and not until it was too late did she realise her mistake.

She had lied.

Fabricated yet another thread in the net of lies that was getting harder and harder for her to control. At the slightest carelessness one of the knots might unravel and bring down the rest with it, and now she had lied without having any idea of the woman's relationship to Pernilla or what that might lead to.

In desperation she let the seconds tick away and tried to act normally while she frantically looked for a solution that could repair her mistake. She quickly considered every imaginable reason why she could have been out there in the courtyard with Pernilla's daughter. Weighed the probabilities against each other, and the seconds hurried by without anything being said. When she had packed all her equipment away and closed up her bag, and all that was left to do was hand over the plastic container for the urine sample, she still hadn't found any way out, but she had to say something.

'Oh yes, now I remember. A while ago I was over here with a friend and her daughter. She was supposed to drop off something for a colleague who lived here, and I kept the daughter company out in the playground, by the swings. That must have been where you saw me. But the girl doesn't live in that building.'

And perhaps she only imagined it, but a tiny smile seemed to play around the corners of the mouth of this woman whose name was Maj-Britt as she silently accepted Monika's explanation with a nod.

Monika said goodbye to Ellinor out in the hall. She quickly scribbled a prescription for a painkiller and gave her some additional instructions. Maj-Britt came out of the bathroom with the urine sample, and Ellinor stared in horror at the red liquid in the plastic container. Monika avoided Ellinor's troubled gaze. The blood in the urine and the nature and location of the pain certainly reinforced Monika's suspicions, but they would have to wait until she tested the samples. It wasn't worth scaring anyone before she was 100 per cent sure. She opened her bag and put the urine sample inside.

'I'll let you know as soon as I have the results of the test.'

The woman had disappeared into the living room, but Ellinor took a step forward and extended her hand.

'Thank you for taking the time to come.'

* * *

On her way back to the car she felt grateful to get out of that flat. She still wasn't sure that her explanation had been satisfactory or had removed all risk. The information she lacked was how well Maj-Britt and Pernilla knew each other, but Ellinor had told her that Maj-Britt never left her flat. On the other hand, Ellinor had gone with Åse when she drove over to see Pernilla. What if Ellinor had told Maj-Britt how they came in contact with each other?

She cast a quick glance up towards Pernilla's empty kitchen window and hurried to her car. She couldn't be seen here right now. Couldn't risk that Pernilla would open her window and shout to her.

She had just set her bag in the back seat, and in only a couple more minutes she would have made it. But fate would have it otherwise, of course. Just as she was about to climb into the driver's seat they appeared on the path from the park, and spotted her.

'Hi, what a surprise to see you here.'

Monika glanced over at Maj-Britt's balcony. The sun was reflecting off her windows and she couldn't rule out that someone might be standing inside. Watching.

Pernilla had reached her now and set the brake on the pram.

'We've just been out for a little walk.'

Monika nodded and sat down in the driver's seat.

'I'm in a bit of a rush. I was just making a house call and have to get back to the clinic.'

'Oh really, who's the patient?'

Suddenly Monika realised that now she could get her answer, and it was better to have her worry confirmed than to continue floating in uncertainty.

'Her name is Maj-Britt. Do you know her?'

Pernilla looked thoughtful and slowly shook her head.

'Does she live in our building?'

'No, across the courtyard.'

'I don't know anyone there.'

Monika's body relaxed. It had all been her imagination. Her nervousness was making her hypersensitive; she had let the woman's comment take on more importance than necessary.

She put the key in the ignition.

'By the way, I talked to the people at the programme today. They will be depositing the money in your account sometime today. I gave them the account number you use to pay your bills.'

Pernilla smiled.

'I hope you know how grateful I am for this.'

Monika nodded.

'I've got to run, sorry. I'm already late.'

'Would you like to come over for dinner tonight? My way of thanking you for all your help.'

To her surprise Monika realised that she was hesitating. How she had waited for this moment. For Pernilla of her own free will to grant her an audience without her having to beg for it. But she was so tired. So exhausted by continually being on her guard and maintaining appearances. She was thinking of taking her sleeping pills early and escaping the evening and the night. But she couldn't say no. She didn't have the right.

'Of course. What time do you want me to come?'

'What time is good for you?'

She was supposed to finish working at five. She

mustn't forget that Pernilla thought she had gone back to work. There was so much to keep straight.

'I get off at five.'

'Shall we say six, then?'

After a last look at Maj-Britt's window she drove back in towards the city. She was already late. Her mother had been waiting a quarter of an hour for her, and Monika knew that she would be sitting with her coat on in the hall, growing more and more impatient with each minute that passed. But first she had to drop by the bank. And the head of the clinic had rung four times and left messages that she hadn't answered. Some of her colleagues had also left messages repeatedly, but she still hadn't called them back.

Somewhere deep inside her something was trying to speak, something that was trying to make her realise that the situation she had created was growing more and more untenable with each hour that passed. But since there was no turning back and there was not a single way she could alter the state of things, it was much easier not to listen. Much easier.

The most important thing at the moment was that the threat she had just experienced had been eliminated, and for the time being she could feel fairly safe. She simply had to take ten minutes at a time. That was all she could ask.

All she had the right to ask.

26

Maj-Britt was standing at her window and watching what was happening down in the parking area. She followed their conversation with interest, although of course she couldn't hear a single word they were saying. But each gesture and facial expression confirmed what she had suspected. That doctor *had* lied to her, but she still didn't understand why.

Ellinor had sat down on the sofa. Saba was standing by her feet and wagging her tail, and Ellinor patted her on the back. Neither of them had said a word since they had been left alone together. Maj-Britt was still dealing with the humiliation of having exposed her incapacity so completely to Ellinor. Not being able to go through even a simple doctor's examination. Ellinor had at least had the good taste not to comment on her obvious displeasure, nor had she tried to make things worse with sympathy or some idiotic claim that she understood how Maj-Britt felt. And that was lucky. Because if she had done that, Maj-Britt would have had to tell her to go to hell, and that was an expression she did not like to use.

Maj-Britt saw the car drive off, and the mother and child went to their door.

Ellinor still showed no sign of leaving. She had completed her duties but was still here; it was always puzzling when she did that. But right now Maj-Britt had something else on her mind and didn't much care.

It was Ellinor who broke the silence first, which was no surprise to either of them.

'Why didn't you say anything about the blood in your urine?'

The mother and her child had gone inside and the main door swung closed behind them. Maj-Britt left the window and went over to the easy chair.

'Why should I? It wouldn't have made it go away.'

There was silence for a while. Water was running through a pipe somewhere in the building, and from outside in the stairwell voices were heard and the sound of footsteps which grew louder and then faded away, only to cease abruptly when the door closed. She looked at Ellinor, who was lost in thought and picking distractedly at the cuticle of her right thumb. Maj-Britt was full of questions, and she knew that Ellinor had the answers. Thoughtfully she sank down in the easy chair.

'How did you know this person, did you say?'

Ellinor abandoned her cuticle.

'Her name is Monika, actually. If that's who you mean.'

Maj-Britt gave her a weary look.

'Excuse me. How do you know *Monika*?'

She pronounced the name with the obvious distaste she felt, and she didn't even have to look at Ellinor to sense how much her remark annoyed her.

'I actually think it was quite decent of her to come over.'

'Of course. A fantastically noble human being.'

Ellinor gave a heavy sigh.

'As I said, sometimes you might think a bit about who deserves your contempt and who doesn't.'

Maj-Britt snorted. And with that it was quiet again. But Maj-Britt knew that if she just waited long enough, Ellinor wouldn't be able to resist telling her. That was the closest thing to a weakness she had been able to find in this obstinate girl. The fact that she couldn't keep her mouth shut. At least not for long.

A few minutes passed.

'I'm not the one who knows her, my mother does.'

Maj-Britt smiled to herself.

'They met at a course a few weeks ago. They went there together in my mother's car.'

Ellinor got up and went over to the window. Maj-Britt listened with interest.

'Do you remember I told you someone died a few weeks ago who lived across the way here?'

Maj-Britt nodded, though Ellinor couldn't see her.

'His name was Mattias. He died on the way home from that course in a car crash. My mother was driving. She hit an elk.'

Maj-Britt stared into space. She could see the father and child outside in the playground in her mind's eye.

'And your mother?'

'Well, it's unbelievable, but she walked away without a scratch. She was in shock, of course, and she has such a guilty conscience because he died and she survived. She was driving, after all. And he had a child and everything.'

Maj-Britt thought some more, watching Ellinor's back as if it might give her some additional clues.

'So that doctor, pardon me, Monika I mean, was she in the car too?'

Ellinor turned round. Stood there a moment and then went back to the sofa. She sat cross-legged and put the embroidered cushion on her lap. Then she suddenly looked at Maj-Britt and smiled. Maj-Britt was instantly on her guard. The little gap she had opened closed up like a clam.

'What is it?'

Ellinor shrugged.

'I suddenly realised that this is the first time we've talked to each other. I mean really talked. The first time you've started a conversation.'

Maj-Britt looked away. She wasn't quite sure that this was a good sign, that she had actually started a conversation voluntarily. She hadn't even noticed it herself. She had done it without thinking, almost as if it had happened naturally. And of course Ellinor had noticed that, the change. For the moment Maj-Britt couldn't decide what it might lead to, whether it was good or bad. Whether it might be turned against her. But she knew that she wanted answers to her questions, so that she would have some sort of compensation if this whole conversation proved to be a mistake.

'I asked whether she was in the car too.'

'No, but she was supposed to be. She and Mattias traded places on the way home, and she rode with someone else instead. The last day of the course was delayed or something, and she was in a hurry to get home, and Mattias offered to stay.'

Maj-Britt took in the information and sorted it as best she could. Attempted to link it with the fact that the doctor had tried so firmly to deny that she knew the fatherless child. And the endless patience with which she had pushed the swing.

She and Mattias traded places on the way home.

'Did they know this Mattias before the course?'

Ellinor shook her head.

'They were all strangers before the course started. That was the whole point.'

And with that Ellinor brought Maj-Britt's thoughts to a conclusion. She had added the one comment that was necessary to link the chain together into an understandable explanation.

'I wonder how she feels, I mean Monika. If they hadn't traded places then she would have been dead now. I wonder how it feels to walk around knowing that.'

To think what a polite attempt at conversation could yield. Her little question had hit the bull's-eye and broken open a peephole right into the insides of that know-it-all doctor. But that was always where the sore points were. Desperately hidden away in the dark, but so easy to get to if you managed to aim the question in the right direction. The only thing that could not be explained was the lie itself. Why had she denied that she knew that child and the mother who had lost her husband because she was still alive?

Unless she had lied to them too.

27

The cemetery was apparently deserted. Monika stood filling a watering can and would soon rejoin her mother by the grave. It had taken Monika only five minutes to stop at the bank, rush in and put the money in Pernilla's account, but she had still arrived late, and as expected her mother had been angry. It had become even worse since she retired. She had all the time in the world to sit and wait. Now every minute had become crucial, and those that went to waste wrought great havoc in her empty calendar. She had never had a particularly large circle of friends, and since she had retired it had become even smaller. She had never met a new husband. Maybe she had never even been interested. Monika didn't know. They never talked about such things. Never talked about anything important at all. They would slip into the meaningless chatter they were used to as soon as they came near each other. They would skid about amongst all the words that never led anywhere and then inevitably slide back to where they started.

Today Monika had hardly been able to control herself when she was met by that peevish glare. With a brusque remark her mother had climbed into the car and then sat in silence during the ten minutes or so that the trip took. And Monika could feel her fury growing. She drove there and back like a cab driver, always trying to adapt herself to her mother's sullen mood and never receiving a thank you, never even a comment that was anywhere near gratitude or appreciation. But the anger was new, it made its way along paths over which she had no control. Had she not been forced into this ferrying role, Mattias would still be alive and everything would be much simpler.

Much simpler.

She left the little fenced gravesite to return the watering can. Her mother was kneeling down, planting heather. Lavender, pink and white. Carefully selected plants.

Monika put down the can and watched her mother's hands gently clearing away some untidy leaves that had settled in the well-tended little flowerbed that surrounded the stone.

My beloved son.

Unconditionally loved and now unconditionally lost, but forever the central point around which everything revolved. A black hole that sucked in everything that could possibly still be alive. Day in and day out supplying new fuel for the attitude that no acceptance was possible, that subjugation was the only option, that everything was ruined and meaningless and would remain so.

A family destroyed.

Four minus two equals zero.

She heard herself saying the words.

'Why did Pappa leave us?'

She saw how the stooped back in front of her flinched. How the hands stopped moving.

'Why do you ask?'

Her heart was thudding in heavy, dull beats.

'Because I want to know. Because I've always wondered but have never got round to asking until now.'

The fingers down by the gravestone regained their mobility and began pressing down the soil around the white heather.

'What made you ask at this particular moment?'

She could hear when it broke. A dull rumble that grew stronger and stronger as the fury she had kept in check for so long tore loose and seized hold of her. The words clogged her mouth, jostling to be first, to escape and finally be spoken.

'Does that matter? I don't know why I didn't ask twenty years ago, but that makes no difference, the answer is probably still the same, isn't it?'

Her mother stood up, carefully and meticulously folding up the newspaper she had been kneeling on.

'Has something happened?'

'What?'

'I just wonder why you have such a disagreeable tone.'

Disagreeable tone? Disagreeable tone! Thirty-eight years old and she had finally worked up the courage to ask why she had never had a father, and the stress just might have affected her tone of voice a bit. And of course her mother's first reaction would be to accuse her of having a disagreeable tone.

'Why don't you ask your father instead?'

She could feel her face growing hot.

'Because I don't know him! Because I don't even know where the hell he lives now, and because you never once tried to help me get in touch with him. In fact, I remember how angry you got when I told you that I wrote him a letter.'

She had a hard time deciding what she was seeing

in her mother's eyes. She had never broached the topic before and had definitely never used this tone of voice. Not in any situation.

'So it's my fault that he left us and never took any responsibility? Is that it? I'm the one who has to answer for it? Your father was an idiot who got me pregnant even though he didn't want any kids, and then when he did it again, it was the last straw for him. He disappeared while you were still in my womb. I already had Lasse, and being a single mother to two small children isn't always easy. But, of course, you wouldn't know anything about that since you don't have any.'

A rhythmic throbbing sound echoed over the cemetery, and it took Monika a moment before she recognised it was her own pulse she was hearing.

'So that's why you never liked me? Because it was my fault that Pappa left?'

'That's idiotic and you know it as well as I do.'

'No, I don't know it!'

Her mother took a cemetery candle out of the pocket of her ample coat and angrily began picking off the plastic wrapper. But she didn't answer.

'Why do we always have to come here to the grave? It's been twenty-three years since he died and the only thing we do together is drive here and light those damned candles.'

'It's not my fault that you never have time. You're always working. Or out with your friends. You never have time for me.'

Always, always, whatever she did. Despite the anger that protected her at the moment, she felt the accusations go straight through her. Sparking the guilty conscience that her mother could play like a virtuoso.

And she was still not finished. Like the maestro she was she could sense the distinct nuance of change in Monika's face. And she wasn't going to waste her chance.

'You didn't even grieve for him.'

At first Monika didn't understand the words.

You didn't even grieve for him.

Like an echo the words ricocheted around trying to make themselves understood, and each time they were repeated something was shattered. Bit by bit everything came crashing down.

You didn't even grieve for him.

Her mother's voice was muffled and she kept her eyes on the candle she was holding in her hand.

'You just went on as if nothing had happened. If you only knew how I suffered, seeing the way you behaved. Almost as if you thought it was good that he was gone.'

There were no words left. Everything was empty. Her feet started to walk towards the car. All she felt was a genuine wish to get out of earshot.

There were woods on both sides and dusk was approaching. The car was parked by the side of a country road. She looked around nervously and didn't know where she was or how she had ended up there. She looked at her watch. In fifteen minutes she had promised to eat dinner at Pernilla's. She turned the car round, guessing that was the right direction to go.

You didn't even grieve for him.

'Could you change Daniella? I just have to make the gravy and then we'll be ready to eat.'

She wanted to go home. Home to her sleeping pills.

Lightning was flashing through her head and it was hard to put all the words she heard into context.

'Could you do it?'

She gave a quick nod and lifted up Daniella. Carried her into the changing table over the bathtub and took off her nappy. Pernilla called from the kitchen.

'You can put on her red pyjamas afterwards. They're hanging on one of the hooks.'

She turned her head and caught sight of the red pyjamas. Changed the nappy and did as Pernilla said. On the way back to the kitchen she passed the chest of drawers. The candle had burned down and his face lay in shadow behind the white urn. He said nothing when she passed by, left her in peace.

'Please help yourself. I'm sure it's not as good as what you usually serve, I'm not very good at cooking. Mattias cooked most of the time.'

Daniella sat in her high chair and Pernilla put an unsalted biscuit on the mat in front of her. Monika looked at the food on the table. It was going to be impossible to eat anything, but she had to try.

They ate for a while in silence. Monika moved the food about on her plate and occasionally put a tiny bite in her mouth, but her body refused to swallow. Each time she tried it got more difficult.

'Monika.'

She looked up. Felt herself immediately on guard despite her fatigue and confusion. It was a risk to be here. Now that she had already lost control.

'I'd like to apologise.'

Monika sat quite still. Pernilla put down her knife

and fork and gave Daniella another biscuit before she went on.

'I know that sometimes I've been pretty unpleasant when you've been here, but I just couldn't manage to be polite.'

Monika's mouth was dry and she had to swallow before she could get any words out.

'You most certainly have not been unpleasant.'

'Yes, I have been, but I've done the best I could. Sometimes it just gets so hard that I simply can't bear it.'

Monika put down her knife and fork too. The fewer things she needed to concentrate on the better. She had to try and pull herself together. Focus. Pernilla had just offered to apologise for something. She had to think of something to say.

'You really don't need to apologise for anything.'

Pernilla looked down at her plate.

'I just want you to know I appreciate that you can still stand to come here.'

Monika raised her water glass and took a little sip.

'After my accident a lot of our friends disappeared. It seemed almost natural, they all just faded away. I always had pain in my back and we didn't have any money either, and most of our friends were still into scuba diving.'

Monika took another sip. It was almost possible to hide behind the water glass.

'Now, after what's happened, I can finally admit that I feel a little disappointed that so few of them bothered to call. All of a sudden it was clear how lonely we've been.'

Pernilla looked at her and smiled, almost shyly.

'So, what I'm trying to say is just that I'm glad we've got to know each other. You've really been a big help.'

Monika tried to take in what she was hearing. Sensed that this was what she had been striving for the whole time, and she ought to be happy now that she had finally received the proof of her success. Then why did she feel this way? She had to go home. Home to her sleeping pills. But first she had to go to the clinic with Maj-Britt's samples. When she was sure that everyone had gone home she would go in there and analyse them. Because she had promised. And you have to keep your promises.

She jumped when the telephone rang. Pernilla got up and went into the living room. Monika sneaked over to the rubbish bag under the sink and scraped off her plate with a piece of clingfilm that was lying on the top.

She could hear Pernilla answer the phone in the living room.

'Pernilla.'

She hid the food underneath an empty milk carton.

'Well, that's to be expected, I don't really know what you want me to say.'

Pernilla's voice had taken on a hard tone and she was silent for a long time. Monika went back to the table with her plate and used her fork to erase any traces left by the plastic wrap. Then Pernilla spoke again and the words made Monika's fear surge up through her confusion.

'Honestly, I wish you wouldn't call me again. What happened happened, all of it, but I think it's a bit much to expect me to be consoling *you*.'

She was apparently interrupted but continued a few seconds later.

'No, but that's how it feels. Goodbye.'

Silence. Everything was quiet. Only Monika's heart refused to adapt itself to the calm. Pernilla reappeared and went to sit down on her chair. At the same moment Monika's mobile rang. It wasn't her intention to answer it, as she began to fumble for the handbag by her feet, just to shut off the insistent ringing. She glanced at the display and saw Åse's name. Her hand shook as she managed to cancel the call. She could feel Pernilla watching her but answered before she could ask the question.

'It was nothing important. Only my mother, but I can ring her later.'

Pernilla pushed away the plate in front of her even though it was still full of food.

'It was that woman who drove the car that called me.'

Daniella dropped her biscuit on the floor and Monika gratefully leaned down to pick it up. So she could be out of sight for a second.

'She was here a few days after the accident too. She came here wanting to apologise or whatever.'

Pernilla snorted.

'I'd taken so many pills that I probably didn't really understand what was going on. I've thought about it quite a lot afterwards. I was sorry I didn't just tell her to go to hell. How the fuck can she think that I would forgive her?'

Suddenly, Pernilla was sitting at the other end of a tunnel. Monika stared at her face, which was surrounded by a surging, dark-grey mass. She squeezed her eyes shut and opened them again only to be met by the same image. And she wondered why the water was running, who had turned on the tap, why it was roaring like that.

'What is it? Don't you feel well?'

She was breathing with quick, short breaths.

'I'm all right, but I have to go now.'

'But I've got dessert too.'

Monika got up from her chair.

'I have to go now.'

Her movement made the tunnel disappear. The roaring was still there but she saw that the tap was turned off, so the sound must be coming from some other flat.

She staggered out to the hall, holding on to door frames and walls for support. Pernilla followed her.

'Are you okay?'

'Yes, but I have to go now.'

She pulled on her boots and coat. Pernilla was holding her handbag and gave it to her.

'I'll ring you tomorrow.'

Monika didn't reply, just opened the front door. She had to go now. Pernilla had asked her to stay but she had to go. She could come back some other day, because Pernilla was her friend and was grateful for their friendship. For everything Monika had done for her. She hadn't told her to go to hell the way she wanted to do with Åse. No, the two of them were real friends now, and you could count on real friends. They never lied to each other. They were there in good times and bad and were always willing to help out.

Pernilla had one friend left, and that was the honourable Monika Lundvall.

If she somehow betrayed her too, Pernilla would be utterly alone.

28

Maj-Britt was standing by the balcony door waiting for Saba to come back inside. The dog had just squeezed out through the gap in the balcony railing and vanished from view down on the lawn.

Maj-Britt had shoved the easy chair over next to the window and had spent most of the past two days sitting there, but nothing very exciting had happened outside. The doctor had visited the widow once. The same day she had seen Maj-Britt and done her disgusting examination, she had shown up again towards evening, but after that she had not put in an appearance. She hadn't called about the test results either, but that didn't make much difference. Ellinor was the one who was waiting impatiently.

Maj-Britt herself experienced the respite as mostly pleasant. The tablets that Ellinor had picked up relieved the pain, and as long as she didn't hear any news there were really no decisions to be made. She stayed right there in the flat doing what she always did, sitting from one silence to the next. The only thing that was different was that the pain in her back was better, and she wasn't eating so much anymore. It wasn't merely the nausea that stopped her. The urge to stuff something in her mouth had been checked, and it was suddenly easy to refrain although she didn't really understand why. Something had retreated when she dared follow all her thoughts to their conclusion. When she approached all the intolerable memories and recognised their repulsiveness, she no longer had to hide from them. Didn't have to flee. They still hurt just as much as she had always known they did, deep inside, and now that she acknowledged it, they couldn't scare her anymore. They were losing their power.

She saw Ellinor coming along the walkway down below. It looked cold outside. Her midriff was bare between her jersey and trousers, and Maj-Britt shook her head. That thin denim jacket wasn't enough for this time of year. But it was apparent that all those little self-assured plastic buttons that decorated it might have stopped the worst of the cold from penetrating. She saw Saba lumber across the lawn to meet her, and Ellinor looked up at the balcony door and waved. Maj-Britt waved back. And she felt something warm inside.

'She's going to come by at two. She said nothing about test results or anything else, but wanted to talk to you in person.'

Ellinor was squatting and untying her boots as she talked. Maj-Britt felt a momentary loathing at the thought of letting that doctor in her flat again, but then she remembered her hold on her and it felt a little better. If you knew where you had each other, everything was so much easier. As long as neither person had the upper hand. That doctor might hold the answers to the mysteries of her body, and she could easily make use of that, but if she did, Maj-Britt had made sure she possessed adequate countermeasures.

No one would ever be allowed to do anything to her again unless she gave her express permission.

It was only a few minutes until two o'clock. Maj-Britt took her place in the easy chair with a view of the parking area, but she hadn't seen anything of the car when the doorbell rang, strangely enough. This was a little miscalculation that she didn't care for, the fact that she hadn't sufficiently prepared herself.

Ellinor went and opened the door.

'Hello, how nice of you to come by.'

The doctor replied briefly, and a minute later Maj-Britt had both of them in the living room. She noticed that the doctor had something in her hand that looked like a small grey briefcase with a cord and some knobs on it.

'Hello, Maj-Britt.'

Maj-Britt gave the apparatus in her hand a suspicious glance.

'What's that?'

'Could I sit down for a moment?'

Maj-Britt nodded and the doctor – no way was she going to call her Monika – sat down on the sofa, placing the strange object on the table in front of her. She took some papers out of her handbag. Maj-Britt didn't take her eyes off her, registering every little movement. She observed with interest that the papers in her hand were shaking a bit.

'So, here it is.'

The doctor unfolded the papers. Ellinor was watching her attentively. Maj-Britt turned and looked towards the window instead. She really did not feel particularly interested.

'Your sedimentation rate is abnormally high, and your blood count is quite low. The sample showed no bacteria in the urine, and I found none after culturing either, so we can definitely rule out any infection in the urinary tract. A kidney stone was another thought I had, but then the pain would have come more suddenly, and besides it wouldn't affect the sedimentation rate.'

She paused and Maj-Britt kept her eyes on the swings outside. What she did *not* suffer from was even less interesting to her.

'So I'm healthy then?'

'No, you're not.'

There was a brief pause when everything was still safe.

'I need to do an ultrasound.'

Still on her guard, Maj-Britt turned her head and met the doctor's gaze.

'I'm not going anywhere.'

'No, we can do it here.'

The doctor placed her hand on the apparatus on the table. Maj-Britt felt trapped. She had made up her mind not to go through any more examinations. Her refusal to leave the flat should have taken care of that, but now this doctor had dragged in equipment that would make it possible. What bad luck.

'And what if I refuse?'

'Maj-Britt!'

It was Ellinor. The boundary between entreaty and exasperation was gone.

Maj-Britt looked out the window again.

'What do you think you might find with this ultrasound?'

It was Ellinor asking about the details that Maj-Britt herself had absolutely no interest in, and the two women began to discuss her possible ailment.

'I'm not sure, of course, but I need to take a look at her kidneys.'

'What do you think it might be?'

Again there was a pause, but all sense of calm was now gone. It was as if the word already lay quivering in the room, before it had even been uttered. Floating in one last moment of innocence.

'It might be a tumour. But as I said,' she added quickly, 'I'm not one hundred percent certain.'

A tumour. Cancer. That was a word she had heard on TV many times and it had never passed by entirely unnoticed. But at that moment she realised that when something was mentioned that might possibly exist in her own body, then it felt considerably different. Then the word came alive, transformed into an image of something black and evil inside. It was almost possible to imagine a monster living inside her that swallowed everything in its path and kept growing bigger.

And yet she was not particularly afraid. It was more as if yet another thought she had not dared follow to its conclusion had finally been confirmed. Because why shouldn't her body have cancer? It would be its last triumph over her futile, lifelong resistance. Lying in ambush and nourishing a growth in order to take its revenge once and for all, to conquer her.

And she realised that she had to know.

'How is such a procedure done?'

Because in some way she did feel the need to have it confirmed.

* * *

The room was utterly silent. Maj-Britt was back in the easy chair. Ellinor leant forward in the sofa with her head in her hands. And in the middle of the room the doctor stood packing up her fancy apparatus which had just reinforced the suspicions that they all clearly shared. Maj-Britt was pleased to confirm that the doctor's hands were still trembling. For some reason it made her feel better to see that.

'As far as I could tell the tumour is still contained within the surface of the kidney, but of course we have to do a contrast X-ray to know for sure. From what I saw there were no signs of metastasis, but that also has to be checked. But it was large, so it's high time to have it removed.'

Maj-Britt felt strangely calm. She looked towards the window again. At the swings that she had looked at for more than thirty years but had never seen up close.

'And if it's not removed?'

No one answered, but after a while she heard a little puffing sound from Ellinor.

'Well, what if it's not removed?'

Now it was Maj-Britt's turn to be silent. She had said everything that needed to be said.

'Maj-Britt, what do you mean by that? You must realise that you have to get rid of it! Isn't that right, Monika? How long can someone live with that sort of tumour if it isn't treated?'

'That's impossible to answer. I have no idea how long it's been growing in there.'

'Well, approximately?'

Ellinor, as usual, was meticulous about details.

'Six months perhaps. Maybe more, maybe less, it

depends on how fast it's growing. As a doctor I must strongly recommend an operation.'

As a doctor. Maj-Britt snorted to herself.

Ellinor's mobile rang and she went out into the hall.

Maj-Britt watched the woman who was very carefully packing up her fancy apparatus.

Six months.

Maybe.

It was hard to tell, she had said.

'You doctors, it's your job to do everything you can to save other people's lives.'

She didn't really know why she said that, but she couldn't help herself. Maybe it was to strip off a little of the officiousness that the doctor radiated. Like goodness personified she stood there pretending to be at the service of all humanity. But she was careful to conceal her own dark secrets; underneath that impeccable surface brooded the same dirty mistakes and shortcomings that all mortals possessed.

Maj-Britt read her reaction at once and it made her want to hammer in the spike a little deeper.

'To make people live as long as possible, remain here on earth with their families and get to see their children grow up. That's probably what you doctors are here for. There's probably nothing that could be more important to you.'

Ellinor was standing in the doorway again.

The doctor bent down and snapped her bag shut, and Maj-Britt saw that she had to brace herself on the arm of the sofa when she stood up. A quick motion with her hand so she wouldn't lose her balance. Without looking in Maj-Britt's direction she went out into the hall. Maj-Britt could just make out a terse conversation.

'Unfortunately there's nothing more I can do until you contact her care centre and go through the required process. They'll arrange the referrals to the hospital for further investigation.'

The front door was opened and Ellinor's last words echoed between the stone walls in the stairwell.

'Thanks for all your help.'

And then the door was closed.

Ellinor stayed on an extra hour even though she had several clients waiting. Maj-Britt didn't say much, but Ellinor's gift of the gab reached new heights in a desperate attempt to convince Maj-Britt to give her permission to ring the care centre. But Maj-Britt didn't want to. She didn't intend to suffer through any more examinations, not to mention any operations.

Why should she?

Why should she co-operate at all?

No matter how painful it was to admit, she couldn't for the life of her come up with anything that was even close to resembling a reason.

29

The woman was a monstrosity. As if she had stepped right out of a horror film. It must be to punish her that fate had set this repulsive woman in Monika's path. It was as though her sharp eyes could see straight through her, see right into her, and for some reason that Monika did not understand, the woman was intent on doing her harm.

She had driven the shortest way home and gone straight into the bathroom without even taking off her coat or boots. There she had swallowed two Zopax tablets. She had written herself a prescription for them at the same time as the sleeping pills but hadn't taken any before.

But she could no longer stand it.

She went into the living room and wandered about, waiting for the pills to take effect. Each second, each instant. It was no longer possible to escape. It was as if there was no room in her body, and at any moment her skin might start to shatter. A feeling that she was about to burst.

And then there was her phone. It kept ringing and ringing, and the noise drove her crazy, but she didn't dare turn it off. It was proof that there was a functioning reality somewhere, and if she completely cut off contact with it she didn't know where she might end up. She just couldn't understand how everything had come to this or what she had to do to put it all right again.

At last.

At last she felt the anxiety loosen its grip, pull in its barbs and dissolve. Letting her breathe. Gratefully she stood in the middle of the room and welcomed the sense of liberation. Stockholm white. That was the colour of the living-room walls. It was odd that in this town it was all right to have Stockholm white on the walls. Almost reassuring in some way. That anything was possible. Just breathe. Breathe calmly and quietly. Nothing else is important. She just had to go and lie down for a bit on the sofa and take time to breathe.

Red brick walls. A cellar. She was in a cellar, but she didn't know whose. She couldn't see a door anywhere. She felt with her hands across the rough wall to find a crack or some sign of an opening, but there was none. Suddenly she knew that there was a dead body sealed up inside the wall, she didn't know who it was but she knew she was the one who had walled it in there. She heard a sound and turned round. Her mother was kneeling and planting an orchid. She had a piece of bread in her hand, which she crumbled up and threw across the floor. *Columba livia. They're best with chanterelles*. And then a train was coming. Pernilla stood in the middle of the tracks and the train whistle grew louder. Monika ran as fast as she could but she never got any closer; she wouldn't be able to save her. She had to make the ringing stop, had to make it stop. Make it stop.

'Hello?'

She had her mobile in her hand. She was standing in her hallway with her coat and boots on but still wasn't quite sure.

'Yes, hi, it's Pernilla.'

The voice convinced her that she was back in reality, but she was still pleasantly high. She was a safe distance from everything that might hurt her or threaten her and not even her body reacted. Her heart was beating with a calm, regular rhythm.

'Hi.'

'I just wanted to hear how you're doing. Your last visit was a bit brief and I thought maybe you'd taken ill.'

Taken ill. Pernilla's words were repeated like an echo. Taken ill. Maybe she had. If she was ill then she would certainly be entitled to a few days' respite from her task, and hadn't she actually earned it? Only a few days? She was so incredibly tired. If only she could get enough sleep then everything would be better. She'd be able to think clearly again, make a plan for how to proceed, how to solve everything for the best. Right now she was too tired. Her brain had taken on a life of its own and no longer obeyed her. If only she could sleep, everything would be better.

'Yes, I've been ill. I'm in bed with a fever.'

'Oh no, maybe you caught it from Daniella, she's not feeling well either.'

Monika didn't reply. If Daniella was sick she ought to be there. It was part of the agreement, but she just couldn't. She had to get some sleep.

'Well, I won't bother you if you're not feeling well. Give me a ring when you're on your feet again. If there's anything you need, just call, if you need help shopping or anything.'

Monika closed her eyes.

'Thanks.'

She couldn't say anymore, and clicked off her phone. With her back pressed against the front door she slid down to the floor. She propped her elbows on her bent knees and hid her face in her hands. The stupor from the pills spared her from fully taking in the thoughts that flashed past. What a fragile line there was between cruelty and care. But what was evil? Who set the rules? Who assumed the right to define a truth that would apply to everyone under any circumstance? All she wanted was to help, fix things, make the unreasonable 'Never again' less ruthless. Because everything *could* be set right if only you made the proper effort. It had to be true! Had to!

She would continue to stand by Pernilla's side; anything else was unthinkable. She would continue to subordinate herself, be on hand as long as Pernilla needed her, put her own life aside as long as necessary. And yet she knew that in the long run it wouldn't be enough. It was Pernilla's husband and her daughter's father that Monika had stolen, not her best friend. She straightened up and she stared sightlessly at the wall opposite. She hadn't realised it before, but that was the solution. Pernilla had to meet a new man. A man who could fill Mattias's place in a completely different way than she herself could ever do. Become a new father to Daniella, take over the burden of supporting them, give Pernilla the love that Mattias's death had robbed her of.

Monika got to her feet and let her coat drop to the

floor. Filled with this new insight she felt everything grow lighter. If she saw to it that Pernilla met a new man, her task would be complete, then she would have fulfilled her obligation. They could still see each other as friends and Pernilla would never know the truth.

Monika's debt to Mattias would be absolved.

She went into the bedroom and squeezed a sleeping pill out of the foil pack. First of all she had to get some sleep. A good night's sleep so that her brain would obey her again. Then she would be ready to start to implement her new plan. Coax Pernilla out of her corner, invite her along on a trip abroad, put classified ads in her name on the Internet and in the papers.

She would fix things.

Everything would be put right again.

She let her clothes drop where she stood. The instant her head hit the pillow she was sleeping soundly, convinced that she had finally regained control.

30

Maj-Britt was sitting in her easy chair in the twilight. The shadows grew darker in the flat and finally merged with their surroundings.

Six months.

At first she felt almost nothing. Six months was only a concept of time. Twelve months was a year and six months was half, there was nothing particularly remarkable about that. She counted on her fingers. October the twelfth. October the twelfth plus six months. That would be April. An autumn, a winter, but hardly any spring.

October the twelfth.

It had been October the twelfth many times before in her life, even though she couldn't remember in detail what she had done on all those days. They had probably passed quite unnoticed like most of the rest. But this October the twelfth would be very special. It would be the very last one.

She had sat there in the easy chair for a good four hours, which meant that the last October the twelfth of her life was already four hours shorter.

It wasn't leaving life that scared her. So much time and so many years had gone by without her having any use for them. It had been a long time since life had offered her anything that she was especially interested in.

But to die.

To be eradicated without leaving a single trace behind, not even the tiniest impression. As long as she had taken the future for granted, the possibility had always been there, it had been so easy to postpone. But starting now her time was limited; it was counting down and each minute was suddenly a perceptible loss. It was absolutely inconceivable that this was the same 'time' that for years had pushed its way forward in such abundance that she had no idea what to do with it. Pushed forward and past, becoming drowned in meaninglessness. She would vanish without leaving a single tiny trace.

Her hands gripped the arm-rests harder.

Whether she gave her permission or not, she would be forced to surrender herself to the great Beyond, to eternity, and no one knew what awaited anyone there.

Imagine if they had been right. If what they had tried to imprint on her with such zeal was true. What if it was there the great Judgement awaited? If it was true, she knew all too well that her reception would not be a merciful one. It took no deep self-examination to realise which of the scales would weigh more. Maybe He would be standing there on the other side waiting, pleased and satisfied finally to have her under His power. Now that her right to choose had been used up and she unquestionably deserved a sort of retribution.

There was no reason to live, but did she dare to die? How could she dare surrender to eternity when she didn't know what it involved?

The ultimate loneliness.
For eternity.
When so much was left undone.

The darkness in the flat took over and her unease grew stronger. With each moment that passed it became more and more obvious. In some way she would have to balance out the scales.

She saw the woman before her, the one who had stood there in her room a few hours ago and pronounced her death sentence, glancing furtively at her thin wrist with its expensive watch, and then with a frightened look hurrying off. Outwardly so irreproachable but so conscious of her guilt. When the next October the twelfth came she wouldn't remember either Maj-Britt or this day. It would all have been lost somewhere in the jumble of other dying patients and days that were no different from any other. In peace and quiet she would be able to continue her life down here on earth, with all the time in the world to absolve her guilt.

Maj-Britt would not be able to do that.

Starting now, each second that passed uselessly was a lost opportunity.

She got up. Saba stood waiting inside the balcony door, and she went over and opened it. There was a light in the window across the way where the man had lived, the one who now possessed the answer which all people down through the ages had sought.

And she thought about Monika again. The guilt she bore.

Two lives, each with too much weight on one side of the scales.

It had suddenly become harder to breathe, and she realised to her horror how afraid she was. She was used to solitude, but to go alone to meet what awaited her . . .

Our Father Who art in heaven . . .

She turned round and looked towards the wardrobe. She knew that it lay hidden on the top shelf, untouched all these years, with the familiar wear on the cover from that time so long ago. But she had turned her back on Him. Said that she could manage without Him and told Him to leave her in peace. Renounced Him. Now she understood at once. With crystal-clear certainty everything was suddenly made manifest. He had only been biding His time. He always knew that she would come crawling back the day the grains of sand in the hourglass unquestionably began to run out. When she could no longer hide in life but stood naked before what everyone knows but pretends to ignore. The fact that one day everything will come to an end. That one day everyone must give up all that is familiar and surrender to what has been the greatest fear of humanity since time immemorial.

He knew that then she would inevitably cry out for Him, begging Him on her knees for His forgiveness and blessing and pleading for His mercy.

He had been right.

He had won and she had lost.

She lay naked before Him, ready for submission.

The defeat was monumental.

She closed her eyes and felt herself blushing. In the colour of shame she went over to the wardrobe and opened the doors. Felt on the shelf with her hand, over piles of sheets and tablecloths and curtains forgotten for years, until she finally felt the familiar shape. She stopped, hesitating a bit; the humiliation burned like fire. And confessing that she had done wrong was also to confess that He had always been right. It increased her guilt even more. She was giving Him the right to punish her.

She found the Bible and took it down. Looked at the well-thumbed book covers. Something was inserted between the pages and without thinking she pulled out what was concealed inside. Not until it was too late and her eyes had already seen them did she remember what they were. Two photographs. Slowly she went back to the easy chair and sank down in it. Closed her eyes but opened them again and let her gaze take in the loving couple. A beautiful spring day. A slim white dress and Göran in a black suit. The veil she had chosen with such care. Their hands intertwined. Their sense of conviction. Utter certainty. Vanja right behind them, so happy for her sake. The familiar smile, the gleam in her eyes, her Vanja who was always there whenever she needed her. Who had always wished her well. And to whom even now she had lied: betraying, condemning and rejecting her.

Too much weight on one side of the scales.

She dropped the photograph on the floor and looked at the other one. Her breath caught when she met the girl's empty gaze. She was sitting on a blanket on the kitchen floor in the house they had rented. The little red dress. The tiny white shoes that she got from Göran's parents.

She could feel the tears coming. Her hands remembered how it felt to lift up that little body, hold her in her arms, the way she smelled. The tiny hands that reached out for her in boundless trust but which she hadn't been capable of receiving. How could she, when no one had ever taught her how to do that sort of thing.

The sorrow she never permitted herself to feel welled up inside her, and the despair she felt was so deep that she couldn't breathe. She dropped the photograph and, clenching her fists convulsively, she raised them towards the ceiling.

'Lord God in heaven, help me. Be merciful to me, erase my transgressions with Your great mercy, cleanse me of my misdeeds and purify me of my sin. Against You alone have I sinned and done what is evil, that You may be found righteous in Your words and impartial in Your judgement. Behold, I was brought forth in iniquity, and in sin my mother conceived me.'

Her hands were shaking.

Six months was too long a time. She wouldn't be able to stand it for so long.

The tears ran down her cheeks and she sobbed out her words.

'I beg Your forgiveness because I commit the evil that I do not wish to commit. Blessed God, grant me Your forgiveness. You must give me an answer! Dear Lord, show Your mercy! Give me courage to dare!'

And she remembered what they used to do when they needed His counsel and consolation. She quickly wiped her eyes, grasped the Bible firmly in her left hand, and moved her right thumb between the closed book covers. Then she closed her eyes and turned to the page where her thumb had stopped, letting her index finger search over the page and choose a verse at random. Then she stayed seated, with her eyes closed and her finger pointing like a spear straight down into the Holy Scriptures. It was now He would speak. Give the message He wanted to show her and which He had made her finger select.

'Lord, do not leave me alone.'

She was so afraid. All she wanted was a little reassurance, a single sign that she had nothing to fear, that she could be forgiven. That He was by her side now that everything would soon be over, that atonement was possible. She took a deep breath and put on her glasses, following her finger to the page in the Bible.

And when she read the verse she understood once and for all that the fear she felt now was nothing compared with that which awaited her.

Her hands shook when she read His Word:

Now the end has come upon you, and I will send My anger against you; I will judge you according to your ways, and I will repay you for all your abominations. My eye will not spare you, nor will I have pity; but I will repay your ways, and your abominations will be in your midst; then you shall know that I am the LORD!

A terror she did not think possible pressed the last of the air out of her lungs.

She had received her answer.

He had finally replied.

31

Her sleep was dreamless. An emptiness where nothing existed. Only a tiresome noise somewhere in the background. Stubbornly it hacked away and demanded her attention. She wanted to slip back into the emptiness, but the noise would not relent. She had to make it stop.

'Hello?'

'Is this Monika Lundvall?'

Everything was so fuzzy that she couldn't reply. She made an attempt to open her eyes but couldn't do it; only her hand's grip on the phone managed to convince her that what she was experiencing was real. Everything was pleasantly diffuse. Her head lay on the pillow and in the brief silence that arose, sleep seized hold of her again. But then more words came.

'Hello? Is this Monika Lundvall?'

'Yes.'

Because she thought that's who she was.

'This is Maj-Britt Pettersson here. I need to talk to you.'

With an effort Monika managed to open her eyes, trying to distinguish enough of reality so she would be capable of replying. It was completely dark in the room. She realised that she was lying in her bed and that she had answered the phone when it rang and that the person who was calling was someone she never wanted to talk to again.

'You'll have to speak with the care centre.'

'It's not about that. It's another matter. Something important.'

She propped herself up on one elbow and shook her head in an attempt to clear her mind. To understand what was happening and if possible find a way out so that she could go back to sleep.

The voice went on.

'I don't want to tell you on the phone so I suggest you come over here. Shall we say nine o'clock tomorrow morning?'

Monika glanced at the clock radio. 3.49. She was almost sure it was night because it was dark outside the window.

'I can't come then.'

'When can you?'

'I can't come over at all. You'll have to talk to your care centre.'

Never in her life would she go there again. Never. She had no obligations. Not to that woman. She had already done more than anyone could reasonably ask. She was just about to hang up when the voice continued.

'You know, when someone finds out that she's going to die she's not as afraid to go out any longer. And if she's been sitting in a flat for more than thirty years, she has a lot of catching up to do. Like spending time with her neighbours, for example.'

The fear was unable to penetrate the fog of the drugs. It stayed on the outside, pounded angrily a few times, and then gave up and stood watch. To wait her out. It knew that sooner or later a gap would open up and then it would be ready to overpower her. In the meantime it made her realise that she had no choice. She had to go there. Had to go there and find out what that disgusting woman wanted from her.

She closed her eyes. So tired, down to her very core. Everything she had was used up.

'Hello? Are you still there?'

The woman most certainly was.

'Yes.'

'Then let's say nine o'clock.'

32

Maj-Britt sat as if paralysed in her chair, unable to breathe. Her thoughts darted like frightened animals trying to escape. For hours she had prayed, beseeching Him for a sign that would show her what she had to do. Time after time she had let her finger race through the pages of the Bible without finding any intelligible answer. In desperation she had asked for clearer instructions and then, finally, the fourteenth time she tried He had spoken to her again. Paul's first letter to Timothy. Her finger had not landed precisely there, but on the next page, but she knew it was because she had been too excited and her finger had missed the right verse. It was 1 Timothy 4:16 He wanted to show her, she knew it.

Take heed to yourself and to the doctrine. Continue in them, for in doing this you will save both yourself and those who hear you.

Thankful for His answer, she closed her eyes. She remembered the verse from the Congregation. An admonition to go out and save your fellow man and thereby rescue them from eternal fire. A good deed. He wanted her to save someone else and thus also save herself. But who was it she was supposed to save? Who? Who was it who needed her help?

* * *

She got up and went over to the balcony door. On the wall across the way the windows reflected black. Only a single lamp was attempting to defy the dark of night. She wanted to open the door and take a quick breath of the outside air. The desire was new and unfamiliar. She placed her hand on the door handle, saw the black windows staring at her like evil eyes and gave up. She left the door and went back to her easy chair.

The Bible felt heavy in her hand. Once again she let her thumb choose a page. He mustn't let her down now, now that she had understood what she had to do but not how to proceed. She was asking for a lot, she knew that. He had already shown His great benevolence through the answers He had given her.

'Only one more answer, Lord, then I shall never again ask You for anything. Just show me who it is You want me to save.'

She closed her eyes. For the last time she let her thumb glide along the closed pages of the Bible. If He did not answer now, then she wouldn't try again. She turned to the page. With her eyes closed she let her index finger fall and then sat still, gathering her courage.

The fifty-second Psalm. He had not let her down.

In a sudden calm, everything fell into place.

There was only one Monika Lundvall in the telephone book.

Maj-Britt hung up the phone. With a strong grip on the Holy Scriptures she took a few deep breaths. She had done it, done as He instructed, and that should have made her feel reassured. And yet her heart was beating hard. Her finger was still wedged in between the covers, and she turned to the page to convince herself once more that she really had the right to do what she planned to do. Despite her promise she had asked Him another question. And He had given His consent. The page she turned to had the word 'Yes' five times and 'No' only twice.

Saba was sleeping soundly in her basket and Maj-Britt tried to take some comfort in the peaceful sound of the dog's breathing. So many nights it had helped her to calm down. The knowledge that someone was there in the dark. Someone who needed her. Someone who would be there when she woke up and be glad to see her. Now the comforting breathing gave her a guilty conscience. Saba would be left behind to meet the same uncertain fate as she would. The only difference was that Saba didn't have the awareness to be afraid.

There were five hours left until it would be nine o'clock. To try and sleep would be wasting time needlessly, and she could no longer afford to do that. She had been given a task that she had to carry out, and God had shown her the way. She knew that Monika would show up. That she wouldn't dare do anything else. Once again Maj-Britt felt her heart palpitating wildly as she thought about what she was about to do.

A good deed.

She mustn't forget that. That it was A Good Deed and nothing more. The threatening tone she had been forced to use to make Monika obey served a higher good! The Lord Himself had shown His approval. It was the two of them now, she and the Lord together. Using fear to prevail was a mighty instrument, but she was grateful at having to subjugate herself. All power was His, and for her all that remained was to prove herself worthy, show that she finally deserved to be chosen. Then perhaps He in His great wisdom would be merciful enough to forgive her.

For thirty years she had imagined death as a last avenue of escape. It had given her strength to know that she could always slip away if she couldn't endure anymore. Having power over this option, she had sometimes toyed with the idea. But that was before, when death had been far out of sight and the choice was still hers. Before her body had secretly invited death in and granted it safe passage, slowly and inexorably to crush her advantage and finally rob her of all choice. Now that death was grinning in her face, it held nothing but burning horror.

Now the end has come upon you, and I will send My wrath against you; I will judge you according to your ways. Then you shall know that I am the LORD!

33

Maj-Britt Pettersson.

The mere name on the letter-box made her feel sick. But she was still safely sheltered, out of reach. She knew that the terror lay in wait out there, but it could not get to her. The tiny white pills had blocked all passages.

She put her finger on the doorbell and pressed it. She had parked the car on the other side of the building so Pernilla wouldn't see it, and like the last time she was here she had gone in through the cellar entrance at the end of the building.

She heard someone inside and then the lock clicked open. She shuddered as she stepped across the threshold; she never would have thought she could be persuaded to return.

She kept her coat on but took off her boots. The fat dog came up and sniffed at her, but when she took no notice it turned and left. She cast a glance into the empty kitchen as she passed, wondering whether Ellinor was there too, but she didn't seem to be. She continued towards the living room. For an instant she wasn't sure whether she was approaching the living-room doorway or it was approaching her.

The monstrosity was sitting in the easy chair and

motioned towards the sofa with one hand. A sweeping gesture that perhaps was meant to be welcoming.

'It was nice of you to come. Please have a seat.'

Monika didn't intend to stay long and remained standing in the doorway. Just get this over with so that she could leave.

'What is it you want?'

The gigantic woman sat quite still and watched her with her penetrating gaze, apparently satisfied with the situation. Because she was smiling. For the first time, she smiled at Monika, and for some reason it felt even more disagreeable than her usual behaviour. Monika was uncomfortably aware of the woman's superior position. The mere fact that she had agreed to come was a confession as good as a written affidavit. Her dazed brain tried to figure out what was actually happening, but she didn't recognise her thoughts any longer. Ellinor and Maj-Britt and Åse and Pernilla. The names buzzed around and stumbled over each other but she could no longer figure out who knew what or why they knew it. And she didn't even want to go near the thought of what would happen if everything was revealed and became public knowledge. But everything was going to be fine. She would just see to it that Pernilla met a new man and was happy again and they would continue to be friends and everyone would live happily ever after.

She had almost forgotten where she was when she heard the voice from the easy chair again.

'I'm sorry I had to resort to such words to get you to come here, but as I said it's important. It's for your own good.'

She smiled again and Monika felt a little sick.

'I asked you to come because I want to help you. It may not seem that way right now, but one day you will understand.'

'What is it you want?'

The woman in the chair straightened her back and her eyes narrowed to slits.

'*Your tongue devises destruction, like a sharp razor, working deceitfully. You love evil more than good, lying rather than speaking righteousness, you deceitful tongue.*'

Monika squeezed her eyes shut and opened them again. It didn't help. This was really happening.

'What?'

'*God shall likewise destroy you forever; He shall take you away, and pluck you out of your dwelling place, and uproot you from the land of the living.*'

Monika swallowed. Everything was spinning. She leaned against the door jamb for support.

'I'm only trying to save you. What's the name of the widow, the one who lives across the way? The one you're lying to?'

Monika didn't answer. In less than a second the thought whirled away and she could only confirm what a fantastic invention Zopax was. It came to her rescue when all her other efforts to solve her problems failed.

The woman continued when she didn't get an answer.

'I don't need her name. Because I know where she lives.'

'I don't understand what you have to do with any of this.'

'I make no assumptions. But God does.'

The woman was insane. She kept on watching Monika, holding her there as if she were nailed to the spot. She clearly felt the woman's eyes worming their way in, dodging her exhausted defences, and finally reaching her very core.

Worming their way in. What a ridiculous expression!

She suddenly heard someone giggling and realised to her astonishment that the laughter was coming from her own mouth. The monster in the chair gave a start and glared at her.

'What's so funny?'

'Nothing, I was just standing here thinking about something and then I thought that . . . it's nothing.'

Someone laughed again but then it was quiet. The true nature of something. A guest from hell disguised as a worm.

When the monstrosity began to speak again her voice sounded angry, as if someone had insulted her.

'I won't tire you with any details, because I can see with my own eyes that you aren't very interested, but you must know that I'm doing this for your own sake. I'll be brief and give you three alternatives. The first is that you voluntarily confess to the widow who lives on the third floor across the way that you have been telling lies and bring her here so that I can hear it with my own ears. The second is as follows. Somewhere in safekeeping there is a letter that I have written. If you do not voluntarily confess, in a week this letter will be delivered to her, and when she reads it she will find out that you were the one who talked her husband into trading places with you on the way home from the course.'

The fear succeeded in opening up a little hole, but

only a little one. So far she was still fairly safe. The pills were in her handbag, but she had already taken more than the normal dosage. Several times over.

'The third alternative is that you deposit one million kronor into the bank account of Save the Children. And that you come here and give me the deposit receipt as proof.'

Monika stared at her. The precise sum and specific request carved out a measure of reality from the insanity. With absolute clarity she comprehended the full import of such an unreasonable demand.

'Are you crazy? I don't have that much money.'

The monster turned her head away and looked out the window. Her chins shook when she continued.

'No, of course you don't. Then it will have to be one of the other alternatives.'

The gate was thrown open wide. She snatched up her handbag and fumbled for the packet of pills, saw out of the corner of her eye that the monster was watching her but it didn't make any difference. She dropped the foil pack on the floor and almost passed out when she stooped to pick it up.

'You can think about it for a couple of days and let me know which one it will be. But it's urgent. The grace of the Lord must not be misused.'

Monika staggered out to the hall and swallowed the tablets. She picked up her boots and sat down in the stairwell to pull them on. She held onto the banister on the way down and found the exit through the cellar. Somehow she had to buy herself some time. Make everything stand still long enough to give her a chance to think and regain control over all that had gone so wrong, slipping out of her hands once again.

The woman was insane and somehow part of the net that had ensnared her. Now she had to find a way out of everything that was no longer possible to comprehend.

She noticed how the Zopax had found its way to the correct receptors in her brain, and she stopped to allow herself a moment's pleasure. Enjoyed the sense of liberation when everything, through a wondrous transformation, was no longer so important, when everything sharp became embedded in something soft and manageable that could no longer do her harm.

She stood utterly still, gently inhaling air into her lungs and breathing. Just breathing.

The sun had peeked out. She closed her eyes and let the rays play over her face.

Everything would be fine. Everything *was* quite fine. Zopax and Save the Children. Everything had a charitable purpose. Almost like the donation fund she was responsible for at the clinic. Which would go to deserving aid groups for children injured in war. Each year they helped hundreds of children all over the world. It was fantastic; they saved them, saved the children. Save the Children. Ha! Now that she thought about it, it was almost the same thing, after all. And no one would ever notice a thing, there was so much in that donation account. She would just have to borrow a little of the money as an emergency measure until she managed to solve the problem in some other way. She had the account number in her wallet, and the bank was open. It was for Pernilla's sake too, of course, she mustn't forget that, so that she wouldn't feel betrayed and deserted and utterly alone. Pernilla needed her. Until she had found an equally good replacement for Mattias, Monika was the only one Pernilla had. And Monika had vowed, on her honour and in good conscience, that she would strive to serve her fellow man with humanity and respect for life as a guiding principle, and now she had a life to save. It was her duty to do everything she could.

The only thing was that in this case she couldn't remember whose life it was that she actually had to save.

34

Maj-Britt sat on a chair just inside the front door. It stood a bit ajar and through the crack she had watched some of her neighbours pass by in the morning hours, hurrying down the stairs and out into the world she had left behind so many years ago. She inhaled the air that streamed in from out there and did her best to try to get used to it.

Ellinor had gone out and bought her a pair of outdoor shoes that were already on her feet, but Ellinor couldn't find a jacket to fit her. It would have to be specially ordered, they said, and Maj-Britt couldn't wait that long. What she had to do had to be done as soon as possible, before her courage failed her again.

Ellinor had kept on trying to persuade her but had finally been forced to give up. She recognised the futility of trying to convince someone who had put all her desires behind her, to undergo a series of complicated operations simply to hold onto a life that had actually ended long ago.

Maj-Britt hadn't said a word about her plans. Ellinor was totally in the dark about the negotiations that had taken place with God. Or the fact that Maj-Britt was in the process of making up for her sins so that she could be forgiven. And then dare to die.

Monika hadn't wanted to understand. Maj-Britt was unsure of how she had reacted. But it didn't make much difference. Whatever Monika decided to do, it would mean that Maj-Britt had performed a good deed. Either she would save Monika from hell by making her stop lying, or, if Monika chose to pay the money instead, it would be thanks to Maj-Britt that Save the Children would be able to help a great number of children to live a more tolerable life.

A little restitution.

Of course it wouldn't be enough, but God had indicated that it would mitigate somewhat the devastating judgement that awaited her.

But she was not forgiven.

She had one more thing to do. Because it wasn't only Monika who had lied.

That's why she was sitting by her front door and peeking out through the crack, trying to convince herself. So that she could approach with tiny ant steps the enormous thing she was about to do.

Those letters she had written.

In order for her to dare to leave this life, all the lies had to be taken back, and she needed to see Vanja with her own eyes to make sure, to be certain that she received her forgiveness. And then she would know. The question kept swirling round inside her: how had Vanja known about the tumour that was growing in her body when she didn't even know about it herself?

She had considered writing a letter in any case, despite the fact that Vanja had said that she did not intend to tell her anything either by letter or telephone.

And if she was only half as stubborn as she had been as a girl, it would be fruitless even to try.

Maj-Britt had to conquer herself. Then Monika Lundvall's confession to the widow or a receipt for the money to Save the Children would be the only thing missing. When she had received proof she wouldn't drag out her dying for as long as six months. She would see to it that things went far more quickly.

It was Ellinor who had arranged everything. For the first time Maj-Britt had picked up her telephone and used the mobile number that Ellinor had left on her nightstand. And Ellinor had been enthusiastic. She borrowed a car large enough and rang to find out about visiting routines. She told Maj-Britt that the woman she had talked to sounded almost glad about her enquiry, replying that yes, of course, Vanja Tyrén was allowed to have visitors, even unguarded, and that she would book one of the visiting rooms.

In the meantime Maj-Britt had been fully occupied trying to prepare herself. For two days she had tried to comprehend what she was about to do, and the fact that she actually intended to do it voluntarily. And she wouldn't even be able to blame Ellinor if things went wrong.

It was an unreal moment when they stood ready inside her front door. Almost as if she were dreaming. Saba stood a bit further down the hall and watched them go out the front door, but she didn't even try to follow because that door was not an exit for her. For her it was a strange opening through which people appeared at intervals and then went up in smoke again. But now her mistress was on the other side, and it obviously made her nervous. Saba came all the way to the threshold and stood there whining, so Ellinor crouched down and petted her on the back.

'We'll come back soon, you'll see. This evening she'll be back again.'

And with every cell in her enormous body Maj-Britt wished that it were already evening and that she could go back inside.

The city had changed. So much had happened since the last time she saw it. New buildings had shot up from green zones and familiar neighbourhoods, transforming her home town into a foreign place. And it had also grown. The entire residential section had spread out over the forest-clad hills to the south, extending the city limits by several kilometres. She hadn't left the town in over thirty years and yet it was totally unfamiliar to her. Her eyes desperately tried to take in all the new impressions, but eventually she gave up and shut her eyes for a while to find some respite. Thoughts of Vanja were constantly on her mind. How she would react. Whether she was angry at her. But all the visual impressions helped her for the moment to dispel the worst of her nervousness.

She dozed for a while. She didn't know how long they had been driving when she woke up as the engine was turned off. They were in a car park. She cast a hasty glance at the nearby compound, taking in the white buildings within a high fence, but couldn't absorb anymore. She had tried to prepare herself as best she could for the attention that she knew her appearance would attract, but now that the time had arrived her discomfort got the better of her. Once again her courage deserted her. The mere thought of having to display herself to Vanja was enough. Having to expose her gigantic failure. Her throat hurt and tears welled up, and was unable to hide them although she felt that Ellinor was watching. The terror she felt at getting out of the car and having to reveal herself to strange people was just as strong as what she felt when she had done her thumb-verses and He had handed down His judgement. Her whole body was trembling.

'There's no danger, Maj-Britt.'

Ellinor's voice was calm and comforting.

'It will be a while yet before we have to go in, so we'll just sit out here in the meantime. Then I'll go in with you and see that everything is in order before I leave you two alone.'

And she felt Ellinor take her hand, and she let it happen. She gripped Ellinor's slender hand and squeezed it hard. With all her heart she wished that a tiny insignificant bit of the self-confidence that Ellinor possessed could be transferred to her. Ellinor, who never gave up. Who, in her stubbornness and against all odds, had succeeded in stepping in to convince her, to prove to her, that there was something called goodwill. And didn't ask for anything in return.

'It's time now, Maj-Britt. Visiting hour is starting now.'

She turned her head and was met by Ellinor's smile. And to her astonishment she saw that the girl's eyes were full of tears.

Maj-Britt's new shoes were walking on wet tarmac. The tips shot out under the folds of her dress at regular intervals but she couldn't look at anything else. The lower edge of a door that opened, a threshold, a black doormat, yellowish-brown linoleum. Ellinor talking to someone. The rattle of keys. A man's black shoes beneath dark-blue trousers in front of her and more of the yellowish-brown floor. Some locked doors along the walls at the edge of her field of vision.

Not once did she raise her eyes but she could still feel all the eyes following her.

The man's shoes stopped and a door was opened.

'Vanja will be right down. You can go inside and wait.'

Another threshold and she managed to conquer this one too. They had apparently arrived. The man's black shoes vanished out the door and bit by bit she raised her eyes to make sure that they were alone.

Ellinor had stopped just inside the doorway.

'Are you okay?'

Maj-Britt nodded. She had made it here and tried to take strength from the triumph. But the ordeal had cost her; her legs wouldn't hold up any longer, and she went over to a table with four chairs that looked sturdy enough to bear her weight. She pulled out one of them and sat down.

'Then I'll wait outside.'

Maj-Britt nodded again.

Ellinor took a step over the threshold but stopped there and turned round.

'You know, Maj-Britt, I'm so terribly glad you're doing this.'

And then she was alone. A small room with venetian blinds pulled down, a simple sofa group, the table she was sitting at and some pictures on the walls. The sounds continued to flow in from the corridor. A telephone rang, a door closed. And soon Vanja would come. Vanja, whom she hadn't seen in thirty-four years. Who she thought had abandoned her and to whom she herself had now lied. She heard footsteps coming down the corridor and her fingers tightened their grip on the table edge. And then she was standing in the doorway. Maj-Britt saw how she involuntarily gasped. She remembered the wedding photograph, Vanja as bridesmaid, and realised how mistaken she had been. In the doorway stood an ageing woman. Her dark hair transformed to silver and a fine network of wrinkles on the face she had once known so well. The concept of time suddenly personified. In a single blow made so palpable that all those things taken for granted that were constantly happening now demanded their tribute, those things that had constantly etched their rings, year by year, whether they were used or not.

But it was Vanja's eyes that almost took her breath away. She remembered the Vanja she had known, always with a gleam in the corner of her eye and a little mocking smile on her lips. The woman she saw before her bore an infinite sorrow in her gaze, as if her eyes had been forced to see more than they could stand. And yet she smiled, and in an instant the Vanja she had once known shone through in that unfamiliar face.

She gave no sign that revealed what she was thinking when she saw Maj-Britt.

Not a sign.

The guard stood in the doorway and Vanja looked around the room.

'Hey Bosse, can't we pull up the blinds a little? I can hardly see my way around in here.'

The guard smiled and put his hand on the door handle.

'I'm sorry, Vanja, they have to stay like that.'

He closed the door behind him, but Maj-Britt never heard him lock it. It didn't seem that he did. Vanja went over to the window and tried to adjust the blinds but it didn't work. They stayed put. She gave up and looked around again. Went over to a picture and leaned forward, looking a little more closely. A view of a forest-covered landscape.

Then she turned round and swept her gaze over the room.

'Imagine, I've wondered for all these years what these visiting rooms look like.'

Maj-Britt sat in silence. For all these years. Vanja had sat and wondered for sixteen years.

Vanja came over to the table and pulled out the chair across from her, looking almost shy as she sat down. Maj-Britt was in a daze. In such a daze that her nervousness was gone. It was only Vanja who was sitting there. Hidden somewhere in that strange body was the Vanja she had once known. There was nothing to be afraid of.

They sat looking at each other for a long time. Completely silent, as if they were searching each other's faces for familiar details. Seconds and then minutes ticked by in inactivity and Maj-Britt's trepidation receded entirely. For the first time in ages she felt utterly calm. The refuge that she had experienced in her youth that always surrounded Vanja was intact; it was possible to relax here, to stop defending herself.

And she thought about Ellinor again: how she had struggled, finally reaching her.

It was Vanja who broke the silence.

'Imagine if anyone had told us back then that we'd be sitting here today. In a visiting room at Vireberg.'

Maj-Britt lowered her eyes. Everything that had poured out of her now made room for something else. The realisation that so much time had been wasted. And that now it was all too late.

'Have you been to a doctor yet?'

As if Vanja could hear what she was thinking.

Maj-Britt nodded.

'When are you going to have the operation?'

Maj-Britt hesitated. She didn't intend to lie anymore. But she couldn't tell her the truth either.

'How did you know?'

Vanja smiled a little.

'I was smart, wasn't I? Making you come here even though I had already told you about it. Because I did in my very first letter. What a person won't do to get to see what the visiting rooms look like.'

The same old Vanja, no doubt about that. But Maj-Britt didn't understand what she meant. She tried to recall what she had said in that letter, but Vanja hadn't said anything, had she? Maj-Britt definitely would have remembered.

'What do you mean, you already told me?'

Vanja's smile grew bigger. Again her old Vanja flashed by. The Vanja who shared so many of her memories.

'I wrote that I'd dreamt about you, didn't I?'

Maj-Britt stared at her.

'What do you mean?'

'I'm just telling you what happened. That I dreamt it. Naturally I wasn't dead certain, but I didn't feel like taking a chance.'

Maj-Britt heard herself snort but she hadn't really meant to. The explanation came so unexpectedly and was so improbable that she couldn't take it seriously.

'You expect me to believe that?'

Vanja shrugged her shoulders and suddenly was her old self. Something in the expression on her face. The more Maj-Britt looked at her the more she recognised her. Time had merely passed and worn out the casing a bit.

'Believe whatever you like, but that's how it was. If you have some better explanation that you'd rather believe, then be my guest.'

Maj-Britt was suddenly angry. She had come all this way, conquering her fears several times over to come here, and now had to listen to this. Then she suddenly remembered that she had also come to ask forgiveness, but she no longer felt like it. Not when Vanja was sitting there making fun of her.

There was a long silence. Vanja clearly didn't intend either to take back what she had said or to offer any further explanation, and Maj-Britt didn't feel like asking more questions. That might be taken as an acceptance of what she had just heard, and she didn't really intend to play along. She really didn't. She had been so sure that the explanation would be satisfactory in some way, though what exactly she was hoping for she didn't actually know. The whole thing had been so confusing, so totally incomprehensible. But this was worse than the confusion; she didn't want any part of this. Especially because not even in her wildest imagination could she have come up with any better explanation.

'I know how it feels, I was so scared myself at first. But then when I got used to it I realised that it's actually quite amazing. That something like that can exist that we didn't know anything about.'

Maj-Britt didn't really feel that way. On the contrary, it frightened her. If Vanja was right, there could be a whole bunch of things she knew nothing about. But Vanja didn't seem to be bothered by it. She sat there quite calmly.

And then she continued the conversation, as if what they had just said was nothing out of the ordinary.

'I've been offered a pardon by the government. In a year I'll be released.'

Maj-Britt was grateful that the conversation had turned to something concrete.

'Congratulations.'

Now it was Vanja's turn to snort. It didn't sound nasty, just a sign of how she felt.

'It wasn't me that sent in the application; it was someone on the staff.'

'But that's great, don't you think?'

Vanja sat in silence for a moment.

'Do you remember what I did sixteen years ago?'

Maj-Britt thought about it. 1989. She had probably been sitting in her easy chair. Or maybe on the sofa, because she was still able to do that back then.

'Since then I've been locked up in here. But actually I only exchanged one prison for another, and I can assure you that at first this was sheer paradise in comparison. Except for all the thoughts that flowed in when it was no longer just a matter of getting through the day without making him angry. Or whatever it was that he felt.'

Vanja looked down at her hands resting on the table.

'A prison sentence is actually the same thing as a fine, it's just that you pay with time instead. And the big difference is that you can always get more money.'

Maj-Britt chose to remain silent.

'It's impossible to survive in here if you don't learn to look at time differently than you did before. You have to try and convince yourself that it really doesn't exist. If you're locked up here you have to transport yourself to another place to survive.'

She tapped her index finger against her silvery head.

'In here. At eight o'clock every evening they lock the door and after that you're alone with your thoughts. And I promise you, some of them you would do anything to avoid. The first year it made me terrified, I thought I'd go crazy. But later, when I couldn't fight against it any longer and just surrendered . . .'

She left the sentence unfinished and Maj-Britt waited impatiently for the rest. Vanja sat silently, staring out into space, and seemed to have finished talking. But Maj-Britt wanted to hear more.

'What happened then?'

Vanja looked at her as if she had forgotten she was there but was glad to see her.

'Then you realise that you can hear quite a bit if you only dare to listen.'

Maj-Britt swallowed. She wanted to talk about something else now.

'What are you going to do when you get out?'

Vanja shrugged. Then she turned her head and sat

looking at the picture she had examined earlier. The forest-covered landscape.

'You know, there's only one thing I think I've longed for out there. Know what it is?'

Maj-Britt shook her head.

'To ride a bike, on a gravel path, through the woods. Preferably in a strong headwind.'

She looked at Maj-Britt again. Smiled, almost with embarrassment. As if her longing would seem ridiculous.

'It might be hard for those of you on the outside to understand how someone can long so much for something like that. Because you can do it every day if you want.'

Maj-Britt looked down at the tabletop. She felt herself blushing and didn't want Vanja to see it. Her own truth was a reproach in this context. Sixteen years Vanja had paid. Maj-Britt herself had thrown away thirty-two of her own free will. She hadn't been near a gravel path. Or a forest. And if the wind was blowing a little she would close the balcony door. She had voluntarily entered her prison and thrown away the key, and, as if that wasn't enough, she had let her body become the final shackle.

'No government can grant me a pardon.'

Maj-Britt was hauled out of her thoughts by the sorrow she heard in Vanja's voice.

'What do you mean?'

But Vanja didn't answer. Just sat there looking at the picture. Maj-Britt suddenly felt that she wanted to offer solace, reassurance, for once be the person who was there for Vanja instead of the other way round. She searched urgently for the right words.

'But what happened wasn't your fault.'

Vanja gave a deep sigh and ran her fingers through her hair.

'If you knew how tempting it's been for all these years to hide behind the argument that none of what happened was my fault. To blame everything on Örjan and what he did.'

Maj-Britt grew more excited.

'But it *was* his fault!'

'What he did was horrid, unforgivable. But he wasn't the one who . . .'

Vanja broke off and closed her eyes.

'Imagine, after all these years I still can't say it. Not without my whole body hurting.'

'But he was the one who drove you to it, he was the one who made you do it. He made you believe that there was no other way out. You wrote to me yourself and explained it all in the letter.'

'But we're talking about years. All those years when I stayed and let it happen. It began long before we had children. I even wrote an article about it once, saying that you should leave after the first time you're struck.'

She sat in silence for a moment.

'I don't know whether anyone can understand how ashamed I was that I let it happen.'

Vanja passed her hand across her face. Maj-Britt wanted to say something but couldn't find the words.

'Do you know what my biggest mistake was?'

Maj-Britt slowly shook her head.

'That instead of finally leaving I chose to see myself as a victim. That was when I let him win, it was like going over to his side and telling him he was right to behave the way he did, because all a victim does is give in, she can't do anything about her situation. I simply couldn't break the pattern that I had been used to from the beginning in my own family.'

Maj-Britt thought about Vanja's home. She had experienced it as a refuge from God's stern countenance, a place where there was always a blessed commotion. Everyone knew that Vanja's father got drunk sometimes, but most often he was happy and never scared her. It was mostly his stupid jokes that could be so tedious. You never saw much of Vanja's mother. She was usually behind the closed bedroom door, and they used to tiptoe past it so they wouldn't bother her.

'Pappa never hit me but he hit Mamma, and that was almost the same thing.'

Vanja looked at the picture again, and there was another pause before she went on.

'We never knew who would be coming home when the front door opened. Whether it was Pappa or that other man who looked just like him but who was a stranger to us. All he had to do was open his mouth and say a single word and we could tell.'

Maj-Britt hadn't known. Vanja had never hinted with a single word what went on at her house.

'You mustn't forget that Örjan grew up the same way I did, with a father who lashed out and a mother who took it. So now I always ask myself where everything actually has its origin. It's a bit easier then, a bit easier to understand why people do things that can never be forgiven.'

It was quiet in the room. The sun had reached the windows and was filtering in through the narrow gaps between the slats in the blinds. Maj-Britt looked at the striped pattern on the opposite wall. Then she took a deep breath so she would dare to ask the question that she felt she had to ask.

'Are you afraid to die?'

'No.'

Vanja hadn't even hesitated.

'Are you?'

Maj-Britt lowered her eyes and looked at her hands in her lap. Then she slowly nodded.

'This is how I usually look at it. Why should it be any scarier to die than to be unborn? Because actually it's the same thing, only our bodies don't exist here on earth. Dying is nothing but returning to what we were before.'

Maj-Britt could feel the tears coming. She wanted so much to find consolation in Vanja's words, but she couldn't. She somehow had to reciprocate, that was her only chance. And all at once she remembered what she had come here to do. So that she wouldn't let any hesitation overpower her, she started telling the story. She didn't gloss over anything and she didn't leave anything out. She put the entire sad truth into words. How it had been. What she had done.

Vanja sat quietly listening. She let Maj-Britt spill out her whole confession without interrupting. There was only one thing Maj-Britt didn't confess, and that was the plan she intended to carry out. The debt she had to pay off.

In order to dare.

Vanja sat lost in thought when Maj-Britt finished. The sun had retreated and the stripes from the blinds on the wall had faded away. Maj-Britt could feel her heart pounding. With each minute that passed, Vanja's silence became more ominous. Maj-Britt was so afraid of what she would say, how she would react. Whether Vanja would condemn her too and not accept her excuses. It wasn't merely the lies. Now that Maj-Britt understood Vanja's loss, the life she herself had chosen seemed a sheer insult. To her consternation she realised that she carried even more guilt.

'You know, Majsan, I don't think you ever understood how important you were for me over all those years, how much it meant to me that I had you.'

Maj-Britt was stopped cold in the midst of taking a breath. The abrupt change threw her off balance.

'I was so sad when you stopped writing without telling me where you had gone. At first I thought maybe I had done something to make you angry, but for the life of me I couldn't imagine what it might have been. I wrote a letter to your parents and asked them where you were living, but I never got an answer. And then time passed and . . . well, everything turned out the way it did.'

What Vanja said was so amazing that Maj-Britt could find no words. How could *she* have been important to Vanja? It had been just the opposite. Vanja had been the strong one, the one who was needed. Maj-Britt had been the needy one. That's how it had always been.

Vanja smiled at her.

'But I never stopped thinking about you. That's no doubt why the dream felt so strong.'

Again they sat quietly for a moment, looking at each other. So much time and yet so little had changed, not really.

'Can't you and I do something together when I get out?'

Maj-Britt gave a start at her words but Vanja continued.

'You're the only person I know out there.'

The question was so unexpected and the thought so disorientating that she had a hard time taking it in. Vanja's words implied so much more, punching big holes in Maj-Britt's solidly anchored image of the way everything was and would continue to be. To think that Vanja wanted to have anything to do with her at all, almost needed her, and of her own accord wondered whether they might do something together when that day came and it was possible.

But it *wasn't* possible. And never would be. When the day came that Vanja would have the opportunity to do something, Maj-Britt would no longer exist. She had made up her mind, after all.

'I have a year left in here and I think I have something important to do during that year.'

Do something together. A little disturbing possibility had opened up, but she would have to quash it here and now. Everything was still so utterly meaningless. She tried to sort out her thoughts as she listened to what Vanja was saying, but they kept wandering here and there, heading down small unknown turn-offs that hadn't existed before. They dashed without permission down the new paths, cautiously testing to see if they would take hold.

She and Vanja?

Try to capture again a little of what they had lost?

Not be alone anymore?

'I don't know what it is yet but I hope I recognise it when it pops up.'

She tried to concentrate on what Vanja was saying.

'Excuse me, I didn't hear you right. What is it you're going to do?'

'That's what I don't know yet. Just that it's something important. It might be that someone needs my help.'

Maj-Britt realised that she must have missed something Vanja had said.

'How can you know that?'

Vanja smiled but didn't reply. Maj-Britt recognised that expression. She had had it many times when they were growing up, and it always made Maj-Britt extremely curious.

'It's probably not a good idea to tell you about it. You wouldn't believe me.'

Maj-Britt didn't ask anymore, because she realised the direction the conversation was headed. She didn't want to hear about any more dreams that came true. Everything was confusing enough as it was.

There was a knock at the door. The man who had brought Vanja stuck in his head.

'Five minutes.'

Vanja nodded without turning round, and the door was closed again. Then she reached out her hand and placed it on Maj-Britt's.

'Keep your stern God if you like, although He scares you out of your wits. Someday I'll tell you a secret, about what happened that time when I wanted to die and almost died in the flames. But if you can't even believe in a lousy little dream coming true then it's a bit too early yet.'

Vanja smiled but Maj-Britt couldn't manage to smile back, and maybe Vanja sensed her anguish. She stroked Maj-Britt's hand.

'You don't have to be afraid, because there's nothing there to be afraid of.'

And then she smiled the smile that Maj-Britt knew so well. Only now did she realise how much she had missed it. Her Vanja who could always make her feel better, who with her fearlessness had helped her through childhood and always made her see things from another point of view. If only she could have the chance to do things over, to do everything differently. Why had she allowed Vanja to disappear from her life? How could she have abandoned her?

You don't have to be afraid, because there's nothing there to be afraid of.

More than anything she wanted to be able to share Vanja's certainty. Leave all the terrors behind and once and for all dare to choose life.

'Oh, how I wish I could believe like you do.'

And Vanja's smile grew even wider.

'Couldn't you just be satisfied with a little "maybe"?'

Saba stood waiting at the door when she got home. Maj-Britt went straight to the phone and dialled Monika Lundvall's number.

Ring after ring echoed over the line before she was forced to accept that no one was going to answer.

EPILOGUE

Snow had fallen during the night. The world lay concealed under a thin white blanket. At least that part of the world she could still see. She had scraped off a spot on a bench and sat looking at her white breath.

One night.

One night she had managed to get through, and now only one hundred and seventy-nine nights were left and just as many days. Then she would be free. Free to do what she wanted. In one hundred and seventy-nine days and just as many nights she would have served out society's punishment for the crime she had committed and she would regain her freedom.

Freedom. The word had previously been such a natural part of her life that she had never even thought about its real significance. Perhaps it was the same with freedom as it was with everything else that was taken for granted. Only with its loss could you gain the ability to really understand its true value.

She had been so envied. A well-paid head surgeon with a fancy company car and luxury flat. A life full of coveted status symbols. The generally accepted proof that she was a successful person, someone important. But each step she had taken to raise herself above mediocrity had distanced her from freedom, because the more she had to protect, the more afraid she had become of losing what she had managed to achieve.

Now she had lost everything. In one single blow all the success she had built up with such effort was shattered, and it was as irrevocably gone as if it had never even existed. Was it really success, if it could so easily be taken from her? She no longer knew. She really didn't know anything. All that was left inside was a vacuum, and she had no idea how she was ever going to fill it. One day when she was forced once and for all to look back on her life, to take stock in earnest with eyes wide open, what would she then find had been of real value? Pure and genuine. If she were forced at that moment to look back, there were only two things. Her overwhelming sorrow at Lasse's death, and her breathtaking love for Thomas. But she had not permitted herself either of these life-changing experiences. She had shut them off, in favour of maintaining appearances. She had let herself be hollowed out so that in the end she had lived as a shadow. She had achieved so much. Oh, what she had accomplished, and, oh, what an effort she had made.

Yet she had lost it all.

Aggravated embezzlement from her superior.

In evaluating the extent to which it was an aggravated crime, they had taken into account whether she had caused her superior significant or pronounced injury.

They had decided that she had done so. The talented and successful Monika Lundvall.

She had deposited the money into the bank account of Save the Children and stuffed the deposit slip in an envelope with Maj-Britt's address on it, and she thought she had posted it. A week later she had found the envelope in her coat pocket, but by that time it was all too late. When she came home from the bank she turned off all the phones, placed both the packet of Zopax and the one containing the sleeping pills within reach on her nightstand and went to bed. Three days later the head of the clinic and a colleague had entered her flat with the help of a locksmith. The bank had called up the head of the clinic. They just wanted to check that everything was in order with regard to the large sum she had withdrawn from the clinic's donation account, and they mentioned her odd behaviour. Naturally they could have been mistaken, but she seemed to be under the influence of drugs. When she awoke in her bed with the head of the clinic and her colleague in the room, the shame she felt was so deep that she couldn't even speak. And although he offered to refrain from filing a complaint with the police if she would only tell him what was going on and what she had done, she chose to keep silent, even when her ability to speak had returned. The daily life that had been hers was already lost. She would never again be able to look any of them in the eye if she confessed to what she had done.

She preferred to face the music.

And in some peculiar way she actually felt liberated after escaping from the absurd reality into which she had locked herself.

Because there were many types of prison. And for

that matter, a person who was imprisoned never needed to have come anywhere near a court of law.

There was a letter from Maj-Britt lying in the hall. With deepest regrets she had begged forgiveness for what she had put Monika through, and wrote that she had tried to call repeatedly to take back what she had said. But Monika never answered. She read the letter over and over. First in anger, but later with more and more sorrow. In vain she had tried to find scapegoats in order to create a way to exonerate herself, but in the end she was forced to admit that there was no one else to blame.

A few days before the trial, a letter came from Pernilla. Monika hadn't been in touch, and in her desperation she had refused to answer phone messages, and finally they had stopped coming. The letter was a sign that Pernilla had found out, and the return address frightened her like a sudden noise in the night. Fingers stiff with dread, she had opened the envelope, and the relief she felt when she read the brief letter was indescribable. She had been forgiven. Pernilla had found out everything, and she admitted that at first she had been both angry and sad. But the person who told her had in the end made her understand why Monika had acted the way she had done, and managed to turn her rage to sympathy. But Pernilla wondered about the money she had received. Had Monika been reported to the police because of the money she gave Pernilla? Or was it because of the money she was forced to send to Save the Children?

Only then did Monika understand that it was Maj-Britt who had liberated her.

* * *

The sun crept over the rooftops and spread millions of tiny sparkling diamonds in the newly fallen snow. Monika wrapped her jacket tighter around her, but it didn't help much. She saw by the clock that she had spent only half of the hour she was permitted to be outdoors, but no amount of cold in the world could make her go in early.

Out of the corner of her eye she saw a door open and someone come out into the courtyard. She didn't look, she didn't dare, she had no idea what rules applied in here for survival. The annihilating feeling of being an outsider and the loneliness she experienced in the midst of all the people at yesterday's evening meal had made her so anxious that she asked to be allowed to go back to her cell early. But it was when they locked the door that she experienced for the first time in her life how it felt not to be able to breathe in a room full of air. She had thought she would die in there. But the only people she could ask for help were the ones who had locked her in, and the torment they were subjecting her to was no careless mistake but a deliberate act. They thought she deserved it.

The impotence she felt had almost killed her.

She sensed that the person who had come outside was approaching, and in a purely defensive reaction she turned her head to get some idea of the possible threat. It was one of the oldest women in the prison; Monika had seen her the day before at dinner. She sat by herself and looked as if nothing that happened in her vicinity actually affected her, and the others in the room seemed to respect her solitude. At first the sight of the woman had made Monika uncomfortable, because of the look in the woman's eyes when they met. As if she were startled, as if she had caught sight of someone she knew. But Monika had never seen the woman before and didn't want to draw attention to herself. That was the way she had planned to get through her time here. By not being noticed.

Now the woman was approaching the bench, and Monika could feel her heart pounding. She remembered the chatter during dinner, the obvious hierarchy, the sense that everyone was acting according to an invisible script in which she had been given no role. And for the life of her she didn't know how she would find her place without getting on the wrong side of someone. She had absolutely no frame of reference as to how she was expected to behave. And yet this was a different type of fear than she had been used to. Inside there was nothing left to harm. Instead it was her body that feared physical pain. That they might assault her.

'Won't you get a bladder infection from sitting there?'

In her gratitude over knowing the answer to the question, Monika's first impulse was to say that it took a bacterium in the urine to provoke a bladder infection, but she bit her tongue to stop herself. It would seem as if she was acting superior.

'Maybe.'

She stood up.

The woman caught a silver-coloured wisp of hair that had come loose and tucked it behind her ear.

'Shall we take a walk?'

Monika hesitated. The woman didn't look particularly dangerous, but to stroll farther away from the buildings alone with her was not appealing. She cast a hasty glance at the door. But she didn't want to go inside yet. Not when there was time left. And she couldn't really say no and stay where she was.

'Sure.'

They began walking slowly across the courtyard. There was no reason to hurry.

'You got here yesterday, right?'

'Yes.'

'How much time did you get?'

'Six months.'

Monika replied politely and quickly to all her questions. So far she was doing fine.

'That's not so bad. The time goes faster than you think when you're bored.'

The woman gave a little laugh and Monika also smiled, to be on the safe side. She realised that she ought to ask a question to show that she was participating in the conversation. Maybe ask how long this woman had been in, but Monika didn't dare. Maybe it wasn't done.

'Sixteen and a half years.'

Monika gave a start.

'But I only have eight months left now.'

She only had a second to be shocked, then she unconsciously slowed her pace. Sixteen and a half years. Not many were given such a long sentence. Only those who had committed really despicable crimes, and apparently the woman she had gone off walking with was one of them. Monika cast a glance back towards the buildings and felt a stubborn desire to go back. She stifled the impulse and tried instead to think up a question of her own. She had to get along with people in here for another six months, after all. It would be crazy to make an enemy on the very first morning.

'What are you going to do when you get out?'

She had done her best to seem easy-going and took a step back in fright when the woman suddenly stopped and turned to her.

'My name is Vanja, by the way.'

She held out her hand.

'It's easy to forget common good manners in here.'

Monika took off her mitten and shook her hand briefly.

'Monika.'

Vanja nodded and started walking again. Monika followed her reluctantly. A little farther up there was a group of people, and that made her feel a bit better.

'What I'm going to do when I get out? I don't really know. To start with I'm going to move in with a friend, an old childhood friend. She's very ill but after this last operation she seems to be on the mend, thank goodness, but they don't know for sure yet. If all goes well maybe we'll take a trip together somewhere, she and I. We'll have to see how things go.'

Monika tried to grasp the time concept of seventeen years. An eternity if you considered that the sentence had to be served in a place like this. Much less serious matters could drive people insane. She knew that from her own experience.

They had turned onto a path between some trees, and when they came out on the other side the open field sloped down towards the end of the world. Soon they would reach the limit of how far they could go. The area was fenced off by a double barrier with several metres between them, and rolls of barbed wire had been attached on top. So that anyone who might consider climbing over them would be ripped to shreds. It was in here that she was confined. Not trusted by society to go outside. Not even in the vicinity, because the safety zone was fifty metres. She cast a glance over her shoulder and made sure that there were still people within sight.

Vanja stopped and shoved her hands in her jacket pockets.

'It's important to have someone waiting for you outside. It's a little easier that way. I know, because I've tried it both ways.'

Monika looked down at the snow. She had no one waiting out there. Maybe her mother, but she wasn't sure. Her mother had called a few times but Monika had never answered. She didn't know if her mother knew where she was now. And to be honest, it didn't really matter.

Vanja took a handkerchief out of her pocket and wiped her nose.

'It's pretty rough in here, so it's not always easy to be the new girl. But it's fairly calm in the section you're in. Get hold of some cigarettes, you'll need them.'

Vanja raised her hand to shield her eyes from the sun and gazed out over the glittering fields that stretched beyond the fence. Monika stole a glance at her.

'Check out how beautiful it is . . .'

Monika followed her gaze out across the landscape and they stood in silence for a while.

'To think that we're so stupidly negligent with everything we have. That we don't understand things better. You and I are actually prime examples of how little we comprehend, otherwise we wouldn't be standing on this side of the fence.'

Monika was inclined to agree, but she wasn't ready to express it in words. Vanja made a little noise that sounded like a snort.

'We think we're the top of the line, that everything's perfectly formed and done with just because we happen to exist at this moment. But the little space of time we're alive on this earth is only a little fart in the universe in the grand scheme of things. I read that we aren't even really completely developed enough to walk on two legs, that there are some suspension thingies inside that haven't yet managed to adapt properly.'

She made a circular motion with her hand over her stomach. Monika wondered which of the body's tissues she could mean, but chose not to ask. Just at this moment it didn't seem so important.

A flock of birds flew across the sky, and Vanja leaned her head back so she could watch their path. Monika followed her example.

'You know, in the Milky Way alone there are two hundred billion stars. That's incredible, two hundred billion, and we're talking just about our own galaxy. It's quite strange to think that our sun is only one of that whole spray of stars.'

The birds disappeared over the woods. Monika closed her eyes and wondered what they were seeing way over there.

'Imagine how afraid people must have been when they were told that the earth was not the centre of the universe. What a terrifying scenario, to walk about here in peace and quiet and know that God created the earth and all the people as the centre of everything, and then suddenly to hear that we are only a tiny flyspeck.'

Vanja took out her handkerchief and wiped her nose again.

'It was no more than four hundred years ago we believed that, but it's all fine to walk about now and sneer at how stupid they were. And we think we're so fantastically enlightened, all you have to do is look around to see how well it's all going.'

Monika stole a look at Vanja. This was undeniably a peculiar woman she had run into, and she realised in amazement that she appreciated the walk. No one she knew ever talked about things like this. If they hadn't been confined inside a barbed-wire fence it would have felt quite refreshing.

Vanja looked at Monika and smiled.

'I usually amuse myself by wondering how many people will have the opportunity to laugh at *us* in four hundred years. And what things that we're so sure of now will later turn out to be bullshit.'

Monika smiled back and Vanja looked at her watch.

'It's almost time.'

Monika nodded and they turned back. Her spirits had lifted somewhat. It felt good to know that there was someone like Vanja in here.

'Do you have anyone waiting for you outside?'

The question made Monika's smile die out. For a brief moment the face that she missed more than anything else floated by. She lowered her eyes and shook her head.

'Are you absolutely sure? I had someone, even though I didn't know it.'

Monika didn't want to be sure, so she chose not to reply. But how could she hope even in her wildest dreams that he would still be waiting? She had made her life's second gigantic mistake when she let him go.

'You can't know anything for sure until it's been proven.'

Monika stopped.

'What?'

But Vanja said nothing more. She just kept walking and the only thing that came out of her mouth was her white, swirling breath.

The will to go on is needed even for the smallest steps. She had read that somewhere, but no longer remembered where or when. She was familiar with small steps; that was all she had devoted herself to since everything came crashing down. But she no longer knew what it felt like to have the will to go on. For so many years she had struggled to excel, doing her utmost to decorate the outside with the loveliest mosaic, but along the way she had neglected what was on the inside. She had become her accomplishments and her possessions, and there was nothing else. When the glorious exterior had been peeled away, all that remained was the emptiness from what she had given up. The opportunity she had thrown away.

She had only one wish.

Only one.

To dare to take that step, she needed courage that went beyond reason. But if she didn't dare, there would never be an occasion to dare to do anything ever again.

And with the courage that only someone who is

truly, truly afraid can summon, she finally picked up the phone.

'It's me. Monika.'

For an eternity there was silence before he finally said something, and she could spill out what she needed to say.

'There's so much I want to tell you.'

And with all her hopes directed at the secret that she so fervently wished would exist somewhere, she said the words.

'Thomas, I'm longing to come home.'